Bomber Patrol

Also by William Stanley

Cloud Nineteen

HEADQUARTERS

Bomber Patrol

William Stanley

Walker and Company
New York

First published in the United States of America
in 1986 by the Walker Publishing Company, Inc.

Published simultaneously in Canada by John Wiley & Sons
Canada, Limited, Rexdale, Ontario.

Library of Congress Cataloging-in-Publication Data

Stanley, William.
Bomber patrol.

Reprint. Originally published: One spring in
Picardy. London : Angus & Robertson, 1973.
1. World War, 1914-1918—Fiction. I. Title.
PR6069.T29305   1986   823′.914   85-26631
ISBN 0-8027-0885-4

Printed in the United States of America

10 9 8 7 6 5 4 3 2 1

On the 19th of March, after a long dry spell, there was rain, with the result that a heavy mist spread over the battle-field. With the coming of night on the 20th the mist thickened and gave the illusion that it muffled sound, for the German artillery fire had ceased....

At 4.45 a.m. on the 21st March, out of the mist, the crash came. Forward and battle zones, battery positions, lines of communications, head-quarters, and back areas to a depth of twenty miles or more, were suddenly deluged with shells, many of them gas ... And massed along the fifty-four miles of front between the Sensée and the Oise rivers ... were fifty-six German divisions, with twelve more divisions behind them ... Opposed to this vast array were the four centre divisions of the Third Army with three in reserve, and eleven divisions along the front of the Fifth Army with three other divisions and three cavalry divisions in reserve ...

from *The History of the Great War:
The War in the Air, Vol. IV*

Dedicated to the local and headquarters staff of the County Antrim Library Service for their assistance in running to earth books I never really expected them to find

I

The Aircraft Park had been growing for nearly three years and now it sprawled across the Amiens road, a small town of wooden huts, workshops and offices ringing the oil-soaked grass of the airfield. Here, forty miles from the Front, the rumble of the guns was drowned by the ceaseless noise of aeroplane engines—repaired engines under test in the workshops, new aeroplanes flying in from England or going off to the squadrons behind the Lines. By air and by train or tender came a ceaseless stream of young men, raw material quickly fashioned into pilots to match the demand of the war machine forty miles to the east. One of them was going the wrong way.

Christopher Robson stumbled as he climbed out of the Crossley tender, and dropped his cane; his cap fell off as he bent down to retrieve it. The driver took his bags from the back of the tender and dumped them alongside the road.

'Recording Officer lives over there,' he said. Then after a deliberately insulting pause he added, 'Sir', before hastily climbing back into his seat without saluting, and driving away. It was the first time he had spoken since they'd left Arras.

There were four pilots, newly arrived from England, ahead of Robson as he waited in the corridor to see the Recording Officer. Their chatter, like schoolgirls before a hockey match, irritated him with its naïve eagerness.

'My dear chap, nobody in their right mind would fly Camels. One gets showered with oil, castor oil at that. And they spin if you reach down to scratch your arse.'

'But a Camel turns faster than an S.E.5. And it's turns that count in a dog-fight. My instructor said so.'

'You'll need to do split-arse turns dodging Emma-G fire at nought feet. My instructor told me Camels get all the dirty work like trench strafing while the S.E.s keep watch at 10,000 feet.'

'You chaps are lucky. I'm going on Harry Tates.'

'I say, jolly hard luck.'

The three of them were looking at their compatriot with the sympathy reserved for the condemned. The R.E.8 Corps Reconnaissance two-seater had had an unfortunate history.

'Is it true the extensions flap before they break off in a steep turn?'

'My instructor said they spin in at the slightest provocation.'

There was a pause, then one commented, 'Apparently, the average life of a pilot is three weeks.'

'Brrr, makes you go all goosey. Do you think we'll get any flying here? Plenty of variety. They've even got a couple of old F.E.s.'

'Brrr, don't mention it, old chap. Night bombers. Imagine landing one of those at night with that filthy brute of a Beardmore perched on your shoulders...'

The door opened, and an orderly beckoned one of them in. The others fell silent.

You'll soon get all the flying you want, Robson thought grimly. And see how you like it at fifty feet with a choked engine, nothing on the clock and the poplar trees by the aerodrome hedge reaching up for you. His eyes watered at the thought. And they would curse the alien sky. Empty one moment, then suddenly vomiting streaks of tracer. Your first warning a splintering strut or the 'flack-flack' of punctured fabric. After a few days of that they would be glad to see the rain soaking into the airfield. If they knew what...

'Mr. Robson.' The Orderly Room clerk beckoned him into the Adjutant's office.

'Robson, Robson, do I know you? Seen you before, haven't I?' the Recording Officer said. Christopher Robson smiled wanly and handed over his movement order. It had not been long, only three weeks and a day, since he had last seen the black patch over the right eye, the white scar that bisected the eyebrow and cheekbone, the black-gloved right hand.

'See too many of you fellers, y'know. Try not to forget a face.' A pause, then, 'Oh!'

It was not until the Recording Officer lifted his head to stare at him, his friendliness replaced by contempt, that Robson began to realize the enormity of his supposed offence.

'Right, the sooner we get rid of you the better,' the Recording Officer snapped. 'I suppose you *can* fly an aeroplane. I dare say the Ferry Flight will be prepared to use you. See Captain Franklin at the Flight Shed. He's got some B.E.s to go home. You can leave at first light tomorrow morning.'

The curt instructions, the cold voice, shattered the illusions that had cocooned Robson since the Major in command of his Camel squadron had told him he was to be returned to Home Establishment, and his words echoed now in his head. 'You're no good to me or anybody else out here, Robson. It's not your flying that is the trouble, it's a vertical draught round your lower extremities.'

Robson's Commanding Officer had been a cold, stiff ex-Yeomanry officer. Because he was basically a decent man he had stifled his anger at Robson's stuttered excuses and had mumbled something about Robson getting more flying time, training, a second chance. Robson's shocked mind had seized on these words, forgetting the reason for their having to be said. Training, more flying time, more time to handle temperamental rotary engines, that was all he needed, that was why they were sending him home.

But the Recording Officer knew and Franklin, the C.O. of the Ferry Flight knew, for the R.O. had telephoned him as soon as Robson had left his office. A pilot only went to Home Establishment after three weeks in France for one reason: cowardice.

'Log book,' Franklin said. Robson handed him his Pilot's log book, his airborne life story. 'You've flown a "Quirk"?' Franklin was referring to the B.E.2c, a reconnaissance aeroplane that was finally, eighteen months too late, being replaced in service.

Robson nodded. He could see Franklin looking at the entries for his time in the Squadron. Nothing to be proud of. Sopwith Scout F.1, commonly called a Camel, 120 h.p. Le Rhone rotary engine, two Vickers machine-guns fixed to fire through the propeller. He'd crashed on take-off twice, engine failure, before he'd even got over the Lines. Two aeroplanes in his first two days. And when he did get into patrol with his flight, there'd been more engine failures, or his guns had jammed, or he'd been shot down. (He never saw the fighter that shattered his petrol tank and sent him hurtling 2,000 feet to an emergency landing behind the Lines.) There'd been a run of lost formation, engine running rough, more jammed guns, lost formation again, then his Flight Commander shouting, 'I won't risk the lives of men in my flight by letting you fly with them. I've just flown your aeroplane. There was nothing wrong with the engine. There was nothing wrong with it yesterday or the day before. You've got the wind up.'

Franklin slapped the log book shut. 'You'll take 5640. Over there. Three of them to go back. I will head the formation. Report back here at eight o'clock tomorrow morning.'

As Robson turned to go, he added, 'Keep off the booze

tonight, Robson. You can cry in your beer when you get home. The "Quirk" is a bloody awful aeroplane over here but they can use them at home. And you've cost us enough already.'

It was too early for lunch and neither of the polarized groups in the bar contained suitable companions. The newcomers, pink-cheeked, new-uniformed enthusiasts were sipping whisky as though they liked it; the others, pilots down from the squadrons to collect new aircraft—men with weather-beaten faces, white-patched about the eyes from wearing goggles—were drinking with the casual abandon of those given the grace of a few hours' release but fully aware of the shortness of their respite. He realized, he could not join either group without becoming a liar, even if he did not say a word. One group would respect him, ask his advice; the others, they knew why a man got sent home after three weeks, they would leave him alone. He turned away and walked out of the mess to his sleeping quarters.

There was a second bed in his room. A mess servant came in loaded with kit, followed by another new pilot.

'I say, sorry to barge in on you like this, but I've just got here.'

Robson grunted. The new pilot—he reminded Robson of one of the prefects at school, fair, curly hair and a blond smudge across his upper lip—fidgeted at the foot of his bed. His cheeks were flushed and Robson could smell the whisky.

'I say, do you know where I can get a glass of water?'

'Water? You'll get some in the mess. I wouldn't drink any that hasn't been boiled. Can't remember anybody ever asking for it.'

'Must have been jolly queer whisky,' the new pilot said, hiccupping. 'Doesn't usually affect me like this.'

'I don't like the stuff,' Robson said. 'Wine is cheaper. Does you less harm.'

'I say, I'm terribly sorry, Sir. I thought you were a new arrival.' Robson had hung up his leather flying jacket and the boy had spotted the tell-tale patch of castor oil on the right shoulder. 'Are you picking up a new Camel?'

'No. I'm flying a B.E. home tomorrow. Don't call me "Sir".'

'Sorry, Sir. I saw your flying jacket and I thought it was only Camels that sprayed castor oil out of the exhaust...'

'I was on Camels. Don't call me "Sir". I haven't been out here much longer than you. Three weeks.'

The new pilot hiccupped and laughed. 'I say, you're an encouraging chap to meet. The story isn't true then...'

'What the hell are you babbling about? What story?' Robson rolled over and sat up on his bed.

'N'nothing. You know, that one about pilots lasting only three weeks over the Lines.' The new pilot grabbed his cap, hiccupped and backed to the door. He hiccupped again. 'I'd better get that glass of water, Sir.'

Robson held his head in his hands. This was a fore-taste of the future. Give him six months and he would be snapping the heads off frightened cadet pilots, living on that patch of oil-stained leather. If only that new pilot knew.

It was being posted to that Home Defence Squadron that had caused all this. If he'd gone to France last autumn everything would have been all right. They'd have put him on something slow and stable, an R.E.8 or a Big Ack W, and he'd have flown reconnaissance flights or spotted for the guns. And by now he would be honourably dead. Instead, he had become a fighter pilot in that comic-opera squadron in Norfolk. Fighters? Home Defence? Three F.E.2s—known as old pushers, flying bath-tubs—a couple of B.E.12s, too slow to be used in France, a couple of trainer-weary Avros, a Pup apiece for the flight commanders, a Camel for the C.O. and a bundle of promises. Oh, his record must have looked marvellous to some ignorant clerk in Bolo House. A pilot with four months' flying with a Home Defence Squadron, fifty-five hours in his log book. That kid suffering from his first whisky would be lucky if he had thirty. No wonder they sent him to a Camel Squadron when the casualties rose.

'I say, Mr. Robson?' The boy was back again, a tall dark-haired second-lieutenant behind him. 'You are Mr. Robson? I thought I saw your name on your bags. This chap is looking for you.' He hiccupped again and fled.

'Hi,' said the newcomer. 'McDonald. Frank. Have you scared the living daylights outa him or did he have one whisky too many in the bar? Sorry to disturb you, feller, but I guess you ain't heard the news. You gotta go to war.'

McDonald stretched himself out on the boy's bed and lit a cigarette, stuffing the paper packet back into his breast pocket when Robson shook his head.

'You got the right idea, feller. You must be the only man in this dump lying on his bed while the bars are open. What are you doing, hiding? It ain't no good, if you are. There's some big push coming off tomorrow or the day after.'

'I thought we had had enough of this big push business last year at Passchendaele.'

McDonald chuckled. 'You got it all wrong, Robson, it's not us that is going to do the pushing. It's the Hun.'

He tossed a paper onto Robson's bed. 'You're posted— same as me.'

Robson sat up. 'Posted? What the hell are you talking about?'

The Canadian looked surprised. 'What did you think you were going on, S.E.5s? You and Mrs. McDonald's boy are going to war against a whole German Army in that relic of the dark ages, the Wright Brothers' second thought, the F.E.2b night bomber. Get your arse off that bed before that damned Scottish R.O. catches you. I've got a tender outside. We've overstayed our welcome, Mr. Robson.' It rained throughout their journey south through Amiens and then south-east along the rutted and crudely repaired road to Roye and on to Catigny. The cloud scudded about five hundred feet above them. The rain and the unending poplar trees conspired with the rolling featureless countryside to confuse their senses.

There were groups of men and a steam roller working on the airfield, four hundred square yards of pasture rimmed on two sides by canvas hangars and wooden huts. A new canvas hangar like a huge marquee was being erected in the middle of a group of five. It was conspicuously white against the mottled camouflage of the others. Nearby, a couple of F.E. aeroplanes sat in the rain, engines and cockpits covered with tarpaulins.

Their driver sucked noisily on an empty tooth. He pointed to the Chinese labourers working on the airfield.

'Jerry was over last night,' he said, 'distributing 'is visiting cards. Dropped them in a long line across the aerodrome and that 'angar copped 'is last one. Proper nasty it was.'

'Anybody hurt?' McDonald asked.

The driver grinned. 'I reckon that's why you gents is here. Mr. Thompson and Mr. McKelvie, two of our observers, tried to keep them off with the guns in their planes. Jerry got them, and a couple of pilots in one of the orficer's huts, and four mechanics in the shed what burned down. Major Timmis, the C.O., 'e's 'urt bad, too. He flew into one of the bomb holes and went arse over tit.'

'It must have been his unlucky night,' Robson said. 'I've tipped one or two on their noses before now.'

'Me too,' added the Canadian.

The driver looked disgusted. 'Not an F.E., you haven't, Sir,' he said. 'The Major was flying in the gunner's seat. It was one of the "pom-poms". 'E was lucky. 'E got tossed out. Only broke 'is collar bone. It was Mr. Sanderson, the pilot, what the engine fell on.'

'My name is Callaghan, "A" Flight Commander and while the C.O. is away I shall be in temporary command. I'm not holding an inquest but the pair of you were supposed to be here yesterday.' Callaghan waved down their protests and stroked away a lank, black curl from over his right eye. Under the faded pilot's wings on the breast of his tunic were the ribbons of the Military Cross and the Military Medal. The voice was slightly nasal, the eyes cynical.

'Forget it,' he said. 'Everybody is the same down at the Depot. Where are your log books?'

Callaghan cleared a pile of maps to one side of the littered desk.

'Canadian, eh,' he said to McDonald. 'Christ, ten hours. You're a bit short of night flying time. Can you do morse?'

The Canadian flexed his wrist in the professional manner, his index finger drumming on the desk top.

'Da—diddy—da da. You're talking to the one man in Moose River Springs that ever built himself a radio.'

'You've been out before?' Callaghan asked sharply.

The Canadian twisted his left sleeve to show the wound stripe and nodded.

'Can you use the lamp?' Callaghan asked, referring to the Aldis Lamp used for light signalling. 'Sure,' said McDonald easily. 'How about you?' Callaghan turned to Robson.

He opened up the log book and Robson's stomach muscles knotted as the Captain's eyebrows lifted.

'If this is your idea of a joke, Robson, we do not share the same sense of humour. What's this about Camels?'

'Yes, Sir,' Robson said miserably.

Callaghan strode to the window, looked out and then turned back to McDonald. He looked furious.

'Get Lieutenant Harris from the mess. The rain is clearing. Tell him to show you the country as far as the Lines. Don't go nearer than five miles. You can take Eight Fifty Two. Be back in an hour.'

'Stand up. Stand to attention.' Callaghan barked after the Canadian had left. 'Now then, Robson. What are you, a deserter?'

'No, Sir. I was at the Depot. Lieutenant McDonald came to my quarters saying that I had been posted here and I was to leave immediately. My orders are there.'

'Stand to attention. You've been in the service long enough not to call a captain "Sir". Why were you at the Depot?'

Callaghan flipped the pages of Robson's log book. 'You've been on a squadron for three weeks.'

Robson stared blindly over the top of the Flight Commander's head. A Kirschner nude, pink lipped and nippled, peaches-and-cream in purple garters, hung behind Callaghan's head on a cupboard door. Robson's mouth felt dry and he stuttered as he replied, 'I was going to fly a B.E. back to Gosport tomorrow morning. The weather held us up. I thought they'd changed their minds.'

Callaghan slammed his fist down on the log book.

'A Camel pilot! Just before the biggest shooting party since last April. Why?'

Robson licked his dry lips again. 'I was being sent home.' Callaghan's face was like a clenched fist. He spoke slowly but with an intensity that made Robson squirm. 'A bloody coward. Why should they send you to me?'

'I was on a Home Defence Squadron. I flew F.E.s there. Day and night.'

Callaghan tore open the envelope containing Robson's movement order.

'Name?'

'Christopher Alan Robson.'

'Number?'

'192933.'

'Robson, Robson. Spell it.'

'R.O.B.S.O.N.'

'Robson, your father's got money, hasn't he.' The voice hardly disguised the sneer, did not disguise at all the hard northern accent. 'Enough to send you to a posh school, teach you to wash your face and eat with a knife and fork. D'ye know what would have happened to you, Robson, if you'd been a private in the line? The poor bastards are tied to a post screaming their bloody heads off, shitting their breeches, Robson, while their mates line up and then shoot them.

'Why, Robson, why? Not because they were any more cowardly than you are, Robson. But because their old man didn't have the cash to make them officers.'

He folded up the log book, replaced the movement order in its envelope and held them out to Robson.

'You're going back to Depot, Robson, to give these orders to the man who should have got them. Lieutenant Robeson, R.O.B.E.S.O.N. You're going home Robson, to live with yourself. If you can. I wouldn't trust one of my observers in the air with you.'

The log book dropped onto the floor before Robson's quivering fingers could grasp it. By the time he'd retrieved it, Callaghan was standing to attention behind his desk. Robson turned, and then sprang to attention, too.

Major Timmis had his right arm in a sling. Both eyes were blackened and a dressing had been taped over a cut on his forehead. His be-ribboned jacket was slung round his shoulders.

'Sit down, Barney. I could hear you shouting on the other side of the aerodrome. Is this one of the replacements?'

Callaghan pushed his chair round for the Major. He sat on the edge of the desk and lit a cigarette. His hand was shaking.

'No, Sir. Depot made a mistake. This man is a Camel pilot being sent home for cowardice.'

'Tut, tut, Barney. We do not send people home for cowardice—not officially. It discourages the others.' He turned to Robson.

'Don't stand there like that, man. We aren't going to eat you—or shoot you. Is this true?'

'Well, yes, Sir, I suppose so, Sir.'

'You surprise me. If you don't know, who does? Don't know the Camel. Never flown one but I'm told it's a nasty beast for raw pilots. I'd a' thought a coward would have killed himself before he got out to France. Has he flown a Fee?'

Callaghan nodded and explained the misunderstanding over names that had brought Robson to the Squadron. The Major nodded and stared at Robson while he filled his pipe with his left hand, waving aside Callaghan's offer of assistance. He broke two matches before the third one lit the pipe.

'Do you want to go home?' he asked. Robson shook his head. 'Then sit down Mr. Robson and tell me how you got into this fix.'

In a daze Robson began. How they had been drafted *en bloc* from the H.D. Squadron to the Pool in France. At that time he had flown a Camel twice: one hour and fifteen minutes' flying time.

His first flight on the Squadron he had been too slow adjusting the mixture control and the over-rich Le Rhone had died on him as he'd crossed the fence. He had landed upside down on the other side of the road. A couple of days later he had done his first patrol. Shocked by the first burst of 'Archie' and let down by a defective pressure valve he had forgotten about his gravity tank and glided back across the lines with a dead engine. On the next patrol, diving to attack a line of transport with bombs and machine guns, they had been bounced by a flock of Albatrosses—or so they told him afterwards. He never saw the aeroplane that shot off his propeller and shattered a centre-section strut. On the patrol after that . . .

He'd been here before. At school. Caught off balance by a catapulted ink blot he had stumbled and swept a bust of their founding bishop onto the floor. The Head had beaten him, his housemaster had beaten him and the following day stumbling from a prefect's cuff he had completed the double by demolishing the bust of their patron, Henry VIII. Given the choice he had taken another beating instead of expulsion.

'. . . And when my Flight Commander found there was nothing wrong with the engine he wouldn't have anything more to do with me.'

'All right. Don't sound so damned sorry for yourself. I reckon you've been damned unlucky. This your log book?'

The Major flicked over the pages to the Home Defence Squadron entries. He shook his head.

'My God. Attacking Gothas in a Fee,' he muttered to himself. 'Five anti-Zeppelin patrols. Did you ever see one?'

'Once, Sir. It was about 5,000 feet higher than me. I did try, honest, but I couldn't get near it.'

'I'm not surprised. Well, Robson, you've been a damned fool but I'm inclined to give you another chance. This squadron is short-handed, and any time now the Hun is going to throw everything he's got at us. As far as I'm concerned you can stay here until the Depot find out they've made a mistake. But I shall be handing the Squadron over to Captain Callaghan in five minutes and it's up to him.'

He turned to Callaghan. 'Well, Barney, he's your pidgin. I suggest you take him up. If his flying is satisfactory, keep him—and make him work.'

The rain had stopped and the black-painted bombers were being trundled out of the hangars by the mechanics. 'A'

Flight was nearest the mess. Beyond the three hangars housing its half a dozen aircraft was 'B' Flight, gap-toothed by the raid of the previous evening.

'We'll take one of the "pom-pom" aircraft,' Callaghan said as they walked across the aerodrome. 'The gun layer sits behind the pilot. So, if necessary, I can grab the controls.'

By early 1918 the F.E., Robson knew, was an anachronism, a relic of a bygone age when aeroplanes were flown by cavalry officers to see what lay over the hill. Designed in 1914 for an engine that was too heavy, then re-engined with the 120 h.p. Beardmore, it had emerged in 1915 as a two-seater fighter to help defeat the Fokker Monoplane, the first single-seater fighter with a gun firing through the propeller. Re-engined again with the 160 h.p. Beardmore and an extra gun it had fought on through '16 and '17 against the superior gun power, speed and manoeuvrability of the Albatrosses and Fokker Triplanes. A year too late it had been taken from the day skies to be used only as a night bomber.

It stood on a stalky undercarriage, its wings a maze of struts and wires. A plywood nacelle stuck out in front of the wings with a gunner in a pulpit-like front cockpit. The pilot sat behind the gunner, twin radiator blocks springing out of his shoulders, and at the back a big six-cylinder water-cooled engine turned a ten-foot diameter propeller beyond the trailing edge of the wings. Wire-braced wooden booms went back in two vees to carry the tailplane and rudder. A triangular spike of a fin like a rhinoceros horn stuck up above the tailplane.

Robson noticed that the one he and Callaghan approached was different from the rest. The nacelle was fatter, the pilot sitting on the left hand side to make room for a one-pounder cannon, the 'pom-pom' gun fired by a gunner sitting to one side and behind the pilot. Like the others, it was painted black apart from the red and blue cockades painted under the wings and the word 'Mimi' in white under the pilot's cockpit.

Robson settled himself in the cockpit, fastened the canvas belt across his lap and turned to look at Callaghan.

'Get on with it,' growled the Flight Commander.

A mechanic raised his arm. 'Switches off.'

'Switches off, suck in,' replied Robson, checking that the engine ignition switches were off.

Behind the wings, amongst the wires and the tail booms, a couple of mechanics strained at the big four-bladed propeller, turning over the pistons of the 160 h.p. six-cylinder Beardmore to suck in petrol. After the propeller had wheezed round half a dozen times the mechanics moved to one side out of the cage. One of them picked up a fire extinguisher. The other raised his thumb. 'Switch on.'

'Switches on.' Robson flicked the ignition switches and began winding the starting magneto.

One cylinder fired, sending a ripple of vibration through the nacelle. A second and a third followed and as Robson switched the throttle open to catch the engine, blue smoke followed by flame spouted from the exhaust.

Robson waved his arm, and the mechanic in front of him darted under the nose to pull the chocks away from the wheels. The old pusher waddled away, lurching as it struck ruts in the field, a couple of mechanics steadying the wing tips.

Dry mouthed, a tense knot tying up his stomach muscles, Robson pointed the aeroplane towards the far corner of the aerodrome and began to open the throttle. A hearty thump from a clenched fist on his right shoulder stopped him.

'You bloody fool,' Callaghan roared. 'Give the engine a burst to make sure the plugs aren't oiled up. Go on, get on with it.'

He tried again, feeling more confident as the heavy

machine trundled across the aerodrome, the rev counter flicking backwards and forwards about the 1,300 mark, the airspeed slowly climbing. At fifty miles an hour he hauled back on the stick and the F.E. climbed slowly away.

This was no Camel popping off the ground like a firecracker with a whirling incinerator a few feet from his feet, spraying him with oil. There was no mixture control, no temperamental rotary to nurse when a few feet above the ground. At 500 feet he risked a glance at Callaghan. The Flight Commander pointed back to the airfield and down.

So it had all been a game, Robson thought as he leaned heavily on the wheel to pull the lumbering old cow round. An act put on before the departing C.O.

'Yes, Major, we'll give him another chance,' until the wounded Major was safely out of the way. Then it would be, 'Get off my aerodrome, Robson. We don't need your type on this station.'

The aerodrome came up to him as he levelled out of the crosswind turn. The F.E. sank slowly as Robson aimed at a spot ten yards beyond the hedge. The engine ticked over, quietly, the propeller, chop-chopping between the booms, the wires whistling. Callaghan's fist hit his shoulder again.

'Take it up.'

Opening the throttle he held the F.E. down and roared across the aerodrome at sixty miles an hour ten feet up, as happy as a boy with a new toy. Callaghan had only wanted to see how he could handle the bomber, what sort of a landing he had been shaping. Even if this F.E. was more war-torn than the one he had flown at home, with its patched fabric, sloppy controls and an engine down on revs, he was content to be flying it.

Callaghan was shouting again. 'Steer due north.' He turned, smiling, but Callaghan was as grim-faced as ever.

The cloud was lifting and beginning to break; the rain-swollen Somme glittered momentarily in a weak sun. At Offoy an observation balloon started to rise. Something on the horizon near the Lines, ten miles away, was on fire.

They went no nearer the Front, but veered to the west to circle Peronne, and then due west over the winding loops of the Somme until Amiens lay on the horizon. Callaghan shouted to him to return.

Before they came in to land Callaghan made him circle the aerodrome at 500 feet. On the eastern side in a clearing of splintered trees was an enormous hill of sand with the much-patched half-wing of an aeroplane resting on it.

'Fly round and come in aiming the nacelle at the cockade on that wing,' Callaghan roared. 'At full throttle.'

He made his approach across the aerodrome from a shallow dive, the airspeed indicator crawling round to ninety-five, with the plane creaking and groaning and its wires screaming as they raced towards the target. Desperately Robson tried to remember whether there was something else he ought to do. The front Lewis gun was not mounted on its pillar. He didn't remember seeing a fixed gun. Each time the wind from the north kept drifting him off the target Callaghan's fist, poised above his shoulder, thumped him. And each time he put on rudder to crab into wind the nacelle moved off the target, and he was thumped again.

A rattle of violent explosions and a flash 200 yards from the target made him freeze on the controls. The F.E. shuddered and seemed to stop in mid-air. A cloud of smoke drifted back over the nose. Before he could react another ripple of explosions rocked the nacelle.

The target was in front of him. A splintered tree raced past just missing the wing. Now the hill of sand loomed above them. Robson could see the splintered spars through holes in the aeroplane wing. He shut his eyes, hauled back on the stick hoping that nothing was broken and realizing simultaneously that the wing was a target and Callaghan had fired the 'pom-pom'. He opened his eyes. None too soon, for the nose pointed to the clouds and the air speed was down to fifty-five. Fervently he prayed that he would not have to take a 'pom-pom' F.E. across the Lines. The thought of that noise accompanying the flash made him shudder.

'Well, the Major said you could stay,' Callaghan said grudgingly after they had landed. 'And there's nothing about your flying to justify my reversing his decision— until the Depot discover their mistake. You'll be flying tonight. Orders come in about seven o'clock. And you mark my words Robson, the Major kept you; I wouldn't. You are on trial. Let me down once, just once, d'ye understand, and by God, you'll be back at the Depot under close arrest. You got that?'

Robson nodded miserably.

'Where the hell has he been?' Callaghan growled as McDonald's aeroplane whistled over the hedge. The oleo legs scrunched in a bumpy landing. Scraps of fabric flapped in the wind from the plane's wings.

Robson realized that Callaghan was angry again but not at him. His face had gone an angry red and then the colour slowly receded into his neck leaving him deathly pale.

'Flight Sergeant,' he shouted to a man in overalls with a sergeant's chevron pinned to his sleeve, 'tell Mr. McDonald to report to my office immediately. And you will personally telephone me about the extent of the damage to his aeroplane.'

He turned to Robson. 'Introduce yourself to Flight Sergeant Watt. Tell him you will be flying "Mimi" again tonight. Her pilot got a bomb splinter in his leg last night. Watt will get hold of your rigger and engine fitter. You may not be interested but I think you should meet, at least once, the oily-handed gentleman responsible for the preservation of your neck.'

Robson waited with his two mechanics for McDonald to taxi back to the hangar.

'I betcha anything you like, Bert,' the engine fitter, Corporal Blythe said to the rigger, Higgins, ''e's been across the Lines. Ten to five in Woodbines. You wouldn't get a Jerry this far over the Lines in daytime.'

'I thought 'e were up to summat when that Mr. 'Arris said to have the guns fitted,' replied the rigger.

'How do you know Mr. McDonald was in a fight?' Robson asked. 'I didn't see any damage.'

'There was a strip of fabric trailing orf the tailplane, Sir,' the rigger said. 'We don't send 'em orf like that.'

McDonald and his gunner, Lieutenant Harris, climbed down from the pulpit-like nacelle in high spirits. Harris was carrying his Lewis gun.

'Say, Robbo, have we had some fun,' McDonald shouted on seeing Robson.

'Sir,' Flight Sergeant Watt threw up a quivering salute. 'Captain Callaghan's compliments, Sir. Will you report to the office at once, Sir.'

'All right, Mr. Watt,' Harris replied. 'I've got a recce report for him. You needn't worry about your bird of prey. Only a few frayed tail feathers for patching.'

'Yes, Sir, and a hole in the port outer strut, Sir.'

'Is there, by God.' They trooped round to inspect the splintered strut. Standing on a trestle Harris poked a pencil through the hole. The line of the bullets' flight passed about a foot over the pilot's cockpit.

'Your mother was praying for you, laddie,' he said to McDonald as he dropped down. 'Must have been some eagle-eyed beetle crusher. I'm going to leave you chaps and hurry on ahead. Our dearly beloved acting C.O. is going to be cross with you, Mac. If I can cook up a recce report for Army H.Q. it may divert some of the wrath of God.'

The two of them watched Harris lope off ahead of them. Then Robson asked McDonald what they had done.

'The cloud was low,' McDonald explained, 'less than five hundred in places, so we nipped across the Lines at nought feet for a look-see. Jerry wasn't expecting company. The tracks are full of men on the move. The balloon'll go up tomorrow, I reckon. We had a go at slowing them up but an unfriendly machine-gun crew took a hand so we decided to get out while the going was good. It convinced me of one thing, Robbo. This night-shift stuff is not for Mrs. McDonald's boy. I'm applying for a transfer to fighters. Right now.'

Captain Callaghan had Lieutenants McDonald and Harris standing to attention in front of his desk while he laid down the law.

'... You are a pair of idiots. You, McDonald, are just too damn green to know what you were letting yourself in for. But there is no excuse for you, Harris. I think you must be out of your mind. I can't afford to lose an aeroplane, I can't afford to lose two officers at a moment like this unless it is in the execution of orders. And you know, Harris, that no F.E. can live in the sky in daylight with the fighters Jerry has now. Even one of their two-seaters could have knocked you down. And as for your stupidity, Mr. McDonald, "nipping up into the cloud", as you called it. Didn't you bloody well learn *anything* at that damn training school? If you must try flying in cloud, McDonald, pick one up high with at least a thousand feet between the base and the ground so that when you come out with your arse where your head ought to be there will be time for you to do something about it.

'As it happens, this report of yours, Harris, has saved your skins—this time. I will not take any further action.

You'll probably get a pat on the back from the General. But don't ever try it again.

'I'm putting you and Robson in "A" Flight, McDonald. My flight. Not because I want you but so that I can keep an eye on the pair of you. Now, get out.'

'Can I make a request?' McDonald asked. Harris plucked at his sleeve trying to pull him away but the Canadian shook him off.

Harris had walked through the Recording Officer's office and was in the orderly clerk's adjacent office when he heard Callaghan's bellowed refusal. The matchboard walls did nothing to hide the fact that the temporary Commanding Officer was refusing Lieutenant McDonald's request for a transfer with some heat. The Orderly Room Sergeant looked up at Lieutenant Harris and smiled. 'I don't think Mr. Callaghan likes fighter pilots, does he, Sir?'

It was dark when Robson stumbled along unfamiliar paths to the mess for dinner. There had been another shower of rain in the late afternoon but now the clouds had lifted a little and a streak of starlight showed to the north. On the far side of the aerodrome there were lights in the hangars silhouetting the emerging bombers. One of them, wheels chocked, wings roped, was having its engine tuned, roaring away at an even note like a demented bumble-bee until some adjustment caused it to subside in a fusillade of misfiring.

It was not cold and the rain had cleaned the air, releasing the fragrance of the coming spring. But as Robson paused at the junction of two paths to get his bearings he felt a claustrophobic oppression. The wind had dropped and there was an eerie silence. Even the Front was quiet tonight. The clouds seemed to be hemming him in, trapping him in company with some terrible catastrophe.

The sound of a pipe tapped on a shoe-heel broke his reverie. The man with the pipe blew through it noisily and began to refill it from an oilskin pouch. Robson could see his outline against the night sky.

'You're new. Just come up today?' the man queried. Robson nodded. 'It must be bad if even you chaps can feel it. I thought it was nerves at first. Sign of having the wind up. Then I realized that there are a quarter-of-a-million men in the adjoining fifty square miles lying under that cloud base waiting to kill and be killed. No wonder it feels oppressive.'

He peered at Robson as they strolled towards the mess. 'Which one are you?' he asked. 'The one who fell foul of Callaghan?'

Robson's stomach muscles tautened. 'What do you mean?'

'Obviously you're not, or you wouldn't ask. Somebody ought to have warned him. Our Mr. Callaghan does not like scout pilots. They are a pet phobia of his.'

'It doesn't sound a suitable attitude for a man commanding a squadron,' Robson replied stiffly.

The other laughed. 'You've been talking to Archie Harris. I can recognize his lecture on Breeding for Command a mile off. Silly ass. There's nothing wrong with Callaghan, or the principle of promoting experienced men from the ranks. You'll soon find that out. And by Christ our new C.O. had to work for it. What's your name?'

Robson told him and in return found his new acquaintance was Tom Cobleigh from Exeter and accordingly known wherever he went as Uncle Tom. By the time they reached the mess he was aware that Uncle Tom was the oldest flying member of the Squadron, nearly thirty, married, two children, agent to a West Country estate, and that on and off he had been in France nearly three years, first with the infantry and then with this Squadron for the past eight months.

'And be careful what you say about me,' he added as

they entered the mess. 'I'll be your Flight Commander tomorrow. Temporarily. Now the Major has gone, Callaghan will have to stay at home most of the time. Wing don't like their Squadron Commanders getting involved in this fearfully dangerous fighting business. It plays hell with the paper work.'

There was no one in the bar apart from a group of four men. Robson asked Uncle Tom about this. He did not say so but it was in marked contrast to his previous Squadron.

'When you've flown eight nights out of ten you'll realize why. This night bombing is really too ridiculous for words. It plays hell with your social life. Come and meet our penguins. One advantage of not having to joust with the herd is that you can drink when and what you want.'

Uncle Tom and Robson joined the group by the bar. Robson wondered whether it was his imagination, or were they looking down their noses at him? Perhaps they were drinking with him because he was with Uncle Tom? Dick Garbutt, the Recording Officer, Robson had already met, and as R.O. he would know how Robson had arrived and why. A man with a heavily scarred face and pilot's wings on his chest over the M.C. ribbon, Robin Armitage, the Armament Officer, handed him a drink. Jordan, the Equipment Officer, pale, bespectacled, and a tall Scottish pilot whose name Robson did not catch, made up the group.

'I thought all R.F.C. Staff Officers were pilots,' Robson said to the Scot who was the Wing Colonel's pilot and had flown in from H.Q. that afternoon. The others laughed.

'Aye, laddie, so they are. An' wi' wings ootspread across their chests to prove it,' the Scot replied. 'Man, the Air Board personally selected me and went down on their bended knees. "Hamish," they said, "will ye no do your duty to King and Country. The Jairman we can cope wi';

the Colonel and the Jairman, No!" So, I fly the Colonel and the Brigadier about their lawful business. Nae mair than an aerial chauffeur. Thank God, he keeps the best stock o' malt whisky in France. Which is more than can be said for present company.'

He drained his glass and to assist in eliminating the Squadron's inferior stock had it refilled.

'Why are we graced with your Lord and Master?' Uncle Tom asked. 'Whatever it is, it will be unpleasant.'

'Aye, you wouldna expect a full-blown Colonel to turn out on a day like this to bring you good cheer. He'll be on about the Big Push, I expect. An' any squadron that flies across the Line i' daylight in Fees deserves all they get.'

'Do you really think the Hun will attack?' Armitage asked. 'Dammit, he's been winning the war for the last two years just by letting us attack him. I don't see what he has to gain.'

'Ach, don't be sich a fule, man. Passchendaele hurt him as much as us. But he can replace them, an' more, wi' his troops from the Rooshian front. It's no a guessing game now. We got a prisoner yesterday an' it's tomorrow. An' they'll be coming frae up there.' He swung round to point a finger at the north-east corner of the mess. 'San Quentin. Ach, man, he's nae choice at all. He has tae fight, or wait for the Yanks and the blockade to finish him off next year.'

'I don't disagree with you, Mac, but I can't see the logic of it. Why should he think he can break through now? We've tried it since '15. The French have tried it. Jerry himself tried at Verdun, and look what happened. A couple of miles of stinking mud changed hands and a million men lost. Why should it be different this time?'

'Ye ken why ye're no a pot-bellied general at H.Q., Dick. Ye're applying civilian logic to an illogical subject. War is no a subject for the use o' logic.'

'Bad time for Timmis to go,' Jordan said. 'This must be Barney's last chance to make a major's star stick to his epaulettes. He'll be driving us with a whip next. You bastards at H.Q. will get your pound of flesh out of this Squadron and a bit extra thrown in for good measure.'

'He's a hard man is Barney Callaghan,' the Scot agreed. 'This is the third time he has been made acting C.O. of a squadron. If ever a man desairved his majority and a D.S.O. yon's the man.'

'What have they got against him, Mac?' Armitage asked. 'He won't be the first man to come up from the ranks to command a squadron. There must be something murky in his copy book.'

'Well now, Mr. Armitage, that's something ye'd best ask the man himself,' the Scot replied coldly. 'It's nothing I'd be ashamed of. The man has more than earned it. He's been out longer than anyone else I know.'

'I think that is why he has a down on scout pilots,' Jordan said. 'He got his wings before McCudden did.'

'Aye, an' a Military Medal for acting as crow bait so that his Flight Commander could prove to the Squadron you could shoot down a Fokker with a B.E. An' that was in '15.'

'I dinna ken who to feel sorry for the most, gentlemen, you or the Jairmans. Barney'll have the bit between his teeth. If you fly more hours and drop more bombs than anyone else I'll no see him losing his Command. Not wi' this Wing Colonel. It was him and Barney that got that Fokker together.' The Scot stopped short as the door of the mess opened and McDonald entered.

'And isn't yon fella the one that was after taking on the Jairman Air Force on his own....'

McDonald walked across to the bar and was welcomed into the group by the Recording Officer.

'It's nice to have known ye, son,' the Scot said after shaking hands. 'Ye must be the only man to take a Fee o'er the Lines in daylight this year. I should send ye're mither a postcard tonight. She'll no be getting anither if ye try it again.'

Jordan fished in his pocket for a mis-shapen piece of metal. He gave it to McDonald.

'The lower starboard boom collapsed as they were wheeling your Fee into the shed. That had almost severed it.'

McDonald gulped his whisky and called for a refill.

'You can get your own back tonight,' Garbutt said. 'We came here in February to stop the Hun from Evreux raiding Paris and our rear areas. Since then we've bombed stations, goods yards, troops and transport, everything but that damned aerodrome. Don't you agree, Mac?'

The Scottish pilot shook his head. 'As ye should be fully aware by noo, Dick, H.Q. very seldom thinks the way mere mortals like you and me do. Maybe it's because it wouldna do if we thought they were human. So although ye have ma sympathy you're no likely to get any support. They have devious minds at H.Q. and here comes the most devious one of the lot.'

The Wing Colonel was tall and stooped, a long, narrow face crowned by close-cut blond hair parted in the middle. The monocle dangling from the button-hole of his right breast pocket swung gently to and fro as he walked across the room with Callaghan. While he waited for his gin and vermouth, McDonald and Harris were introduced and congratulated on their audacity in going over the Line in daylight, warned not to do it again and complimented on the information they had brought back. Then the mess servants left the room and the doors were shut.

'Gentlemen, during the coming days you are going to fight as you have never fought before,' the Colonel said screwing his monocle into place. Someone at the back let out a realistic groan and everyone laughed. 'Thank you. I'm not much good at speechifying but if it amuses you I have achieved something.

'The Hun is desperate. Our blockade is starving him, our battles last year have thinned his ranks and the coming summer will see ever-increasing American forces fighting alongside us. But now, thanks to the treachery of the Bolsheviks, the Boche can bring those forces from the east to the Western Front. This he has done. We are about to fight the biggest battle of the war. The fight of a mad dog gambling everything on forcing a victory before our growing power crushes him completely.

'You will, I am sure, bear yourselves gallantly. For we, and especially you, are not just the eyes of the Army but its shield in defence as in attack. Good luck, gentlemen.'

Releasing his monocle from his eye the Colonel raised his glass and drained it with a theatrical flourish. The others did the same. The Colonel moved round the group for a few minutes and then, bidding them all good night, stalked from the room with Callaghan at his heels.

' "Once more into the breach, dear friends." ' Dick Garbutt quoted. 'Do Wing Colonels have speech writers, Mac?'

'Ye know what Trenchard woulda' said. Aboot the same as he said to 59 Squadron when they lost six Harry Tates in one fight. "Go and do ye're work properly and give the Hun Hell." Ah, well, as a speech I find it grows on me—after a fashion and after a dram or two.'

The Recording Officer asked where they were going now in such a hurry that the pair of them could not stay to dinner. The Scot collected his flying jacket, helmet and gauntlets. He laid a bony finger against his nose and winked.

'We're going to see the Navy Fours up at Mons,' he replied, referring to a Royal Naval Air Service D.H.4 day bomber squadron.

'I'm no sure o' the quality of their cooking but they've a most superior brand of Scotch. And for why should we spend oor time wi' the lads on the night shift. Och, ye poor sinners . . .'

'Flamin' Fours,' Uncle Tom broke in. 'Gulping for breath and freezing to death for three hours at 20,000 with all the ambitious Huns in the neighbourhood hammering at you. What sort of a life is that.'

'Aye, laddie, but when they're doon they can drink the night awa'. That ye canna doo . . .'

'What do you really think about this big push of Jerry, Sir?' Callaghan asked the Colonel as they walked slowly back to the H.Q. R.E.8.

The Colonel giggled. It was a nervous affliction, as meaningless as another man's absent-minded scratching. His face was coldly serious as he said to Callaghan, 'I don't like it, Barney. I don't like it one iota. Everything is running against us. The Line is thinly held in places, too bloody thin. And you can trust Jerry to know exactly where those places are. We're not up to strength yet after last year. I don't see how we can be until the Yanks turn up. The French are worse than we are. I don't trust them an inch. Oh, they'll fight, all right. For Paris, for France, but not to help us.

'And Jerry is no fool. He knows that time is running out for him. Once the Yanks are here, once they've been blooded as we have and know the ropes, once all that happens he'll have to break. We must hold fast this year. If we do, you'll be home before midsummer next year, although I do hear that Haig is still optimistic about finishing it off this year.'

'I heard that last year, before Passchendaele.'

The Colonel glanced at his watch. A couple of mechanics materialized out of the gloom and stood by the engine of the R.E.8.

'In the meantime you've got to fly every hour you can. There's a whole army over there. Drop a bomb anywhere, you can't miss. I'm sorry I can't let you go for the Jerry airfield at Evreux. You can get your own back another night.'

'Eighteen F.E.s against an army?' Callaghan said. 'They were a joke in '16.'

'I know, I know, old chap. But you'll be getting Handley Pages soon—provided we get the engines, provided there are no more strikes, provided the blasted Navy doesn't pinch them. It can't be long now. Where the hell is Mac?'

The tall Scot loped towards them.

'I don't like men flying after they've been drinking,' Callaghan said. 'I'll take you, or I could get you a tender.'

'Rubbish. You've got more important things on hand. What we'll do is take one of your "pom-pom" Fees and I'll fly it. You can get someone to fly the R.E. over tomorrow. And don't forget, Barney, you're the Commanding Officer now. I can close my eyes to the occasional trip; no more than that.'

2

An hour and a half later Callaghan was talking to Robson. 'I want you where I can keep an eye on you. As you don't know the area we'll take the "pom-pom" and I'll go along as your gun layer. The bloody fools at H.Q. never look at the observer's name on the reports.'

They were standing by the F.E. that Robson had flown that afternoon. A shower of rain had washed clean the wings. It had gone now but raindrops glittered at the intersection of the streamlined R.A.F. wires that rigged the structure. In the flickering light of a petrol flare iridescent streaks of oil shimmered in a puddle.

'You saw what I did this afternoon,' Callaghan said as they leaned over the gunner's cockpit. There were about a dozen clips of shells in racks at the side, and the breech of the gun seemed absurdly massive in contrast to the plywood nacelle. The wired wings with their spindly booms swayed gently and creaked in the light evening breeze. 'I can elevate it five degrees either way,' Callaghan continued, pointing to the gun, 'but there's no traverse so you have to aim the nacelle at the target—just as you would your Sopwith bloody Camel. We'll go up around St. Quentin. Steer about forty-five degrees. With this thing you really need a railway engine or M.T. for a target. You can create more havoc with the Lewis gun on horse traffic.'

He looked up at the cloud base. 'Let's hope we can pick up the light from the firebox on a loco. We'll need it. The clouds will be too low to use flares.'

'Why?' Robson asked.

'Oh, for God's sake use your mother wit.' Callaghan snapped. 'You fly over the target, drop a flare and then turn to attack in the light. With the cloud at 500, and the turning speed of a barge like this old bus, the flare will be on the ground and out before you get round.'

The mechanic by the propeller called out, 'Switches off.'

Robson fingered the ignition switches. 'Switches off,' he confirmed. 'Petrol on. Suck in.'

The mechanic threw his weight at the propeller. The engine wheezed round sucking in petrol and air. Once, twice ... six times. The mechanic ducked clear of the booms.

'Switches on.'

Robson flicked the ignition switches down. 'Switches on,' he replied, and cranked the handle of the starting magneto. The engine coughed twice, spat a tongue of flame from the exhaust, and was silent.

'Switches off,' the mechanic called, cursing in an audible meaningless monotone.

'Relax, man, it's not going to bite you,' Callaghan snapped in Robson's ear. 'These water-cooled jobs are always pernickety after a spot of rain.'

'Switches on. Contact.'

Robson barked his knuckles as he twirled the magneto handle. The engine fired lumpily, first two cylinders, then three; the nacelle quivered and rocked as if alive. A sheet of flame sprang from the exhaust, and the shuddering that made Robson think the engine was jumping from its mounting died away to a smooth quiver as the engine ran on all six cylinders. He eased back the throttle.

They bounced and jiggled across to the far corner of the field, the superb long-stroke undercarriage of the F.E. doing its best to smooth out the farmland ruts.

Robson's gloved finger rattled the morse key controlling his identification lamp on the underside of the nacelle. Three petrol flares in a line across the aerodrome burst into yellow flame. Robson licked his lips as he opened the throttle smoothly, his ear straining for the stutter of a failing engine that would land them among the trees rushing towards them. The first flare went by under his wing. His booted feet were slow to correct. The F.E. was turning away from the flare. He pushed hard on the rudder pedal, easing the stick forward a little to get the tail up.

Not too much.

He remembered his instructor in the Home Defence Squadron. 'The F.E.2b, gentlemen, has the finest undercarriage of any aeroplane flying. There is no excuse for bad landings. But should you happen to perform one, then the engine—a quarter of a ton, give or take a pound or two, of best Scottish cast iron—will move smartly forward and occupy that part of your anatomy that usually houses your kidneys.'

But they were off before passing the last flare and sailed over the treetops with ample room. These F.E.s, Robson remembered, had 160 h.p. Beardmores. The one he had flown in the Home Defence Squadron had had a war-weary 120 h.p. engine.

A ragged trail of cloud whipped by, reddened by their exhaust flame. Callaghan punched him on the shoulder and signalled that they were high enough. The altimeter indicated 800 feet.

Now Robson had time to look around. The darkness was intense enough to be felt as he gingerly eased the big bi-plane on course for St. Quentin. As his vision improved he found he could see the horizon. Beneath him was a black desert with occasional pools of light. There was no sign of activity as they approached the scarred earth of the Front Line. Callaghan seemed to be able to see and even to know where they were because he kept issuing changes in direction. Robson's right shoulder began to feel sore from the repeated punching and his left leg muscles were complaining from having to hold on rudder to stop the F.E. from turning. He would have to get the rigger to cure that if he was going to continue flying this machine, he thought.

Something Callaghan called a 'lighthouse' slid beneath them, a flashing light continually morsing its recognition letter.

The clouds were higher near the Line and they got up to nearly a thousand feet. Robson fought off the onset of panic as the ground below was flooded with white light, but it was only a German parachute flare. Some sleepless machine-gunner searched for them, but the streaks of tracer climbed slowly towards the cloud well behind and to the left of them. Callaghan pointed out the lights and loom of St. Quentin and directed Robson to fly in a big loop round to the east and north in order to hit the railway line from Valenciennes and Le Cateau.

The weather was beginning to deteriorate now and the cloud was getting lower. A trailing shower of rain stung their faces and soaked the fur-lined collars of their flying suits. Robson wriggled his frozen toes in his flying boots, too nervous to stamp and yet afraid of losing all feeling on the rudder bar. A mile to the left a storm of fire surged up from the ground machine-guns firing tracer and slow-moving multi-coloured fire balls—flaming onions as they were called. A line of small flashes marched across the darkened earth. One of their number was dropping 25 lb. bombs. They turned towards the attack.

A second string of flashes triggered off an enormous explosion. A tongue of flame reached up towards the cloud and then settled down to a fierce fire on the ground. In the light reflected back from the low clouds two black F.E.s flew sedately round and round, and the observers could be seen leaning out of the front cockpits hosing the ground below with their Lewis guns. As they came on the scene a spear of tracer spitted one, but the F.E. seemed to continue unharmed, magically absorbing the bullets. Then it started to dive, the curve steepening as it flew slowly into the ground. The flame and the explosion came as a shock after that stately descent.

Callaghan shouted, pointing to the invisible gun position as lines of tracer came up from it seeking the second F.E. now sweeping in to revenge its colleague. The light of the fire was reflected on the wings tingeing them with pink.

Crack! Their F.E. bucked as Callaghan fired a long shot with the 'pom-pom' to distract the German gunners away from the illuminated bomber.

Robson suddenly realized that there was more than the reflection of the ground fire on the other F.E. A small snake of flame trailed away from the engine, and got brighter as the F.E. left the reflected glare for the safety of the surrounding darkness. The tracer followed it. Then, realizing that its work was done, switched to Robson who was watching the doomed bomber, oblivious of Callaghan or the tumult about him.

The F.E., now only a slow-moving flame in the darkness, turned sharply towards the Lines and began to descend. The explosion was like a bright yellow star in the light of which the F.E. came apart like a badly made toy. It was visible for a moment as the booms broke up and the nacelle came away from the wings, and then it became just an oily-red fire in a copse.

The instrument panel in front of Robson abruptly disintegrated into pieces of broken glass and metal, and another bullet ricocheted off the 'pom-pom' barrel and creased his arm. He was suddenly aware that they were flying slowly across the ground-fire not more than fifty feet above the tree-tops. Callaghan was punching his shoulder, and shouting. Every machine-gun in the German Army seemed to be firing at them.

His mind was a blank, incapable of instructing his limbs. They were sailing through a sea of flame. The wings were translucent red. He could see men running about on the ground below. The aircraft rocked in the blasts as the ammunition in the burning dump exploded. He hunched his shoulders together and huddled his body, contracting into the smallest possible target, and in that position he flew out into the cover of darkness.

Slowly the instincts implanted by his training asserted themselves. He opened the throttle gingerly and picked up speed. Not before time, for the F.E. was shuddering on the brink of a stall. Tentatively he tried the controls. Then he turned to Callaghan for instructions, hoping that the Squadron Commander would know where they were and where they should go.

He did. He was still going to St. Quentin and the railway line.

'It'll be worse than that at St. Quentin,' Callaghan shouted. 'You need more speed. Get up to cloudbase level and dive in when I tell you. At full throttle.'

Robson's eyes were getting used to the darkness again. There was a long, straight road running east and west towards the darkened mass of St. Quentin. Mont D'Origny Road, Callaghan shouted to him. It was packed with transport, nose to tail. But as they were about to turn along it a line of flashes showed that another F.E. was working its way along the road with 25 lb. bombs. Ahead they could see the railway line from Le Cateau and the mist steaming up from the marsh by the St. Quentin Canal.

It was not only mist. A fire-box door opened for a moment to redden a plume of steam and, directed by Callaghan, Robson pushed the nose down and headed in a shallow dive towards the oncoming train. But his frozen feet seemed unable to stop the nose from swinging from one side of the track to the other. Callaghan's first bursts missed the engine but the third hit a wagon in the middle of the train. A couple of machine-guns opened up as they swept along the long line of coaches. A couple of bullets clanged into the massive crank-case of the Beardmore.

They circled and came in again at forty-five degrees to the train. Callaghan was scoring hits now. He hit a coach —making the train split into two—then he hit the track in front of the locomotive. Finally he scored on the train's boiler so that they flew through a great plume of steam.

Again they went around to attack the stationary train. But after one 'pom-pom' shell had blown sparks from the embankment the big gun fell silent leaving only the fixed Lewis gun. The 'pom-pom' was jammed.

Still Callaghan would not go home. He made Robson fly in a huge figure-of-eight a mile long centred on the town. They dodged machine-gun fire and flaming onions. Occasionally, for no reason that Robson could see, Callaghan told him to fire the Lewis into the darkness and the mist that was soaking up the horizon. Soon he was too cold, too frightened and too bewildered to care what Callaghan was doing. There were no instruments functioning. He had no idea whether the engine or the radiator had been damaged and his befuddled mind did not appreciate the menace of the mist coming up from the sodden earth. The gale whistling through the shattered windscreen had so numbed his face that, flying through the occasional shower of rain, he could sense the impact of the rain but could feel no pain.

His flying grew more and more ragged as the cold crept up from his feet and down into his chest. A steeple poked out of the mist leaning over at an angle. It took him an age to recognize that the steeple was vertical and that the F.E. was not. The mist-shrouded tree-tops reached up for them as he struggled with the controls to pull the bomber out of a spiral dive.

Full right aileron, right rudder, ease back on the stick.

The wires were whistling as the speed built up. He realized he had over-corrected. The nose pointed up into the darkness, and noise in the wires had died away. The whole aircraft shuddered on the brink of a stall as he heaved the nose down again. The exertion of manhandling the heavy aeroplane brought him back to life. Slowly he got the F.E. back into level flight. He was sweating, and could feel the sweat freeze on his face. Callaghan pointed to the west.

It was time to go home. The compass was intact, but spinning wildly. Callaghan shouted a course to steer. Robson had no idea how he knew. Slowly, in fits and starts, holding the aeroplane steady until the compass settled down, he was able to edge round on to a course of 270 degrees—due west.

The mist was showing up the ground contours, lying like water in every dip. The patches of greyness outlined trees, silhouetted a village and lay in low-lying meadows like a pond. Ahead of them he saw the loom of a light flashing, only the glow of it illuminating the mist.

Callaghan shouted an identification letter to him, as the aerial lighthouse appeared. Gingerly, Robson eased round on course for their aerodrome and slowly began to realize that sooner or later he would have to grope through that mist and find the ground—and the numbness brought on by cold was replaced with terror. In his imagination he saw the woods around the aerodrome, the columns of poplars guarding the road on the south side, and the blackened gash in the copse to the west where someone had crashed and set the trees alight. He felt sick.

But the aerodrome was on high ground, and fairly well drained, and the mist was thinner. When Robson flew over, morsing his identification letter on the light beneath the nacelle he had no difficulty in seeing the line of flares as they were lighted.

He flew over the aerodrome, losing height slowly, then

turned to the left in a wide sweep which was intended to bring him back to the downwind end of the flare path. But once he had turned, the flares were no longer visible, only the flat top of the mist lit by an internal glow.

After his second attempt at finding the flare path a red rocked soared up out of the mist. Callaghan leaned over towards him. He had taken off his flying helmet and now he plucked off Robson's.

'Do as I tell you,' he shouted. Robson's eyes began to water now they were unprotected from the slipstream.

'Use your compass. Get a bearing on the flarepath.'

They flew over the aerodrome again. The flares were coming up now at regular intervals of about a minute. Robson huddled down in the cockpit, watching his compass, drawing confidence from the big frame of Callaghan leaning over him.

'Right. Make a wide turn. Don't let your compass spin. Slowly, damn you ... Get well down wind of the field ... Line up on the red flares ... Check your compass ... Make sure you are on the right heading ... Throttle back.'

The mist came up to meet them, swirling, the diffused glow from the flares thickening and thinning like something alive. A patch of trees was suddenly revealed and as suddenly fell behind them. A road appeared, then some houses. The Very lights, fired from the aerodrome, came nearer, red fireworks soaring up through the greyness, falling, reddening the mist, disappearing.

'Throttle back ... Keep it straight ... Hold it there ... Let her sink. And say your prayers, sonny.'

Trembling with fear and cold Robson froze on the controls as the F.E. sank slowly into the mist. The greyness turning to darkness ... To grass. A flare flashed past. They hit the ground with a shattering crash, the oleo legs on the undercarriage squealing and clattering. They were airborne again, bounced back ten feet into the air.

'Cut that bloody throttle,' Callaghan screamed, thumping Robson's left shoulder. The engine noise died away. They hit the ground again. And again. The wheels knocked a flare pot spinning starting a miniature grass fire behind them. But they were down. Over to the right the hangars blazed with light. It did not seem possible that they had not seen them.

'You ought to say a bloody prayer,' Callaghan shouted, 'anything else but a Fee would have gone arse over tip.'

'I'm sorry, Sir,' Robson said.

'Save your breath. You'll learn. And you ought to know the airman's motto by now. If you can walk away from it it's a good landing; if the aeroplane is the right way up it's excellent.'

The mechanics were waiting for them by the hangar. Together, the four of them walked round the aeroplane watching the steam boil off the radiator. A bullet had punctured a header tank. There were holes in the wings. One of the rigging wires on the left-hand boom was broken and something in the undercarriage had been strained by that landing.

'Better make your report out now, Robson,' Callaghan said as they walked towards his office. 'There'll be no more flying tonight.' He sounded angry, as if he regretted this fact. The Flight Sergeant had just told him that, in addition to the two aircraft lost in the attack on the ammunition dump, another two had landed further north. One of them had a badly wounded observer. The mechanics were in for a long night.

'Report, Sir? I don't know where we've been or what ... I thought you ...'

'Robson, you are a Second Lieutenant in His Majesty's Army in the Field. There's a war on. There'll be a big battle soon. You've been fifty miles into the enemy's territory. Don't you think our H.Q. should know what you have seen?'

Callaghan pushed the report form in front of Robson

and went on talking while he sat behind his desk going through a pile of papers.

'Oh for God's sake, Robson, haven't you ever filled a report in before? Squadron number first, then F.E.2b, number A 854.

'We crossed the line, here, just north of Stancourt. Quote the map reference number. Did you see the troops moving out of the village into the Line? Mention that. Then the dump went up here. Map reference again. That's where Harvey and Johnson got hit...'

Callaghan stopped talking to light a cigarette. He glared at Robson through a haze of smoke. Only his red-rimmed eyes and his smoke-blackened face betrayed the fact that they had just landed. His black hair had been smoothed back into place and his tie was straight and the old tunic pulled back into shape.

Robson felt ghastly. He groped for a grubby handkerchief to wipe his eyes as Callaghan continued, 'You young bastards take the biscuit. You are here to take part in a war not to act the fool. We have few enough machines to spare without people like Harvey and Johnson getting themselves killed. We are night bombers, depending on darkness for safety. Get a fire like tonight and you might as well try attacking in daylight. Never fly straight and level. And never, never lose your head and go in to get your revenge. It didn't do Harvey any good for Johnson to get himself killed...'

Suddenly Robson remembered Harvey, a tall good-looking boy with a wisp of blond moustache and an enormous curved pipe. He was one of those who had complained loudly earlier in the evening in the mess because they had not been allowed to attack Evreux aerodrome in revenge for the raid of the previous night.

'...The road from Mont D'Origny, you must have seen that. Motorized transport nose-to-tail going into St. Quentin ... Then the trains. We made a mistake attacking that troop train. Twenty coaches, put that down. We should have had a go at the goods train in front. It might have been carrying ammo. Or gas. I've a fancy to turn some of Jerry's gas on his own troops. Did you see the troops in the station? Put it down ...'

On and on he went while Robson wondered whether or not they had been on the same flight.

When, eventually, Callaghan dismissed him he walked back to the mess with Garbutt, the Recording Officer, leaving Callaghan to his paper work. Garbutt explained why Callaghan had insisted on spending so long over St. Quentin without bombs and with the 'pom-pom' out of action. Nobody slept or did any work while a bomber was overhead. Callaghan had a theory that if you could keep a succession of single bombers flying round a town dropping the odd bomb at random they would do more harm to Jerry than a successful mass raid.

There was a party working up in the mess. It was not often, Garbutt said, that they stopped flying early enough to get a drink, and with a shock Robson realized that it was only ten o'clock.

Uncle Tom Cobleigh looked at him for a moment and then thrust a glass of champagne into his hand.

'You don't look like a whisky drinker,' he said. 'And if you intend to stay with us for long you'd better keep that way. This stuff is cheaper and you'll feel better in the morning. Knock it back quickly and get out of that flying gear. We have visitors and the Mess President is glowering at you. It's your face. Wash it, it's filthy.'

'What happened to McDonald?' Robson asked. 'I don't see him.'

'He's all right. They got lost. It is one of our Mr. Harris' failings, not knowing quite where he is. Not that he could be blamed on a night like this. They crossed the Line at the wrong place, flew slap over some machine-gun nests and got a severe puncture in the engine room. They only just managed to get back across the Lines before the pistons parted company with the connecting rods. The French are driving them back.'

Robson had no real desire for a party. His eyelids seemed as heavy as lead and he was shivering all over. He took off his flying suit and fur-lined boots, washed and lay down on his bed, tired to his innermost fibre but completely unable to sleep.

The room was lit by a paraffin lamp suspended from the ceiling. The swaying of the lamp, the ever-changing flame on the wick, threw a golden light that moved slowly —flickering like a fire, like a red glare reflecting from the clouds, turning night into day. Night bombers into day bombers, Robson thought drowsily.

Aeroplanes silhouetted against the fire-lit clouds, old pushers, F.E.2b aeroplanes pushed along by clattering six-cylinder Beardmores at eighty miles an hour. Engines developed from a 1912 German model in a 1914 design aeroplane. Flying straight, diving gently, there wasn't room to do anything else—diving at eighty-five miles per hour towards the machine-gun posts so positioned that at least one of them could get in a no-deflection shot. You were threaded into a line of tracer, pretty, flickering lights, glittering specks of lead and steel and copper. You were skewered on a rod of iron and like a toy you slipped down to the bottom and like a toy you fell apart. Or burned. Leaving nothing. A wing fluttering leaf-like, moth-like, bearing your own candle of flame. Inflammable dope, dry linen soaked in oil. Cellulose acetate rots the pretty girls. Their teeth drop out. Burns. The wing, dope-soaked, burns. Then there's nothing, nothing but fine grey wood-ash coating the mist-dampened groundings. And a fire; oily, red, consuming the cast iron and aluminium; buckling the polished copperwater jacket of your 160 h.p. Austro-Daimler Beardmore.

'Robson, Robbo, quit squawkin', you'll put the fear o' the Lord into Jerry. Come on, wake up, feller. There are girls in the mess. Real live genuine female-type girls...'

Robson opened his eyes and focused them with difficulty. McDonald was darting about the room. A piece of plaster, the lint pink with dried blood, was stuck across the bridge of his nose. He had a bruise the size of an apple on the right side of his forehead.

'What happened to you?' Robson asked. He felt terrible. His mouth tasted foul and a hammering pain in his forehead threatened to burst his temples. He was sweating and his mind was still half-merged in his nightmare of being burnt alive in the air.

'That goddamned idiot, Harris. You'd reckon he'd know his way around after a month. Never again. From this day forth, Mrs. McDonald's boy will do his own navigating. We flew right over the most goddamned heap of machine-guns in the whole of the German Army. I was scared, I can tell you.'

He did not look scared, Robson thought, as he skipped about the room leaving a trail of discarded garments.

'Didn't cha' hear what I said, feller?' McDonald squatted at the side of Robson's bed, his clean tunic open, knotting a fresh tie. 'There are women in the mess. Girls, you remember, are fascinating things shaped like this.' He sketched an hour glass shape with his hands. 'Some ambulance-driving outfit working with the French. Ain't that just like the goddamned French to get our women to drive their ambulances.'

3

Callaghan and Garbutt joined the party just after Robson and McDonald got there. Callaghan—there had been a signal from H.Q. authorizing him to put up the crown that signified his majority—had just completed his office work. His report on the night's operations had gone off to H.Q. with the pilots' reports. Three new aircraft and new air crew had been indented for to replace those lost —two pilots and two observers, and replacements for the wounded. He had written the letters of condolence by hand in the neat copperplate handwriting hammered into him by the Army's schoolmasters. 'The Air Board can send the news by telegram,' he had once said to Garbutt, 'but no damned clerk is going to type my letters to the next-of-kin. And don't tell me I sound like an Army Manual. Next-of-kin sounds better than parent. Parent better than father and mother. Thank God, they weren't married.'

'Next-of-kin is a useful euphemism,' Garbutt had murmured. 'Why not say they've passed over—or gone before?'

Callaghan had spent an hour with Flight Sergeant Watt. There were four engines to be replaced, and two radiator blocks to be replaced including one from the 'pom-pom' aircraft. One of 'B' Flight's aircraft had a main spar severed in the bottom port wing just outboard of the booms, and 'Mimi' needed a new instrument panel. The engine would have to come out anyway. Boiling away all the water was not likely to have improved it.

Out of his eighteen aeroplanes Callaghan would be lucky to have ten by the following evening.

'How did you get on with the new man, the wrong Robson?' Garbutt asked as he spotted Robson, McDonald and Harris—his left arm in a sling—approaching the bar. 'You kept the poor sod out long enough.'

'I should send him home before he kills himself and some poor bloody observer. But I'm damned if I will. He's so damned scared he can't see where he's going and he handles the controls like a pump handle.'

'Aren't they all like that when they first come out?'

'Maybe. But I'm damned if I'm going to make it easy for Robson. There are too many like him at home. Killing pupils they're too scared to teach properly and knocking off young women in the bars at night with their talk about wounded heroes fresh from the Front.'

'I don't think Robson is like that.'

'No I don't suppose he is. Now. Give him a month at home and he will be. What chance has he got to be anything different? He's been out here flying Sopwith Camels and night bombing on our mighty battle plane, the F.E.2b. Unless he puts a bloody great sign on his chest, "Sent home with cold feet", he'd have to play the returned warrior. Better to keep him here until he gets himself killed. Which shouldn't be long.'

> 'Après la guerre finie,
> Soldat Anglais parti;
> Mam'selle Fransay boko pleurry
> Après la guerre finie.
> Après la guerre finie,
> Soldat Anglais parti
> Mademoiselle in the family way
> Après la guerre finie.'

McDonald was singing as they lurched through the darkness, the mist wetting them as much as though it was raining. Harris, his tie and collar undone, lay on one of the mess doors carried by Robson and McDonald under the supervision of Uncle Tom.

'Oh, my aching back. Let's have a break,' McDonald said, 'you big fat Limey bastard.' He kicked the door lightly. 'First you get me lost, then you get me shot down. I carry you out of a cocksucking trench and now I carry you home. What a bloody observer.'

'I thought one was not supposed to drink after being wounded,' Robson said.

'That's exactly when I would want a drink,' Uncle Tom said.

'That's why he said he was drinking soft drinks—champagne,' McDonald said. 'What do we do tomorrow, Uncle Tom?'

'Today,' Cobleigh corrected him. 'At oh nine thirty hours, you two are on a funeral party. The chaps who got it the other night. New arrivals always finish up at funerals. Teaches them to mind their P's and Q's, and gives them respect for their elders. "A" Flight, by numbers. One, grasp the door. Two, lift. Wait for it. On the word of command. Sl-ow march.'

Uncle Tom cupped his hands and blew a passable rendering of the Last Post as the other two staggered on with the inanimate Harris.

'But,' McDonald said firmly, 'Lieutenants Robson and McDonald, pride of the youth of the Old Countree and her Dominions overseas, have a date for lunch.'

'Impossible. No women at funerals, and you can't have a date without girls.' Cobleigh continued his rendering of the Last Post, 'Ta, ta-a-a.'

McDonald's foot slipped on the greasy turf as they reached their hut. He dropped his end of the door and shot Harris head over heels onto the ground. Harris stood up holding his hand to his head in a statuesque pose.

'You have no respect, you ignorant colonial peasant, for the sick and wounded.' He brushed the dirt from his tunic with his good hand and turned into the doorway. 'I shall walk the remainder of the way,' he added. 'There are others out there. Their need is greater than mine.'

McDonald threw a clod of earth at Harris' retreating back and, sitting on the doorstep, pulled a bottle of champagne from his tunic. He peeled off the foil cap, and levered out the cork with his thumbs. 'I give you a toast: Mesdames Sorensen and Hart of the Lafeyette Ambulance Corps, with whom, old chap'—he waggled a finger at Uncle Tom—'we shall lunch tomorrow, funeral or no funeral.'

A bright, wavering light pierced the mist from the direction of the Line. A second or so later the concussion and the noise hit them. A rumble like a million kettle drums rattled the window panes.

'Jesus H. Christ,' McDonald said, the champagne frothing unheeded over his hand.

'Poor bastards,' Uncle Tom said. 'The big push is on. I wouldn't count on that lunch. And you're spilling good champagne.'

The sun was still trying to pierce the mist as Robson and McDonald walked towards the *estaminet* that stood at the Roye-Noyon crossroad.

It had been a dispiriting morning. Two chaplains had arrived by tender from Wing H.Q., one Church of England, the other Roman Catholic. The bodies of the men killed in the air raid and that of an observer who had died from wounds the previous night, had been segregated into two heaps on the back of a lorry. The mist had wrapped itself around them—bodies, priests and firing party—in one self-contained group by the graveside. Globules of water, condensed from the fog, stood on the greatcoats of the living while the coffins containing the dead had been lowered into the ground. And in the background was the constant rumble of the guns firing in the battle to the east.

The mist coiled among the trees and conspired to increase their unease, now dampening the noise and then, by a trick of the wind, bringing it nearer so that some of the men, straining to distinguish whether or not the battle was coming closer, had started at the rattle of rifle bolts from the firing party. As soon as the bodies were in the ground, and the last hasty words mumbled over them, the chaplains had departed in their Crossley for the doubtful safety of Wing Headquarters.

Now, McDonald produced a silver flask cased in leather, and handed it to Robson. It was like drinking dynamite, cold liquid explosive that ignited in the stomach and flashed a train of fire up into the throat.

'That's how I figured it would be,' McDonald said as he watched Robson coughing and spluttering. Then he drank —with the same results.

The village clustered round the crossroads was dirty in the way that only a French village could be but there were no hens pecking round the cottages. The traffic that had rolled up and down the long straight road had taught the villagers the fate of stray food in the presence of armies.

But the *estaminet* was clean enough and the presence of half-a-dozen French Artillery Officers in blue uniform emphasized that the aerodrome was in a French Army Area. The two pilots had just decided, after a second glass of rough, red wine, that the new German offensive had cost them a lunch with the two drivers when a Ford Model-T ambulance 'tuf-tuffed' into the yard.

'Shan't be able to linger, I'm afraid,' one of them said as they wriggled out of greatcoats and unwound voluminous scarves, stamping their feet in front of the fire like a couple of coachmen from an earlier era. 'This damned mist, it's worse than rain. 'Scuse our language, I'm afraid we swear like men now.'

By now the two girls were unwrapped. They wore khaki uniforms cut like that of a British Army Officer with khaki skirts down to mid-calf, and shirts and ties of the same colour. Small Red Cross cloth badges were stitched on their upper arms. Although the uniforms were clean and pressed they bore the marks of long service. McDonald did the introductions: Mamie Sorensen from Oatesville, North Dakota—practically next door to Moose River Springs, he assured Robson, give or take a border and five or six hundred miles—and Madelaine Hart, of Hampshire, England. Madelaine, the elder, a brunette in marked contrast to the blonde Swedish features of Mamie, was doing the talking.

'We have to be back by one o'clock,' she said, 'ready to move off sharpish. Jerry has broken through south of St. Quentin and unless this fog lifts so that you boys can have a crack at him he'll come a long way.'

One of the Artillery Officers asked something in French. Robson thought he was asking about the German attack. Madelaine told what she knew. He shrugged his shoulders philosophically at her reply and called for another bottle of wine.

'Food and wine, *mes enfants*, and *vite*,' Madelaine said. 'And if you two have ordered egg and chips I shall scream the house down.'

'I like egg and chips,' Mamie said.

'But when she says eggs, she means a half-a-dozen to start,' Madelaine replied.

Robson laughed. It seemed to be the first funny thing that he had heard since he landed in France. It seemed unbelievable that he should be sitting next to a girl who, despite her uniform and command of French, might have stopped off at a country pub after a day's hunting. The obvious envy of the French Officers helped, and the rumble of the guns counterpointing the clatter of traffic outside intensified the element of absurdity. The lunch he had been dreading turned into an enjoyable party. Even the weather joined in because as they finished their trout and prepared to tackle a *coq au vin* the sun finally broke through the mist and flooded their table by the window with warmth and light.

There was something familiar about the two girls and lunch was nearly over before he recognized it. Mamie Sorensen was telling them how they had disposed of an unpopular senior member of their group, leaving the unfortunate woman stranded with an unserviceable car in the rain on a road about to be swept by the routine artillery strafe when Robson remembered and recognized the attitude. It was like being back in the mess on the Camel Squadron listening to the old hands—the ones with three months' service at the Front. There was the same calm indifference to the pettiness of seniority, the confidence of men who had fought their battle with fear and, having won, had lost their respect for appointed authority. These girls too had been through their baptism of fire. For two years now they had ferried wounded up and down the roads of France.

They talked lightly about the reasons that had brought them to this place in France, so lightly that Robson was certain each one hid deeper feelings than circumstances allowed them to show. No one within firing range of the Lines talked about patriotism or the need to be of service. They were devalued words, robbed of their dignity by those at home who could use them without risk.

Mamie Sorensen, so she told them, had followed a fiancé out and discovered that the world outside a small American town had a greater selection of men from which to choose. And seeing them melt away on the Somme, like a summer ice on the prairie, she had found it impossible to return. She swore like a man and laughed to hide the tears that threatened to dampen the party.

Madelaine, half French herself, had watched her husband go and had had him exchanged for a War Office telegram and a letter of condolence from the King after the first Ypres. Then, like Mamie, she had entertained the succeeding victims until she revolted. It was, she said, a case of either chauffeuring an ambulance and paying for the privilege, or making shells for thirty bob a week. And there were women who needed the thirty bob.

All too soon their hour of grace came to an end. They drained the wine and paid the bill.

'We must do this again, sometime,' Robson said to Madelaine as they walked to the ambulance. McDonald and Mamie Sorensen were some way ahead talking about the delights of the North American Midwest.

Madelaine held him back, putting her hand on his arm.

'I'm glad you enjoyed it, Christopher. I did too.' Robson realized how long it was since anyone had used his Christian name.

'I heard them talking about you in the mess last night. You've had a rough time.' The pressure of her hand increased as he stiffened. 'No, let me finish. I know what you are going through. I was the same, and since then I've seen a lot of girls crack and go home. It doesn't do any good. Going home, I mean, even if you can honourably do so. You have to go on living with yourself.'

He kicked a pebble, moodily reluctant to be dragged back from the present to the future.

'You know how it is if you heard them talking. Our C.O. thinks I am yellow. Perhaps he is right. But he will not give me a chance. One more slip and he'll have me sent home.'

'You must do what I did. There's one emotion that is stronger than fear. You have to learn to hate.'

'What, believe all the propaganda that gets fed to people back home. The baby-stabbing Boche. What do you think I am, Madelaine?'

'No, that's no good. You can't hate a nation, not well enough to overcome fear. You can't hate something abstract. It has to be some one, a man you can see and touch.

But not too close. You go and talk to the men in the trenches. To them the Germans are only soldiers like themselves condemned to live in mud and squalor. They hate the men who don't have to live in the Line—they hate the Staff. You might try that Squadron Commander of yours.'

'Callaghan? Don't be silly. My God, if anyone is entitled to despise someone like me, he is.'

Madelaine shrugged. 'Just remember he is going to get you killed or crucified. He hates your guts. You have to do the same.'

They paused by the ambulance. Mamie was already at the wheel. McDonald was cranking the engine.

Robson smiled at her. 'You might be right. I'll try it.'

A dozen D.H.4a, day bombers, flew over a couple of thousand feet up, flying east, noses cocked skywards as they struggled to gain the altitude that might delay their interception by fighters. Robson shuddered, imagining himself crouched in one of those cockpits watching dials on the instrument panel and the wing tips of his neighbour and listening for the change in engine note that would indicate the engine defect that would make him abandon the flight.

They flew on but he still heard the noise of their engines and felt the fear they took with them.

Madelaine kissed him on the cheek and broke his reverie.

'Hate him,' she whispered. McDonald had got the engine running. 'Hate him. Make yourself survive to spite him. But remember that hate is corrosive stuff. It can kill what it is preserving. Keep it in the back of your mind that this is something you are doing deliberately. It's a lifebelt—and when you can swim you can throw it away. God speed, Christopher.'

She bent down and kissed him again, on the lips this time, and the Ford chugged away.

They set off to walk back to the aerodrome, and McDonald said, 'I wonder what that bastard Callaghan has got lined up for us tonight.'

4

The tender had just arrived from the Pool with replacement pilots and observers when they got back to the aerodrome. A small group of newcomers, conspicuous in their new uniforms stood outside Callaghan's office watching the activities with half-concealed eagerness. A couple of re-engined F.E.s stood outside one of the hangars having their new engines run up, while a group of mechanics swarmed over a new aeroplane, as conspicuous with its freshly doped surfaces as the newcomers by the C.O.'s office. Robson and McDonald, with the assurance of twenty-four hours in the Squadron, stopped Flight Sergeant Watt and asked him who was getting the new aeroplane.

The Flight Sergeant scowled at them. 'None of ye, Sir, if I'm having my way. I wouldna let one of my officers fly a pool machine till it's been checked over to ma satisfaction. Man, if you knew what I know about them Pool mechanics ye wouldna touch yon thing wi' a barge pole. Mebbe tomorrow night—if we ha' the time. By the way, Sir, Major Callaghan was after the pair o' ye. I'm thinking it might be wise if he found ye shortly. Ye ken what I mean.'

Self-consciously they pushed their way through the new arrivals, into the office. Garbutt rolled his eyes at them and winced in mock terror.

'For God's sake, boys, don't start him off. Once he starts shouting, those lads outside are likely to scatter all over France.'

Inside the office, Callaghan and a clerk were working on a large wall map of the area. A piece of string had been coloured in half-inch alternate bands with red ink and they were pinning it in place. It bulged ominously westwards away from St. Quentin.

'Well, don't let me interfere with your efforts at entertaining our Allies,' Callaghan said as they saluted. 'That Ambulance Unit works with the French Army. Let them entertain their own women. If you two could spare me a little of your time I've got a job for you.'

Robson began to stutter an explanation. They had had permission to go off to the *estaminet*. But Callaghan cut him short.

'If I remember rightly, Mr. Robson, your multifarious career has included flying an R.E.8.'

Robson nodded.

'Good. I want all the aeroplanes I can get, and Watt is crying his eyes out at the thought of using the replacement we got before he has torn it apart and put it together again. The Wing Commander decided to take our other "pom-pom" aircraft the other night. He left it up at Mons. Perhaps he didn't like flying in the rain. Or that Scotch Soak he calls his pilot took on too much Navy rum. Take McDonald over there in the R.E. and bring it back, without stopping for Naval hospitality. I don't believe in mixing booze and flying. Understand? I want you back here before dark. Well, what the hell are you waiting for—a medal?'

Then as they turned to go, both of them trying to squeeze through the door together, he called to them, 'Don't forget you need ballast for solo flying in both the F.E. and the R.E. And, Robson, remember that is the Wing Commander's personal aeroplane. He'll be bloody cross if you bend it but not half so bloody cross as me. So no bloody skylarking.'

'Skylarking,' McDonald said. 'In a Harry Tate. I tell you, Robbo, that man has got a queer sense of humour.'

McDonald, helmet in hand, gazed sadly at the odd-looking aeroplane in which they were about to fly north. Robson walked round it as an instructor had once told him to. He was not sure what he was looking for but it put off the moment when he had to fly it. He remembered the stories he had heard about them. The first squadron to fly it had lost so many men in accidents that they had eagerly reverted to the almost defenceless B.E. Then there was the instruction he had read somewhere that on no account was the observer to stand up while the R.E. was gliding in to land, because the extra air resistance of the man's body could precipitate a spin. It was known too, that the petrol tank would split in the inevitable crash and pour petrol over the red-hot air-cooled cylinders...

But he had flown one once. For three-quarters of an hour.

He nodded to the mechanic by the propeller who was shuffling his feet, eager to get back to the hangar and the work that was waiting for him. Until it was finished he was on duty.

'Have you got the map, Frank?' he asked McDonald.

'Yeah, not that we should need it. It's about twenty miles. We'll steer due north until we hit the Amiens–St. Quentin Road. Can't miss that. Then fly along the road until we hit it.'

'All right, but you watch out. I've no desire to fly this thing over St. Quentin in daylight. They say the service in Jerry's P.O.W. camps is shocking.'

'Yeah. We've no guns either,' McDonald said ruefully.

Robson settled himself in the strange cockpit trying to remember what it had been like three months earlier. He raised his thumb to the mechanic.

'Switches off. Petrol on. Suck in.'

The mechanic began to pull the big four-bladed propeller round. In front of him Robson saw the exposed tappets depressing the valves and releasing them, heard the engine wheeze as it sucked in petrol and air.

'Switches on. Contact.'

They flew north at a thousand feet. McDonald was in his element, startling Robson time and again as he spotted aircraft, calling out a warning and then identifying them as friendlies, mostly before Robson had even seen them. They were nearly all Camels and S.E.s flying east to the battle. The S.E.s climbing, the Camels low down to attack the advancing Germans on the ground. A squadron of D.H.s went over already 5,000 feet higher, sixteen of them tucked up tightly in a fighting formation. Once, three R.E.s laden with 25 lb. bombs under the lower wing, came over to investigate the stranger flying north. Everyone else was either heading for the Line or returning to re-arm.

As they flew on, even Robson began to relax. The sun shone through scattered clouds. At cruising speed the plane rattled along, slightly nose down like all its type but without requiring any attention other than slight pressure on the rudder. Robson had no intention of veering off to the east.

As it happened, he had over-corrected the tendency to turn to the right or else the wind had freshened because they hit the long straight road further west than they had intended.

McDonald shouted the name of a village to him but Robson did not understand the Canadian's French. And looking at the shattered remains surrounded by a sea of old shell holes he doubted McDonald's navigation. It was about here, he thought, that the old Front Line ran at the beginning of the Battle of the Somme in '16. He shuddered. He guessed that they were well to the west of where they should have hit the road.

They were flying east now with the wind behind them, racing up the right hand side of the road as they dropped down to 500 feet. Below them the road was thronged with troops and transport moving up to the Line and a sparse line of ambulances, red crosses painted on the canvas hoods, were heading back to the Base Hospital.

Something flared ahead of them, attracting Robson's attention.

'Sausage—Observation balloon,' MacDonald bawled. 'Hope it was one of theirs.'

In that moment they had flown into a different country. The once-crowded road became abruptly empty except for an occasional ambulance or car. A flash of flame registered in the corner of Robson's eye. A gun battery. Hastily he edged the R.E. over towards the road out of its line of fire.

McDonald thumped him on the back and pointed over to the left. Burning buildings, a plume of black oily smoke. Cockades: red, white and blue-ringed aeroplane wings stacked in a pile. A couple of engineless and wingless fuselages stood together like plucked chickens. It was a dump of broken aeroplanes. Beside the blazing hangar Robson saw a familiar black shape. It was the all-black 'pom-pom' F.E. They had arrived. He throttled back and dived, keeping their speed well up as he sensed McDonald dodging from one side of the rear cockpit to the other.

'Where the hell have they all gone?' the Canadian shouted.

Apart from the wreckage and the F.E. beside the burning hangar there were no aeroplanes visible. Even more strange there were no men about. No mechanics came out of the hangars to see if it was one of their aeroplanes that had returned or to stare in curiosity at the stranger.

McDonald pointed to the hangars again. 'Look at those holes. They've been bombed.'

They saw a Crossley tender turn off the road into the aerodrome and stop. Four men in naval uniform got out and turned towards the circling R.E. and began waving their arms.

'Somebody is glad to see us,' Robson said as he straightened the R.E. and slowed down to glide in to land. 'Sit down,' he shouted to McDonald, remembering the stalling habits of the R.E.

Three of the men were back in the tender. It began to move, circling round to run alongside the R.E. when it landed, Robson guessed. He could see the fourth man through the flickering blades of the propeller, running, waving both arms in a swinging motion as though he was doing physical jerks. Robson wished he would move further over. The man had more confidence than he had in his ability to keep the R.E. straight. In fact the man seemed determined to run into them. At the last moment as they whistled in over the hedge the man threw himself flat on his face. Robson began edging the stick back, suddenly aware that he had come in much too flat, and the peculiar shape of the Harry Tate's fuselage meant that the nose should have been pointing much higher. The field looked too small. He put his hand on the throttle ready to go round again. The R.E. showed no sign of settling.

A geyser of mud, stones and grass erupted beyond his left wingtip, buffeting the aeroplane. Another rose straight in front of him. A stone skittered along the cowling and bounced off the windscreen over his head. And now the R.E. bucked sideways as there was an explosion on the right. Another to the left blew it straight. One wheel touched and they swung to the left, bounced back into the air. They were heading straight for the burning hangars.

'Get out of here! Hit the throttle,' McDonald roared. 'It's shell fire. Jerry is shelling the goddam aerodrome. Hit it, Robbo.'

Mechanically Robson obeyed, pushing the throttle forward. But the engine seemed loath to pick up and the wheels touched again. There was dust and dirt everywhere. Another stone hit him in the face.

But the engine was slowly picking up revs, shuddering and vibrating. They were down on power but slowly they staggered off the ground and flew clear of the cloud of mud and smoke.

Robson was deaf and blind now to whatever was happening back on the aerodrome. They were in greater trouble, fifty feet in the air with insufficient power from the engine and the whole aeroplane shuddering and vibrating on the brink of a stall.

'What the hell are you doing?' McDonald screamed. 'Get the hell out from here. Not that-away, you're heading for the Line.'

'Can't help it,' Robson shouted back. 'There's a bit chipped off a propeller blade and a couple of cylinders have gone phutt. For Christ's sake, sit down.'

Robson did not dare move or take his eyes off the angle the nose made with the horizon to look at the airspeed indicator. His feet were frozen on the rudder and he tried to relax his grip on the control stick, to hold it lightly the better to distinguish from the shuddering structure the quivering of wings on the point of a stall.

He became aware that they were gaining height, slowly. The tree-tops he had seen in the periphery of his vision were no longer there and the angle from which he viewed the ground was different. If the aeroplane stayed in one piece they had a chance.

Now he let the nose drop slightly and risked a glance at the airspeed indicator. The needle was flickering around the sixty m.p.h. mark and rising. He pushed the nose down further and gingerly eased the R.E. into a gentle turn. Turning at too low an airspeed could kill people. McDonald gave his shoulder a relieved squeeze. He risked turning his head to shout, 'Stop breathing down my neck and look for E.A. We must be near the Line.'

They had lost height in the turn and the trees were coming up at them again. He coaxed the aeroplane up to nearly 100 feet before he again risked turning his head to shout to McDonald to tell him they were going back.

The Canadian pointed over the power wing. 'There's a field that looks flat,' he yelled. 'Put it down there and we'll walk the rest of the way.'

Robson shook his head. He remembered what Callaghan had said about this being the Wing Commander's aircraft. There was nothing wrong with it that Flight Sergeant Watt could not put right. It was covered in mud, shell fragments had torn a rent in the lower wing and a corresponding hole in the top wing just outboard of the centre-section struts. The torn fabric fluttered and snapped in the slipstream. A plume of oily smoke leaked from the split left-hand exhaust pipe. The Triplex windscreen was starred. Worst of all was the vibration that blurred the bracing wires and centre-section struts.

He turned towards the flat field and by the time he had coaxed a little more height they were almost over it. McDonald thumped his shoulder and pointed down, but Robson shook his head. He had a choice between an unknown and a certainty. The certainty was what Callaghan would say if they returned without the Wing Commander's aeroplane. Gingerly he eased the nose round on to a southerly course. The frying pan was better than the fire.

Flight Sergeant Watt was waiting for them when they landed. Looking at the mud-caked aeroplane, the wings drooping from slack bracing wires, the cloud of pungent, oily smoke shrouding the overheated engine, he clicked his tongue against the roof of his mouth.

'D'ye think I've no enough work wi' them flaming things oot there, Sir. Man, could you no ha' left it where it was.' He shook his head and walked away. Then, turning he said, 'Ye'd best see the Major quick, Sir. He'll no be expecting to see ye. The wee Navy fella telephoned a whiles back and said ye'd crashed into a wee wood. The Major was stampin' an' swearing aboot like a mess-trooper. Ah reckon he was thinkin' aboot what yon Wing Commander would be saying.'

McDonald was leaning against the port wing tip, a broad grin on his face as he crumbled the mud from the fabric.

'Oh boy, if your mother could see you now,' he said to Robson. 'All you need is a banjo. Ladeez and Gennelmen, pray silence for the original, the genuwine, the one hunnerd per cent unikew, the only one in the worrld, the Flying Minstral.'

And as Robson slowly walked off towards Callaghan's office McDonald capered round him plucking an imaginary banjo and singing 'Way down upon the Swanee River'.

There was an early dinner in the mess that night. The bar was shut and after the tables were cleared the mess servants were dismissed. For once Callaghan was late and a variety of possibilities for his absence, ranging from simple blasphemy to the wishfully obscene, were bandied about as everyone sat there waiting and smoking and waiting. No one seemed to know what had happened or officially that anything had, but that did not stop the conjecture. Robson and McDonald were quizzed repeatedly about what they had seen earlier in the day. The older hands were frankly incredulous and dismayed that an airfield twelve miles from the Line could have been shelled at the end of the first day of a battle. It meant that the breakthrough that the Allies had fought for through three bitter months in '16 on the Somme and in '17 at Passchendaele had been made by the Hun in twelve hours.

Robson had seen nothing, but McDonald claimed he had seen ground fighting as they'd turned for home. Pieces of information gleaned from the Orderly Room clerk were quickly magnified and embroidered as they waited. The early meal and the absence of Callaghan suddenly as-

sumed a new importance. There must have been an un-
paralleled disaster further north. Everyone was suddenly
aware that they were in the French Army Area, isolated
from their colleagues. Suppose the French broke? If the
Line had been broken what was to stop the Hun splitting
them off from the Fifth Army? They, the French, would
pull back to protect Paris. The British Armies would fight
for the Channel Ports.

Robson sat amid the hubbub and conjecture and wondered what had happened to Madelaine. He remembered
the widely-spaced ambulances on that road and imagined
her on a similar stretch with the shells bursting around
her. There was nothing impersonal about a shell, he now
realized. Each one was aimed.

Uncle Tom slipped into the seat beside him, his pipe
waggling in his mouth as he spoke.

'Hello, young Robbo, how did you like your first taste of
shell fire? My God, but you are an expensive feller to have
around. A Fee last night and a Harry Tate today. I dunno
that we can afford fire-eaters like you around. You'll have
to watch your step or you'll be having a permanent piece
of French real estate—rent free.'

'What *is* happening? Does anybody know, or are we
waiting for the Hun to shell us out?'

'We've had a nasty knock,' Cobleigh replied. 'And it
will get worse before it gets better. But it has happened
before. It'll happen again before this bloody war finishes.'

The door swung open suddenly, and Callaghan strode
in. A hush fell on the waiting group. The map Robson
had seen in Callaghan's office was pinned to the wall and
there were quiet whistles from the older hands when they
saw how the red tape bulged eastwards beyond St.
Quentin.

'Three miles in one day,' someone said near Robson. 'I
don't believe it.'

Callaghan was reassuring. The Hun had brought in

fresh troops from the Eastern Front now that Russia was out of the war, but he had not broken through. The Allies had had to give some ground, but everyone knew how difficult it was to keep up the impetus of an attack. The Squadron's function was to make that task harder by hitting the Hun's supply lines which would help stop the flood of supplies essential for his offensive.

Half a dozen of the more experienced crews were to go as far as Le Cateau to bomb the station. Others were to have a roving commission from St. Quentin to the St. Gobain Woods. Robson found himself with an experienced observer, a red-faced beanpole of a man, Tim Latimer, wearing the uniform of the Lincolns with a couple of wound stripes on his sleeve. They were detailed to fly along the St. Quentin–Mont D'Origny road dropping parachute flares to observe the traffic, and to disrupt any they found. They were to carry a dozen 25 lb. bombs. Everyone was warned that if the weather was good they would be doing a second and perhaps a third sortie that night.

Latimer had been with the Squadron four months. He was plainly disgusted at having to explain to Robson how they would do the reconnaissance. As they approached the aeroplanes lined up outside the hangar he pulled a heavy pewter case from his left breast pocket and lit a cigarette with a 'Tommy' lighter, drawing deeply and exhaling twin plumes of smoke like a cart horse taking a hill.

'Patricia'—the name was stencilled in white letters by the pilot's cockpit—differed from the 'pom-pom' fitted F.E. that Robson had used the previous night. The nacelle was slimmer. The pilot sat in front of the engine and in front of him the nacelle extended into something like a hip bath for the observer. There was a Lewis gun on a pipe mounting, extra drums of ammunition round the sides and in the floor was a tube through which Latimer would drop the flares.

With nightfall the cloud had returned and there was a smell of rain in the air. Latimer lit another cigarette from the stub of the previous one.

'You need some height to use these flares,' he said looking up at the clouded sky. 'Or else the flares hit the ground before you've seen anything. Don't get underneath them or you make yourself a target.'

They had to wait, for the aeroplanes going to Le Cateau took off first. Latimer lit a third cigarette. The half-finished one expired with a fizz in a puddle rainbowed with oil droppings.

'And try to hold it steady while I'm dropping them. If we get one stuck in the tube, we'll both be wearing wings tomorrow morning.'

The last of the Le Cateau bombers flashed its letter and trundled along between the flares to lift off into the darkness laden with two 112 lb. bombs. Robson turned to the mechanic by the propeller and raised his thumb.

'If we get caught by a searchlight don't turn away,' Latimer added. 'These barges are too damned slow to escape. Turn into the light and dive.' He patted the Lewis gun drooping on its piece of pipe. 'A squirt from this will soon put the light out. Or you can use your own gun. Watch you don't get blinded and dive in. It's easy to do on a night like this.'

Robson nodded and began the evening ritual. 'Switches off. Petrol on. Suck in,' he called to the mechanic.

Latimer was sitting on the edge of his cockpit. He threw away the remains of his third cigarette.

'You're in a hell of a hurry, aren't you?' he said with a twisted grimace that might have been a smile. 'Don't let that bastard Callaghan get under your skin. He's trying hard for his D.S.O.'

Only when the engine was ticking over with its deep-lunged stutter did Latimer button up his flying suit and pull on his helmet and goggles and to Robson's dismay he stayed sitting on the edge of the cockpit, steadying himself on the Lewis gun mount, while they taxied across the aerodrome and lined up with the flarepath. As they trundled over the rutted turf Robson reflected on Latimer's remark. Was this another man using Madelaine's way of fighting fear—by hating Callaghan? But if Latimer after four months was still afraid, what chance had he, Robson, of conquering his fear? Latimer took him north of St. Quentin, picking up the Amiens–St. Quentin Road and turning east to fly along it. Robson saw no sign of life or fighting where he thought the new Line was, but he could imagine the men below frantically repairing trenches or digging new ones, and the challenge and counter-challenge as men, cut off during the day, straggled back to fight on the following day, and he wondered what he would do: struggle back to fight and risk being killed the next day, or accept the harsh monotony of life as a prisoner-of-war.

A searchlight lit the sky beyond the port wing, looking for them as they approached St. Quentin. Robson veered away further north. Latimer pointed behind and turning, Robson could just make out clusters of sparks in the sky.

' "Archie," ' Latimer shouted, and put his fingers to his nose.

A stream of multi-coloured lights floated slowly up towards them and on up into the clouds. Flaming onions, Robson thought. Nobody seemed to know what they were but they were best seen—like these—from a distance.

Suddenly, St. Quentin, 'Archie', ground lights, all disappeared, for the searchlight and the firing had made Robson instinctively climb and now they had flown into the base of the cloud. He eased the stick forward, felt the beginning of a turn to the right and pushed on the rudder bar to correct it. The turn seemed to stop and then start again. A cold breeze slapped the side of his cheek. They were side-slipping. The altimeter was unwinding and the noise of the rigging wires rose to a shrill scream.

They came out of the cloud like a thunderbolt, the nose down, wings tilted at a crazy angle. A searchlight shone above Robson's head as he struggled to right the aeroplane. Latimer's face was a pale blur turned beseechingly back at him.

He braced his feet on the rudder bar and threw all his weight and the strength of his shoulders on to the joystick. The engine howled. He dared not take his hand off the wheel to pull the throttle back. Something black and heavy, a drum of ammunition, flew out of the front gunpit and sailed overhead. He waited, muscles tensed, for the scream of a racing engine as the propeller shattered. But nothing happened and slowly, painfully slowly, the left wing came up and he was able to ease them out of the dive.

Firelight was reflected off steam ahead of them, lights glittered on marsh and railway track. It was a train and they were low—200 feet.

A searchlight lit up. It pointed straight at them and was followed by a stream of tracer, an intermittent stream of white light that seemed to die out just before hitting them. Latimer was standing up at the front firing his Lewis down the beam. Bullets plucked at the fabric on the right wing. The light went out and the tracer fell behind them as they hurtled over the train at ninety miles an hour.

A few minutes later climbing back towards the cloud base they saw lights moving along the Mont D'Origny road. The cloud was lower, barely a thousand feet high, trailing tendrils of rain and each time they struck one Robson pump-handled the stick forward. He could hear Latimer cursing him as he prepared to drop the parachute flare.

They were too low. As the brilliant light lit up the

countryside Robson could see marching men, long lines of horses pulling guns and ammunition limbers. Streams of tracers laced the sky without coming near. He saw plunging horses as the flare, still burning, drifted onto the road.

Then it was out, and in the darkness he could see nothing.

Latimer was shouting at him. 'You look for the river. The Oise. Don't cross. Jerry airfields. "Archie". They'll knock hell out of us at this height.'

Another flare blossomed, but died quicker than the first. Then a third floated down. A searchlight sought them from the right, sweeping low across the road lighting the occupants better than their flares had done. It caught them, rendering the wings translucent and bringing a cone of tracer in its wake.

Instinctively Robson turned—away from the lights and the gun fire. Too slowly. Bullets clanged on the engine, and one cylinder cut out.

Another light struck up on the far side of the road and fastened onto them. Latimer was firing at it—without effect. He disappeared into his cockpit. The aeroplane lurched.

'I've dropped the bombs,' Latimer shouted as he reappeared. 'Get out of here.'

But Robson was lost, trapped like a fly in a web of blinding light that sapped the mind and paralysed the eyes. The compass was spinning like a top. He did not know which way to go.

'Dive on one of them,' Latimer roared. He turned the Lewis onto the nearest light, but the ammunition drum was empty and seemed to be jammed. As the big bomber turned slowly in a storm of tracer bullets Latimer hammered away at the jam.

'Use your gun,' he shouted as Robson lined up with the beam and dived. The light seared into Robson's brain, blotting out everything. Gunfire and ground alike were absorbed in the great eye that was fastened onto them sucking them onwards and down. Robson's left hand groped for the trigger of the fixed Lewis only because Latimer, a silhouetted gnome, bellowed at him to do so.

The gun fired barely a dozen shots before jamming, but it was enough. The blinding glare was replaced by darkness—an absolute inky blackness—there was nothing, no plane of reference, no horizon, nothing but Latimer beating on the cowling in front of him screaming, 'Pull out, pull out.'

For the second time that night Robson's shoulders ached as he struggled with the joystick, hauling back with all his strength. But his night vision, killed by the glare of the searchlight, was coming back and he saw tree-tops and then a glimpse of water, marsh perhaps, and a brief glimpse of men kneeling with rifles at their shoulders, aiming up at them. He gave a final heave on the stick and the F.E. pulled out of the dive, one wheel thumping a tree-top before they climbed away.

Latimer guided him round onto a course to the west. The compass was still spinning. Keeping low, listening to the strange note of the wind over torn fabric, waiting for the change in the noise of the engine, Robson hastened back over the Line. They had sighted the first friendly lighthouse and had altered course for home before he realized that Latimer was perched once more on the edge of his cockpit. There was a field dressing tied round the lower part of his right arm. He leaned upwards towards Robson holding out his arm.

'Tie a bloody tight knot in that, old boy,' he shouted, grinning all over his face. 'And thanks for everything. A "blighty" one for sure. Maybe I'll get that pilot's course now. Callaghan will have a job to stop it this time.'

'You're supposed to damage the equipment and lower

the morale of the German Army, Robson—not mine,' Callaghan said wearily. Light rain pattered on the office roof as Robson wrote his report. Latimer had dictated his reconnaissance report to one of the clerks and had made sure, in signing it, that there was a substantial smudge of blood on the form. The bullet had gone through the muscle just below the elbow and he had gone, white and happy, to have it dressed.

'All right. You went there, I'll say that for you. A damn queer way round, if you ask me, but I dare say that was Latimer. But you didn't bomb anything or do any sort of a proper count of what's moving along that road...'

Callaghan looked at his watch. It was nearly eleven. Even the soft light of the oil lamp could not hide the furrows in his face. It had been a bad night so far.

Latimer was wounded and for nothing better than the already known fact that there was heavy traffic on the road. The bombers that had left for Le Cateau were not yet back. One of the roving commission F.E.s was down in the Oise with the water washing the blood from its pilot crushed under the engine. Tom Cobleigh had limped into a nearby airfield ten miles to the north with a red-hot engine, half a radiator and a dead observer; and one of the new pilots, flying the replacement aeroplane for practice, had misjudged his landing and lay with his observer under a broken poplar by the road.

'All right. Get yourself some coffee. We are going back there. Just as soon as this damned rain stops,' Callaghan said savagely.

'We?' said Robson.

'That's what I said, Robson.' Callaghan stood up. 'And while you're about it tell that Canadian friend of yours to watch his step. If I catch him trying to pull strings at H.Q. it will not be a scout squadron he'll get, but a boat home. He can play with those glamorous toys when he has earned his corn and not before.'

5

It was nearly midnight before they took off. The rest of the Squadron had left nearly an hour earlier but Callaghan had waited for the return of the machines from Le Cateau. Four of them had got back, and a fifth was down safely at an aerodrome further north with nothing worse than a hole in the main petrol tank. Then Callaghan had had to see them off on a second trip, and only three had made it this time. The fourth had returned with a misfiring engine ten minutes after taking off and Robson, still remembering the gunfire and searchlights of the first trip, saw Callaghan in earnest discussion with Flight Sergeant Watt soon after it landed.

Then it was their turn to take cover, as aeroplanes from the airfield they had been south to destroy, flew over. The flare path was doused but Jerry was after bigger game. It was as important to stop supplies from reaching the defender as it was for the attacker.

By the time they took off, Robson was wet and shivering from cold and fear. The aeroplane still stank from the patches doped on over bullet holes collected from the previous flight. Watt had clicked his tongue when Callaghan had insisted on using it.

As they droned towards the Line again, Robson became uneasily aware that something was wrong. The engine note, the feel of the aeroplane, was somehow changed, although he could not pinpoint a cause. He was not even sure whether there *was* change or whether it was his imagination. He was wet, and sitting in the open cockpit the wind chilled him despite the fur-lined suit. His back was warm—the radiators saw to that—but his arms and face were so cold that it seemed a sudden movement would snap something. How Callaghan stood it, right in the nose, hunched down in a cockpit with no windscreen (it would have interfered with the Lewis gun) Robson could not understand. But he was too concerned with his own misery to care.

Then he began to think about the ignition switches. There were two of them: two magnetos, two sets of wiring and in each cylinder two sparking plugs. Two sparking plugs gave good combustion so if you switched off one plug for a few moments the engine would still run though with slightly reduced power. But oil would collect in the dead plug. If you then switched that plug on and cut off the other one you immediately got an engine that seemed to be on the point of failing. It coughed and spluttered and blew clouds of black oily smoke from the exhaust pipes. When he had been an eager young pilot in the Home Defence Squadron fretting for a posting to France, doing this had been a favourite ploy among the older pilots, to put the fear of God into passengers, especially aged passengers of senior rank.

Fear and misery lent Robson's mind a new desperation, a new cunning. He was haunted by the memory of the two burning aeroplanes from the previous night and how he'd nearly followed their example a few hours ago. The position of the main petrol tank, just behind his seat, sandwiched between him and a hot engine, haunted him too. The red-hot exhaust pipes and the web of wiring to the sparking plugs were just under the emergency tank slung beneath the top wing. He could picture vividly what would happen if that was hit—the plume of vapour, the spark, the flash, the flame like a blowlamp playing on the wooden tail booms and rigging wires ...

Callaghan thumped the cowling in front of him. A lighthouse was flashing over to starboard. They had drif-

ted north. Robson put on right rudder until Callaghan
was satisfied with the new course. Instinctively, despite his
preoccupation, Robson waited until the compass had
stopped spinning and memorized it.

The fingers of his left hand rested on the leather-bound
padding of the cockpit rim. A flick of a switch, that was
all that was needed. He could see the glitter of the Crozat
Canal with lights like fireflies spangling the ground. Camp
fires. They were coming up to the Line.

There was nothing to it, Robson thought feverishly.
Switch on the dead oily plug, switch off the good one.
The engine would leap and buck in its mounting. Even
Callaghan would not push on over the Line with a faulty
engine. And he would not really be shirking. He had been
out once already tonight. The mist was getting up too.
Christ, he was cold.

Anyway there was still something wrong with the aeroplane. The engine revs were down and the speed was low.
Robson's fingers moved as though they had a will of their
own. He slipped his hand out of its thick fur-lined glove.
There must be no chance of error, no flicking off of both
switches. His frozen fingers fumbled for the switches, and
hesitated. There was something wrong with them. One
up and one down. No wonder the revs were down. Half
the job had already been done for him.

Knowing there was nothing wrong with the plane Robson could not bring himself to reverse the switches, but
it took him ten minutes to pluck up enough courage to
rest his hand on the coaming again and put the offending
switch right.

The cloud was lower and the ground mist thicker by
the time they flew along the D'Origny road. Nevertheless,
Callaghan was not convinced that the reconnaissance was
impossible. Not only was the burning time of the flares
reduced but the mist reflected the light back at them,
and in between the low cloud and the mist the Germans

could see them. The streams of tracer got closer with each pass and the tattoo of flapping fabric frayed Robson's strained nerves. Under his breath he cursed Callaghan for his arrogance, for his stupidity in going on.

The searchlights improved with practice, picking them up quicker on each turn. Callaghan made Robson climb into the cloud, fly straight for a few minutes and glide down with the throttle closed. Each time Robson remembered the first occasion, the disorientation, the tilted sky and the camp fires like the stars over his head. But because Callaghan was there he did what he was told, and it worked. Three times they dropped out of the cloud to scatter horses and limbers with well-aimed bombs, but on the fourth occasion they ran straight into machine-gun fire that seemed to erupt just beyond the nose of the nacelle. The Lewis showered sparks and ricocheting bullets, the windscreen disappeared and suddenly there was a strong stench of petrol as the auxiliary tank up in the top wing was shattered.

Robson did not wait for instructions but broke off in a great wide turn into the darkness south of the road.

They were about three miles beyond the right side of the Line, or where they hoped the Line was, when the petrol ran out. Callaghan stood up in the front cockpit.

'Undo your strap,' he ordered, his voice suddenly loud in the comparative silence. The wires thrummed and a few score holes each whistled in a different key. 'Better to break something being thrown out than squashed by that heap of iron.'

He pointed down at a double row of poplars protruding through the thin mist. It was a road.

'It's probably packed with troops,' Robson shouted back.

Callaghan grinned. 'I'll soon sort that out. Get ready to make the steepest gliding turn you've ever made. Ready. Steady. Go.'

Callaghan thrust the last of their flares down the chute.

Robson hauled on the stick and kicked the rudder as though he was handling a bus, pushing the nose down hard to avoid stalling. Even so the flare had almost died as he levelled out and started pulling back the nose to slow the F.E. down to landing speed. But it stayed alight long enough for him to see movement on the road. Men and machines taking cover from what they thought was a Jerry bomber. Any minute now, they'll be firing at us, Robson thought. Thank God the French made their roads straight.

He aimed for the centre of the road, slowed down as much as he dared and let the F.E. sink down into the mist. He guessed the road was about twenty, maybe thirty, feet wide between trees and the F.E. had a wing span of forty-seven feet.

With a great snapping noise the bomber started to turn left and dropped. Another snatch to the right pulled them straight. The nacelle bounced a couple of times and suddenly seemed to pick up speed. Robson glimpsed eyes, tin helmets, mouths gaping from the side of the road, bodies frozen by their speed. Trucks, limbers, steaming horses, flashed by. Then the wingless and tailless nacelle, speeding along like a three-wheeled racing car, turned in a graceful gentle curve to the left and crashed with a great noise of splintering plywood into an ammunition limber.

The next thing Robson knew was that his head was being propped up and something hard, a wheel hub, was sticking into the small of his back. He opened his eyes. Callaghan was crouching beside him, wiping the mud off his face with a dirty scarf.

'Dammit, Robson, you get so much practice at crashing you'll soon have forgotten how to make a proper landing,' he said. 'It's a good job you woke up. The locals were in favour of leaving you. Drink this.'

The neck of a bottle of Scotch rattled against Robson's teeth and he gulped down the fiery liquor again and again until it dribbled out of the corner of his mouth.

A tall scarecrow of a man wearing a private's uniform leaned over the two of them, a pair of blue eyes blazing out of red-rimmed sockets. It was only when he took the whisky bottle from Callaghan that Robson noticed the three cloth stars of a captain on his shoulders. He carried a rifle slung over his shoulder and chalk-grey mud patterned his uniform from boots to cap.

'Can he walk?' the scarecrow asked, tilting the bottle to his own lips. 'He'd better. We'll be pulling out in a couple of hours. Where's your base?'

Callaghan told him as Robson hand-over-hand pulled himself upright on the wheel that had supported his back. Callaghan waved a hand. 'Captain Thetford is our St. Bernard,' he said. 'Lieutenant Robson.'

The Captain nodded and sucked a drop of whisky off his moustache.

'I'll make a bet with you, old man. You won't make it back tonight. Jerry is swarming over like fleas on a fat dog's belly, and they're damned good soldiers. So they ought to be. Three years fighting on the Eastern Front, having it all their own way all the time, no wonder their tails are well up. This damned mist doesn't help. No matter how many you shoot they still keep coming. We're still in contact with the French over there,' he waved the bottle south. 'But God knows where our left flank has gone. God knows how it will end.'

He stared gloomily into the mist but Robson noticed that the red-rimmed eyes were never still. They flickered from a group of sleeping soldiers to the sentry on the bank above, then to the east as though his eyes had some special property to see through the mist, then back to the men clearing away the wrecked bomber and on to a man stripping and cleaning a Lewis gun, to the east again and then to a man with his boots off, massaging his feet.

'I never thought anything good would come out of the Somme battles,' he said quietly as though communing with himself. 'I thought tanks would be a wash-out. The Cambrai show seems to have convinced Jerry that they were dud. Because if he had a squadron of tanks right now he could take his pick—straight through to Paris or right turn for the Coast. Then we'd be in the soup, old man.'

He sucked at his moustache again. 'How are you chaps going to stop them?' he asked suddenly.

'Us!' Callaghan and Robson replied in unison. 'What is wrong with your artillery?' Callaghan said.

Thetford shook his head and waved an arm in a wide sweep.

'Look at us. A thin line of outposts every hundred yards for half a mile. Quarter of a mile to the right and there's nothing—as far as I know. Can't have artillery lying about all over France. Get captured. So it's going back—looking for something solid to rest on. No, when it happens it will be up to you chaps. Can't you drop bombs on them? I can tell you, heavy machine-guns won't stop them.'

Callaghan pulled his lower lip. 'We couldn't guarantee to hit them with bombs. Not unless they stayed in a nice straight line on a road...'

Thetford belched and laughed. Callaghan went on, 'We've got a gun that might do. A "pom-pom", a one-pounder. It would blow a track off a tank or wreck a truck. But you couldn't operate an F.E. in daylight. We had a bad time last year trying to do just that. It would be murder to try now.'

'Then you had better fit it to a machine that can, old chap. Or else there'll be a lot of murderin' done 'tween now and the end of this year. Stay where you are, I'll see if we can drum up transport for you.'

Thetford strode off into the darkness and reappeared a few minutes later.

'Can you manage to walk a couple of miles?' he asked. Robson nodded. 'Right, there's a crossroad about that far back. A Frog Ambulance Section is evacuating wounded through there sometime in the next hour. You should get a lift from them, if you hurry up. Here, take this,' he thrust the half-empty whisky bottle into Callaghan's hand. 'You'll probably need it. Good luck.'

Robson would have moved off immediately but Callaghan made him sit down again. He poured the whisky into a half-empty water canteen, sipping it until he had the strength right. Handing the canteen to Robson, he said, 'Sip that slowly and get your strength back. Walking on this stuff is going to be like walking over ploughed land. Wet plough-land.'

He went over to the wrecked nacelle of the bomber for the two Lewis guns. A second trip brought half-a-dozen ammunition drums and a couple of small packs with which he could carry them. Splotches of blood on the chalk stains showed that their previous owners had no longer any need for them.

Robson glared at him. The immediate shock of the crash, the ghastly feeling that his muscles had turned to water, was fading but as he regained his strength he became more aware of their situation and the whisky that was bringing the strength and awareness back to him made him irritable.

'I don't think Jerry is going to bother about a couple of old guns,' he said to Callaghan. 'So do we have to festoon ourselves like pack mules. Or are we just following Army tradition?'

Callaghan smiled grimly as he took an ammunition drum, wiped the mud off it carefully and fitted it to the Lewis gun.

'Good. The whisky is getting your dander up. Sit down. Take another swig.'

He lifted his wrist to peer at the luminous dial of his watch.

'We move off in five minutes,' he said, fitting a drum to the second gun. 'Yes. I was brought up to believe that losing your rifle was the worst crime a man could commit. I was a soldier before I became an airman. But that is not why we're going to carry them.

'That Captain doesn't know a thing except that he is going to be attacked again in the morning from one direction or another. But he did warn me that the fighting is different now. More like it was in '14. Or in the Boer War or up on the Frontier. India, that is. It's fluid again. Not sitting in trenches waiting for a shell to blow you to Kingdom Come—although there's still plenty of that. But you can't rely on Jerry coming at you from your front. We are carrying these guns in case we have to fight.'

He nodded his head at Robson and the pair of them set off down the road each one with a pack carrying spare ammunition drums slung over one shoulder and with the Lewis barrel propped over the other.

'You should worry,' Callaghan growled before Robson could say anything. 'An infantry man carries sixty pounds on his back when going in to attack.'

It was an old road and for three years it had carried loads never envisaged by the men who had built it—and during that time it had been repaired by men for whom there was no future beyond the coming day. Forced labour had filled in the pot-holes that gaped where the roadbed had broken, and at some time British Pioneers, Chinese labourers or Annanese peasants had refilled the same holes after the frost had lifted up the road metal and the rains had washed it away. On both sides the traffic, gun limbers, ammunition wagons, ambulances, trucks, buses, all the

visible logistics of war, had squeezed the roadbed outwards. The poplars which had been spared by quick re-
treats, the straightening of salients, and the gunfire, were
being strangled by road metal.

It was not an easy road to walk along, not in the dark
with the continual movement and the mist hanging like
smoke head high. The road pulsed like a vein in a body.
Men were moving up all the time, while others lay at the
roadside asleep still gripping their rifles. Ammunition
carts, ration carts rattled by and stragglers kept appear-
ing cautiously from the fields. Occasionally they passed a
couple of walking wounded, their bandages emphasizing
the dirt on them, eyes red-rimmed, plodding on with the
terrifying intentness of men who, having been lost, now
see a way out provided they can keep ahead of whatever
it is pursuing them.

Robson's left foot slipped on the crumbling edge of a
deep puddle. He lurched into Callaghan and as the weight
of the Lewis ammunition swung the small pack forwards
he tripped and fell. Callaghan dragged him to his feet,
swearing at him for his clumsiness and haste. He strained
to see the luminous face of his watch and insisted that
they sat on the fallen bole of a poplar.

'You are pinning too much on what that poor bloody
foot-slogger said. The chances are his information was
twelve hours and a battle out of date. I don't expect to
find any ambulances but sooner or later we must stumble
on a Battalion H.Q. The buggers can't run that fast.'

He lit a cigarette bending down to shield the flame
from his lighter between cupped hands.

'Three o'clock in the morning. Hour and a bit to first
light. Don't fall asleep. You'll feel worse when we move.
Where would you be, Robson, if you hadn't volunteered
to be a gallant birdman? Bed, I suppose, or were you one
of the home-with-the-milkman-boys?'

Robson took off his helmet to wipe his forehead. The

fur lining made it too warm to walk in and now he had a splitting headache. He sipped the dwindling canteen of whisky-and-water while he considered Callaghan's question. The answer was simple enough but he disliked the sneering tone of Callaghan's words.

'Oh, I'd be asleep. Unless I was on the test-beds working on a new engine. After I left college I spent a couple of months working on new diesel engines for submarines. While I was waiting for my papers.'

Callaghan's cigarette end glowed a brighter red.

'A college trained engineer. What the hell are you doing here? You should not have been allowed to join. I suppose you had to come here to be a hero.'

Robson took a long drink from his canteen. 'That wasn't the answer,' he said and got up to start walking again. It was better to force his creaking muscles into movement. He had no intention of telling Callaghan that he'd hit on the truth. After his conduct and his disgrace, the truth would have seemed too laughably incongruous.

'Some woman give you the white feather?' Callaghan asked, falling into step with him. 'Some silly bitch gave me one in the Strand in '16. I'd just spent a month in hospital while the quacks dug a couple of lumps of "Archie" out of my thigh. It was the first time I'd been out in civvies since 1914. Stupid women. Stupid civvies. They don't know what it's like.'

They walked on in silence, each sunk in his own thoughts. After ten minutes or so the smell of frying bacon floated in from the right. A figure on horseback materialized between two trees.

'You men. Halt,' a crisp voice shouted. 'What are you doing here?'

'Look at the polish on those riding boots,' Callaghan sneered. 'Must be a H.Q., of a sorts. We're as good as home.'

He stepped forward towards the horseman. 'Major Callaghan, Royal Flying Corps, in sore need of breakfast and transport...'

The poplars round the airfield were just visible in the grey pre-dawn light when Callaghan and Robson arrived by motorcycle and sidecar. Light from the open front of the hangars showed that the mechanics had been working all night.

Callaghan uncoiled himself from the sidecar as they stopped outside his office. Robson eased his aching backside off the pillion seat.

'See the driver gets something to eat, Robson,' Callaghan said. 'Find Flight Sergeant Watt. He'll arrange it. And tell him I'll be in the office. I want a report on our state of readiness. Then you'd better get some sleep. I've an idea we are going to have a busy day.'

The light flicked on in Callaghan's office as Robson walked wearily towards his quarters. Old iron guts, Robson thought savagely, trying to prove that, without him, the war was lost.

There was a light on in the mess and he walked in, half hoping to find some breakfast. The whisky he had drunk was sour in his stomach and his head ached. There were still a few people round the bar. Uncle Tom Cobleigh and McDonald, a couple of pilots from 'C' Flight, Dick Garbutt and Armitage, and a few of the newly-arrived pilots and observers.

'Hello, Robson. Glad to see you back,' Garbutt said. 'Have a drink.' He drained his own. 'I suppose you did bring the Major back?'

Robson nodded.

'Pity. In that case I'd better get over and join him. H.Q. have been raising Cain.'

Uncle Tom handed Robson a glass of whisky. 'We thought you were a gonner,' he said.

'Not much chance of that,' snapped one of the 'C' Flight

pilots. The left sleeve of his tunic was split from cuff to shoulder and his wrist was bandaged. 'Not as long as you stick to chauffeuring our gallant Major about the sky.'

'That's enough of that, Fenner,' Uncle Tom said. 'We've all had a rough night.'

'I'm not blaming Robson,' Fenner snapped back. 'I envy his personally conducted tour of the Front. You can say what you like, Uncle Tom, but the casualty rate for R.F.C. Majors is bloody low. Popping that stupid gun at locos outside St. Quentin is a bit different to flying those damned egg boxes up to Le Cateau and back. Come on, Tony.'

The two of them drank up and left.

'Take no notice of them,' Uncle Tom said. 'They lost Peters, their Flight Commander tonight.'

'It's fatal to fly with a leave pass in your pocket,' Armitage commented dryly. 'You look a bit pale round the gills. Have another. If Callaghan wants to take you up again, good luck to him. We seem to kill off new pilots like flies.'

'And old ones. I never thought Peters would cop it,' somebody said. 'I thought he was indestructible. This was his second time out, wasn't it?'

'He came out last January,' Uncle Tom said. 'With 57 Squadron on the Rolls F.E. Got his M.C. after bloody April.' Robson knew that the F.E., fitted with a Rolls Royce engine, had fought on as a fighter in 1917 long after it should have been retired. He also knew that April 1917 had been the worst month of the war for the R.F.C.

'No wonder he thought he was indestructible,' Armitage said. 'But when your number comes up, that's that. Remember his fishing stories. He could tell 'em.'

'Last summer he used to sit for hours with the locals fishing in the Somme: a nice bloke,' Uncle Tom said, closing the file on Captain Peters, M.C.

Robson could feel his head spinning. He could hardly

keep his eyes open and their voices crackled at him from distant shapes in the gloom. It had been a bad night, he gathered. The Le Cateau flight had run into bad weather. Two of them were back, two of them were down on the right side of the Line, one was missing—and Peters was dead.

'One of the new fellers from the Pool was saying that there's a rumour we're going to get Handley Pages,' McDonald said suddenly. 'Now, there's a ship and a half. I reckon I'd toss my chances of a scout squadron into the ash-can if we got them. Two Rolls engines and a ton of bombs. Yes sir, that's a ship and a half.'

One of the new observers mentioned he had flown a Handley Page before he came out to France. McDonald started to quiz him about the big twin-engined bomber that was slowly trickling into service. One of the new pilots chipped in to say that the R.F.C. were not getting them, but day bombers, a new improved version of the D.H.4. The observer disagreed and they began to wrangle about the merits of day bombing versus night. Armitage and Jenkins departed to see Callaghan. Some of the new pilots were arguing about whether or not it would be possible to use the F.E. to bomb by day as well as by night, using the clouds as cover. Uncle Tom continued to lean against the bar. He looked incredibly old in the dim light as though the crude hut was a natural growth that had incorporated him in its structure.

Robson sat down in a convenient armchair. Uncle Tom, drinking steadily without speaking, framed in the rectangular outline of the bar, seemed to waver and flicker like a bioscope film of a play. The voices of the others sounded like the tinny jangling of a piano. The rumble of gunfire momentarily stopped the conversation. It was dawn.

Robson was asleep, twitching and shivering like an old dog dreaming in front of a fire.

*   *   *

They were all in the mess just after eleven, bleary eyed, drinking scalding hot coffee, and complaining. Something was afoot. All the F.E.s were out in front of the hangars and the mechanics seemed to be even busier than usual. Rumour swept through them like wind blowing over corn.

Things were so desperate that the Squadron was going to do a mass daylight raid to try and hold the Hun ... The General was coming to inspect them ... They were to be given the King Harry speech ... 'Once more into the breach, dear friends' ... No, the St. Crispian one...

'The Squadron's moving north. Jerry is attacking Ypres again.'

'Jerry has got his own tanks. We're going to bomb them before they smash through the Lines.'

A few people who had heard about Robson's landing during the night came up and asked him what things were like. They were mostly observers wearing their own regimental uniform, men who had served in the Line before being seconded to the R.F.C. They listened to him, asked a few questions and went away with pursed lips and a frown.

'My batman got it from the Orderly Sergeant. We're pulling out. The Hun has broken through.'

'Twenty miles in three days? Don't be so damned silly. Look how long it took us last winter...'

'According to my man we're going to drop gas bombs. Give the blighters a drop of their own medicine...'

'Gas bombs. I got it from one of the ack emmas. Have to use a Fee. Pilot and observer in front of the wings. See...'

Callaghan came in. The Squadron was going back. Right back. Thirty miles or more east and further north. Maison Vert, north of Amiens. All aircraft were to be off the field by midday. A skeleton group of mechanics would stay on to make four damaged aeroplanes airworthy. Anything not flyable by four in the afternoon was to be burned. The Hun was no more than six or eight miles away. By nightfall the airfield would be either a battlefield or swept by shell fire.

'I have to go to H.Q. immediately,' Callaghan said. 'Captain Cobleigh is in charge in my absence. As Mr. Robson has not yet landed a squadron aeroplane without damage he will take me there in an effort to divert his destructive tendencies. Aircraft will take off in flights, armed but without bombs. There will be no unauthorized flying towards the Line.'

With a glare at McDonald after the final sentence he swept out.

'How do you do it, Robson?' Fenner said. 'Think of the peasants while you're swilling champagne with the Brass Hats.'

'Mind yer manners,' said an Australian beside him. 'They might be giving the joker a job on the staff.'

'Go to hell,' Robson said. No one, except McDonald, noticed him slip away after Callaghan. No one was saying much. They were stunned by the bald announcement confirming what the majority had thought but had resolutely refused to believe to be true. One or two had begun to look over their shoulders through the window facing east. The drum roll of gunfire was acquiring a personal interest.

'Sir,' Robson saluted as Callaghan turned to him. 'I wish to be excused from flying you to Headquarters.'

'Why?'

'If the job is a sinecure, Sir, then one of the old hands should go. If it is to do with learning the countryside, one of the replacement pilots...'

'Shut up, Robson, unless you want me to return you to the Pool. You were given an order. It is not my habit to discuss the reason behind my orders with my junior officers. And Robson? You, a veteran of three days on the Squadron, should note that two of those replacement pilots were out last night and managed to return without smashing their aeroplane. You will be outside the sheds in thirty minutes, eleven-fifty. Bring your overnight kit only. Your batman can deal with the rest. And Robson, flying with me is *never* a sinecure. Got it?'

Callaghan's mood was still black when they met by the 'pom-pom' F.E., 'Mimi'. He stowed a battered leather case in the observer's seat under the breech of the gun. Telling the mechanics to start the engine and warm it up he drew Robson aside.

'You are a rotten pilot, Robson,' he said as they walked up and down out of earshot of the waiting pilots and mechanics. 'You've got the worst case of cold feet I've seen for many a month. If I was doing my job properly I'd send you back to the Pool. Back home before you kill yourself and somebody else. Don't start denying it. I've seen it before. Dammit, man, I can feel it from the way you push the Fee round the sky. You jerk the controls about as if you were working a pump. God only knows how you got a Camel off the ground and back again.'

Robson opened his mouth to protest.

'Let me finish, damn you. I'm keeping you for one reason; no, two. I don't like cowards and I'm damned if I can see why you should go home to a cushy billet while better men than you have to slog it out over here. Secondly, I think you are a born survivor. You must be, with your luck.

'So you are not flying me to H.Q. I am flying you. It's time you realized how an aeroplane should be flown. Maybe it'll save your life sometime. Here.' He handed Robson a map with the flight track to H.Q. drawn in pencil.

The gunner's cockpit of 'Mimi' was uncomfortable and cramped. Robson's shoulders rubbed on the stuffed leather padding rolled round the rim. Slightly ahead of him and offset to the left was Callaghan. The breech of the 'pom-

pom' gun protruded between his legs. He shuddered, remembering the stories he had heard in the mess about breech failures. The shells were in clips along the sides of the cockpit. An Aldis optical sight protruded past the windscreen. Clamped underneath it was a fixed Lewis gun with a canvas bag to catch the spent cartridges. A spare drum dug into his right thigh. The nacelle vibrated with the pulsations from the engine as it ticked over, the big propeller revolving so slowly that each blade could be seen. Each made a 'thwacking' noise as it whirled past the tail booms.

Callaghan waved a hand. The mechanics darted in to remove the wheel chocks. Robson gripped the cockpit sides. It was a long time since he had flown as a passenger and he had not liked it then. He was going to like this even less.

With a blast of engine power Callaghan moved off, heading for the downwind corner of the field. The rest of the squadron, twelve of them, were warming their engines. Robson answered McDonald's wave with a flutter of the hand. Harris was sitting on the side of the gunner's cockpit. Behind them, Uncle Tom Cobleigh was waiting to go.

The wind was from the south-west towards the poplars fringing the road. Off to one side of their take-off run there was a gap where one of the F.E.s had failed to get off carrying a 112 lb. bomb. Callaghan took a quick look around, waggled the controls, and opened the throttle.

Halfway across the field the nose came up and the squawking of the oleo legs stopped. They were airborne. Callaghan pushed the nose down again and skidded the old bomber round to the left and headed for the gap in the trees, the airspeed accelerating as they hurtled over the field a few feet off the ground.

The trees raced up towards them, rising above them gaunt and leafless. Robson gulped and shut his eyes as

Callaghan took them through the gap. A staff car swerved wildly across the road and was gone. Ahead of them was a small wood and a half-ploughed field. The ploughman astride his big white horse stared across at Robson open-mouthed. The nose was turning now towards the north-west. Their wheels seemed to brush a hedge. Two trees shading a farmhouse whipped by. A skidding turn, and the skeleton arm of a tree reached out for them and fell back. A converging course took them back towards the road. The driver of a Crossley R.F.C. tender stared back at them, missed a bend, and went through a hedge still staring.

Something black seen out of the corner of his eye attracted Robson's attention. No wonder the driver of the tender had crashed, he thought. For strung out behind them in single file, black beetles, wheeling in line astern, were the remaining eleven F.E.s of the squadron...

Roye, red brick, grey stone and timber, a cluster of roads converging, loomed up. They went round it, flicking between the isolated cottages on the outskirts. Soldiers waving; cars stopping; a couple of horses rising in their traces; washing; white faces, stupefied; a man bending over a stream, falling, the act frozen on the retina. Robson would never know whether he ever hit the water. A train loomed up and disappeared as they flew through the plume of dirty steam. A shattered village, still littered with the debris of a two-year-old skirmish, whipped by them, a church steeple and the remains of a church. They flew straight for it until it dominated Robson's mind. As it towered above they skidded to the left through the shattered nave. Robson turned. The steeple lay directly behind them and the following aircraft were split-arsing about the sky to dodge it.

They flew over a roofless cottage, disembowelled. There was a bed, complete with rotting linen, a sideboard and a chair, but no wall where the stairs had been.

'Where are we?' Callaghan shouted at him. Robson pointed at a little town just visible over the roof of a farmhouse ahead of them. He glanced across at the wildly spinning compass.

'What course are we steering?'

Robson shook his head again completely bewildered.

'Don't look at that damned thing,' Callaghan roared. 'Use the sun. North-east, I make it. Look at your map. That was Nesle.'

A railway line bridged the road. Callaghan eased back the throttle and suddenly zoomed up to 500 feet. As he levelled out he threw the F.E. into a steep right-hand turn shaking his fist at the following aeroplanes as they veered in all directions. He was grinning as he turned to Robson.

'You thought I didn't know they were there,' he accused. 'If you are going to stay alive you have to start seeing other aeroplanes before they see you. How many other aeroplanes did you see? How many can you see now?'

Robson gazed around wildly and finally pointed to the black F.E.s now in squadron vee formation heading north-west.

Callaghan scowled at him and started to point. A squadron of de Havillands flew over 5,000 feet above them. An R.E. away to the east plodded towards the Line and ahead of them three S.E.5 fighters climbed eastwards.

'H.Q.,' Callaghan yelled. 'And if your pal, McDonald was as good as he thinks he is he would have stayed in that tight turn with us. If we had been a Hun he'd be dead.'

The Headquarters of the Wing was in a small chateau unmarked by the war externally but inside blighted with official green and brown paint on the walls of the partitioned offices. Robson ate a solitary lunch in the H.Q.

mess. His confidence had not been improved when Callaghan pushed him in and told him to make himself inconspicuous because he was not supposed to lunch there. He seemed to be the only one there with a rank lower than a captain. Afterwards his coffee and a substantial balloon of brandy were served in a spacious lounge overlooking an ornamental garden. He took a copy of *The Times* from the previous week and hid behind it in an armchair. There had been, he read, a major German attack on the Western Front. The Allies had inflicted enormous casualties on the enemy and, while the battle still raged, informed circles were confident of the outcome. He remembered the weary men sleeping by the roadside the previous night, and wondered...

Voices from a couple of chairs behind him woke him.

'I told the feller he was a damned fool. Wanted me to leave my horse behind. I told him, "You've got the wind up. You fill that infernal stink box up with my kit and the groom, and I will ride the horses." Feller's not an officer. He's a mechanic.'

'Did you hear Callaghan shouting at the Old Man?'

'Callaghan?'

'The ex-ranker feller that took over Timmis' night bomber squadron.'

'Remember him now. He was in 20 Squadron in '15. Got involved in that bad business with his young brother. They shot him, didn't they? Poor show. Didn't do Callaghan any good. In fact, I never thought he'd ever get a squadron.'

'No choice, old boy, not with Timmis catching a packet. Senior Flight Commander and all that. My God you should have heard him. Squadron moving back to Maison Vert. Too far back for Mister Callaghan. Sounded like a real fire-eater.'

'Probably still after his D.S.O. Be useful after the war to paper over the blot in his book.'

'My dear chap, don't be so ridiculous. Men like Callaghan as officers after the war ...'

Their voices died away. Robson stared at his newspaper without reading. No wonder the bastard was so keen to get in so many trips in a night.

6

'War is sure hell,' said McDonald striking a theatrical attitude. 'And you haven't seen the worst yet. The ack emmas are in tents pitched in the orchard. They're nearer the garbage pit than we are.'

There was nothing particularly green about Maison Vert, the farm from which the aerodrome took its name. Farmhouse and outbuildings made three sides of a square with a pond in the centre flanked by a steaming midden. Crudely camouflaged bell tents had been pitched between the trees of the orchard and beyond them, climbing a gentle slope, were the canvas hangars flapping in the evening breeze. The black-painted hut in which Robson and McDonald were standing showed few signs of its previous occupants. There was the inevitable piano and a large brick fireplace flanked by two broken armchairs. One of them had a hole, perfectly circular, about two inches in diameter, burned into the leather.

'Very pistol,' McDonald said poking his finger into the stuffing. 'There must've been one hell of a binge before the fellers pulled out.'

'A year ago,' Robson said.

Half a dozen rickety chairs and a table completed the furniture. Over the fireplace a fine slab of timber had been let into the wall but it was chipped and scarred by cigarette burns and under the dust were the rings left by countless glass bottoms. At the far end of the room the bar, empty-shelved and dust-covered, added to the sense of desolation.

The noise of aero engines took them outside. A flight of three R.E.s, lower wings laden with light bombs, appeared over the hump in the middle of the aerodrome that effectively hid the buildings of the squadron on the far side. Although they were airborne as they came over the rise none of them climbed. Wheels still rotating, they raced towards the mess to skim the roof with the observers fingering their noses at the newly arrived night bombers. A piece of mud from a wheel or tail skid splattered on Robson's shoulder as the pair of them cringed from the noise and slipstream.

They had barely recovered when three Bristol Fighters followed. Sheltering in the doorway this time Robson could see fragments of mud dropping away, the four 25 lb. Cooper bombs under the wings of the leader—and another observer fingering his nose at him.

'Two squadrons on the other side of the field,' McDonald shouted in his ear. 'I hope their C.O.s realize I am a light sleeper.'

Robson squinted up at the departing bombers and their escort, climbing now for height.

'If they're going to do that often,' he said, 'I hope they've got those bombs tied on properly. As night bombers it should be easy to cure them of disturbing our sleep. Where are we supposed to rest our heads?'

'Flight Commanders and the Major billet at the farm,' McDonald said. 'Peasants like us are in Nissen huts. We've got a room with four beds in it but we can take our pick. The other places are for two new guys. The R.O. reckons they'll be here tomorrow. You'll be bunking down on bare boards tonight. Mrs. McDonald's boy did himself some scouting in his battle-plane a couple of hours ago and there is the great grand-daddy of all traffic snarl-ups along the Amiens Road.'

'What about food? I'm ravenous. There was too much gold braid and too many red tabs at H.Q. for my appetite.'

'There's a field cooker over by the farm. We eat at the farmhouse tonight. Of course,' McDonald polished his finger nails on his lapels and blew on them, 'if you could bear to be parted from your comrades and your beloved goddamned C.O. we could eat in Amiens. I'm told the Godbert restaurant is highly recommended. Followed by a bed with one of those soft downy French mattresses— maybe a soft downy *fille* to go with it...'

'You're nuts. Amiens is twenty kilos away. And what about the war?'

'The hell with the war, Robbo, the Squadron is officially stood down tonight. And Messewers McDonald and Robson have been ordered to Amiens for the buying of mess furniture. We have a tender laid on. We can go tonight or tomorrow morning.'

Robson lunged at him, shoving him bodily out of the hut.

'Of all the long-winded, jaw-breaking colonials, you take the biscuit. We've wasted a quarter of an hour.'

They got into Amiens at dusk after rashly bribing their driver to make it a fast trip.

There was something unreal about the city. For an hour after they had dropped their overnight kit at the hotel Robson walked McDonald about the streets. Here were lights, shops selling mundane things like groceries and meat, clothes and bed linen. Men and women, civilians going about their business, jostled the uniformed men. Factories blowing whistles and hooters disgorging pale-faced, tired workers. There was so much noise from the bustle and throb that the ever-present rumble of gunfire that accompanied their lives on the aerodrome could not be heard.

Even the railway station took on an extra dimension, Robson thought, as he watched a line of people shuffling past the booking office. It was an escape route, not just a bird-infested, bombed-out echoing hall.

A line of ambulances moved slowly into the station and

Robson turned away. He could not stand the sight of the wounded being carried or allowed to make their own way, stumbling onto the ambulance train.

'That goddamned Major of ours kin say what he likes but I reckon Jerry has put the wind up some of the boys back here,' McDonald said, gesturing behind them at the ambulances. 'They must be clearing out the hospital...'

The squawk of a klaxon horn immediately behind startled them into leaping sideways. The leading ambulance had crept up behind them, and leaning over the wheel, her face freckled with spots of mud, was Madelaine Hart.

'My God, if I were a man I'd be in the R.F.C.,' she said to them. 'Every time we meet you are either drinking or on your way to get a drink.'

'Yes, Ma'am,' McDonald replied as he saluted. 'And you'll excuse me saying so, Ma'am, but every time we meet you your face is dirty.'

She put her tongue out at him. 'And what's the matter with you?' she said to Robson. 'Cat got your tongue?'

Stuttering with pleasure, Robson at last managed to ask whether she and her friend could join them for dinner.

'La, sir, but we are honoured,' she said raising an imaginary eyeglass. She put her hand to her mouth in mock horror. 'I'm afraid we have nothing to wear. Nothing fit for the company of officers and gentlemen.'

'Who cares,' McDonald said. 'If it bothers you we won't behave like gentlemen.'

'In that case, we accept. Provided you can persuade your friend. He looked doubtful. Mamie is about three back down the line.'

After McDonald had gone whistling down the line of ambulances Madelaine turned to Robson.

'You haven't said that our muddy uniforms will be good enough for you. Or are you worried about not being a gentleman?'

'I, I'm not as quick witted as Frank,' Robson stuttered. 'Perhaps it is because I like my beautiful women with mud freckles on their faces.'

Madelaine cocked her head and looked at him with mock severity.

'H'm, you worry me. If I didn't know how difficult it is to find one I'd have said you have been practising on the local young ladies. How is that beastly Commanding Officer treating you?'

'He doesn't exist for the next twelve hours. Or the war.'

'Good, we accept your invitation. But I warn you. We've eaten nothing but biscuits since early this morning. You will be taking out a couple of wolves.'

A chorus of klaxons blared behind them. Madelaine's ambulance was blocking the road. The girl in the Ford behind was whistling and waving. The klaxons kept blaring. Robson felt his face reddening.

'Eight o'clock, Godbert's restaurant,' he said as the Ford jerked forward and 'tut-tutted' away.

McDonald was already in the bar with a group of pilots when Robson, glowing from his first civilized bath in weeks, came downstairs. They were fighter pilots, McDonald explained, part of a Camel squadron newly arrived from further north. He had already sounded out the Flight Commander with them, a Canadian captain, about the chances of getting a transfer. The Captain stared hard at Robson and said, 'Have you got a brother on Camels?'

Robson flushed and felt his stomach heave. Were those dreadful weeks on the Camel going to be flung in his face again? Like a waterlogged body in a shell hole the past refused to stay down. He shook his head.

'Queer. You must have a double. Or you did have. The feller I saw didn't shape up as if he was going to last long.'

'Robbo is our expert with the "pom-pom",' McDonald chipped in. 'We've got a couple of Fees fitted with them.

Hangover from '17. Him and the C.O. go out knocking-off locomotives.'

'What is it, a one-pounder?' one of the pilots asked.

Robson nodded.

'You can keep them. The Navy had a queer kite made by Beardmores on test while I was at Ayr. The breech failed. Made an 'orrible mess in the cockpit. Right between the gunner's legs. Absolutely ruined his interest in women.'

'We've had that happen,' Robson said, remembering the stories he had heard on the Squadron. 'But it's mostly misfires and jammed cases. I doubt whether we'll get any more.'

'Fees?' someone said. 'I should damn well think not. Animated bird cages. They should have been scrapped in '16.'

'Pity, we'll need them,' the Captain said. 'Not your bath tubs, I mean the gun. I hear Jerry is starting to use his own tanks.'

'Tanks? You can keep them, sport,' an Australian said. 'A mate of mine was at Bullecourt. They went in without artillery support 'cos there were tanks to take them through the wire. None of them got off the start line. Don't talk about tanks to anyone in that Brigade.'

'I watched them at Cambrai,' retorted the Captain. 'They went through Jerry like a dose of salts; you wait till your mates have had to stand up to tanks. Christ, if we'd done that job properly and had a couple of dozen in reserve we'd have cleared Jerry out of France in a week.'

'And now the Hun has got his own, I am sure we need a gun like the one-pounder in an aeroplane. A sort of flying field gun. Machine-guns are no good. I killed a Hun at Cambrai who found that out. He'd fired all his ammo at a tank and it didn't seem to know he was there.'

'Maybe you've got something,' McDonald said with a spasm of excitement. 'Maybe we could fix something up when them Jerry tanks get going. We could take a Fee over with your lads as close escort...'

The others burst into peals of laughter. Taking a F.E. over the Line in 1918 in daylight, escort or no escort, was certain sudden death.

'Easier ways to commit suicide,' someone commented.

'...The Harry Tates go over every day,' McDonald protested amid renewed laughter.

'...Yeah. And look at the casualty rate on them ... You're off your chump, old fruit.'

'I wouldn't let you do it, Frank,' the Captain said. 'Even if your C.O. agreed, which I doubt. But we'll need a plane with a gun like that. Sopwith is making a special armoured Camel for trench strafing and Jerry has got the Hannoverana. What we want is something like a Bristol with a big gun.'

'Not like a Bristol,' someone argued. 'The wings pull off already. For Christ's sake shut up, Skipper; if the C.O. hears you he'll put one on a Camel and that will be the end of the ring-a-rang-aroo.'

On the way back to the hotel Robson had had the foresight to call in at the restaurant and tell the head waiter that he was bringing two starving girls in at eight. On the waiter's advice he had ordered there and then, watched by a grinning McDonald.

Half apologetically he explained to the two girls what he had done. He need not have had any doubts. They flatly refused to take a drink before the meal, explaining that when they had said they had not eaten since early morning they had been telling the absolute truth—apart from wine and biscuits at midday.

Madelaine grinned impishly at Robson. 'I can see I shall have to watch Sir Christopher here. I have seen this masterful-man act before. A man of experience. Dinner ordered, wines prepared. Champagne for ladies, red wine for the men. You didn't learn that studying engineering. Confess.'

'My father was a very broad-minded man,' Robson said by way of explanation.

'More than mine is,' Madelaine said. 'You should hear him when I go home on leave. "Painted hussies dancing with officers in public places." Public places means any hotel in London other than Brown's.'

A strand of dark hair had escaped and blew about her forehead. Was it the candlelight Robson wondered, or the wine, or the company that hid the crows-feet about her eyes with their blue-shadowed weariness.

'And what about your sisters,' Madelaine asked. Robson had told her he had two, and a brother. 'How did your broad-minded father treat them?'

Robson grinned. 'After his own fashion, quite well. They were taught to read and write. The youngest went to Girton. She got married in her second year so she didn't take her finals. She could twist the old man round her little finger. But while they were at home they had to be in by ten o'clock. Unless of course they were escorted by suitably vetted young men.'

Madelaine finished her glass and deliberately took the bottle of wine and refilled it. 'Why the devil, once she'd got to university, didn't she stay the course?'

'There was a war on, remember. I don't suppose she felt that there was time to wait.'

'Poppycock. It's because of the war she should have taken her degree. She might be a widow before you can say "Jack Robinson". So she threw up the chance of being qualified to become a camp-follower. My God, you should see them. Lonely, bored young women, living in hotels, nothing to do but watch and wait. No wonder so many of them have a few drinks and stop waiting.'

'I don't think my sister would do that.'

She laid a hand on his. 'I'm sorry, that was a beastly

thing to say. But I have seen it happen. I know. I've been through it myself.'

'Were you one of those women that chained themselves to railings? What do they call them. Suffragettes?' McDonald asked.

Madelaine grinned at him. 'No, I wish I had been. The lecture is not over. Your cruel Canadian mind has unmasked me. Everything I said was hindsight. It has taken a war and a dead husband to make me realize that most of the trouble we women get into is our own fault.'

'No frontiers to plough and seed with young men,' Mamie said.

'My dear girl, we have frontiers enough,' Madelaine replied. 'If it had not been for the war I might have been sitting on one, helping my Lord and Master climb up to the command of his regiment by toadying to the Colonel's Lady and putting a delicate ladylike foot in the face of anyone coming up behind us.

'Suffragettes! Father would have had a fit if the name was mentioned in the house. And Mama would have taken us aside and pointed out that no young man, no nice young man, would waste his time on a girl who occupied her mind with such matters.'

'My father says that women will get the vote when the war is over,' Robson said. 'He also thinks the country will go to the dogs.'

'That's noble of him—after all we've done in the last four years,' Madelaine retorted. 'We'll want more than the vote. We can drive buses, make shells—and if we can run an army like the W.A.C.s we can run a business. But,' she lifted her glass to him again, 'people like you will stop us.'

'I don't see that.' Robson felt indignant. 'I would have thought that the war has brought women and men closer. I don't ever remember my father and mother discussing things such as we are discussing.'

'So how the heck are we going to stop you women from getting what you want?' McDonald demanded.

'Because, my irate Canadian friend, when this is over the men who have fought, those who survive—and I don't mean just the men who were not killed—will want to go back to 1914. For years to come, the era before the war will have a golden tinge. The "never-never" years of might-have-been.'

'Not all of 'em,' McDonald said. 'When I was a gravel-basher I trained with some miners—from Northumberland, I think they were—and some Cockneys from London. They won't want to go back to '14. And what about our gallant C.O.? D'ye think he wants to go back to a bob a day as a mechanic?'

Madelaine held her glass out for the last of the wine. 'That was a marvellous meal. All I want now is coffee, lots of coffee.'

She clicked her fingers. 'And I would love to dance. A dreamy, dreamy waltz. Frank, your miners and your Cockneys will be just like the others. When they go back to the bankrupt world of the future they'll remember the fun, and dream of what they might have done with four years of wasted youth.'

She turned to Mamie. 'I think we should go to Babs. Is she on duty tonight?'

The American girl shrugged her shoulders. 'What's the difference. Henri will be glad to see us—provided we bring the cognac. Gee, I don't see how she stands that guy. He looks at me and I wonder whether I put on clean lingerie. Ugh, he gives me the creeps.'

'With two missing legs, what do you expect him to do, stand to attention and sing the "Marseillaise"?'

'Yeah, I know. I'm a hard-hearted son of a bitch. But he still gives me the creeps. It'll cost you two bottles of cognac, boys. Let's go.'

* * *

Babs' place turned out to be a studio four stories up looking across towards the canals that intersected Amiens. It was cold despite the fug, and the noise of chattering voices almost drowned the gramophone in the corner. Henri sat in a rocking chair, a blanket covering his mutilated legs. A souvenir of Verdun, he told McDonald.

Behind them half a dozen couples danced to the music of a gramophone. Another group drank and talked and flirted. Turkish and Virginia cigarette smoke boiled around the single bulb hung from the high ceiling. The talk almost drowned the music. Mamie came up and linked her arm in McDonald's. She nodded at Madelaine and Robson waltzing to 'Sweet Seventeen'. 'Your pal looks to be badly smitten,' she said. 'I hope he knows what he's doing.'

'He's free, white and nearly twenty-one,' said McDonald. 'He's all right, I guess. Too many sisters and too much mom, I reckon. She won't bite him, will she.'

'Don't get me wrong, buster. I'd go bail for that little lady anywhere, anytime. Just warn him off from going in too deep. She'll not let herself get too involved with another man. She talks as if this war was a cakewalk to freedom for women. She has paid her entry fee, and nobody will get to first base with her until this blasted war is over.'

She yawned. 'Dammit, Frank. I hate to do it but I've got to get some sleep. I need my eight hours even if Madelaine can manage with four.'

'You are a fraud, Christopher,' Madelaine murmured in Robson's ear as he manoeuvred her through the other couples filling the floor. 'No one could learn to dance like this with his sisters.'

'It's like riding a bicycle. Once learned, never forgotten.'

'I can't imagine you on a bicycle,' Madelaine teased him, 'I...'

The music died with a squawk as someone lifted the

arm off the record. The chatter stopped and they stood listening. From the street below they could hear whistles blowing.

'It's an air raid,' someone said.

'It's only Fritz doing his rounds,' a man said. 'Put the music on again.'

'Messieurs.' Henri rocked himself out of his corner. 'This room is twelve metres long by five metres wide. The roof is glass. You will kindly put out the light and leave.'

'What about you?' McDonald asked Henri as they began filing out of the darkened room.

The man's teeth gleamed as he smiled. 'I like the dark, my friend. I shall sit here and watch the moon come up.'

The four of them huddled in a shop doorway arguing about what could be done. Robson and McDonald wanted the two girls to take over their hotel rooms as there was no chance of getting a cab while the raid was on.

The street was deserted now. It was a fine starlit night with a moon low down on the horizon. Half a dozen searchlights waved about in an ineffective way.

'Sure is funny,' McDonald said. 'How goddamned useless those searchlights are when you're on the ground. Now if we were up there and they were Fritz's lamps I'd bet my bottom dollar they were looking for me personally.'

'Listen,' Robson said. 'They're coming back. Two of them. Two engines each.'

The unsynchronized throbbing of the two engines, *'pour vous, pour vous, pour vous'*, was getting louder as the bombers, after circling the town, came back with the moon behind them.

'Gothas,' McDonald whispered, 'from Etreux. They must be giving Paris a rest tonight.'

'I wish you men would stop being so damned calm and technical about them,' Madelaine murmured. She was shivering as she huddled closer into Robson's arms. 'They terrify me. If I was at the hospital now I could pull the bedclothes over my head and pretend they weren't there.'

The guns on the outskirts of the town were firing now. Momentarily one of the bombers was caught in the beam of a searchlight, and two streams of tracer lanced at it. Sparks glittered well above the Gotha. The guns were firing high. From somewhere in the town a couple of machine-guns took up the attack. The searchlight went out and the other groped in vain.

'They are after the railway station,' Robson said. 'Where is it?'

'Couple of blocks ahead of us,' Mamie replied. 'Is that bad?'

'Not good,' McDonald said. 'They'll be heading into wind. If they get the line right the bombs could overshoot. We should get out of here.'

'I am not moving,' Madelaine said firmly.

An army tender squealed to a standstill in front of them. A couple of nurses waved to them.

'Room for two. Hurry.'

Madelaine refused to move from the imaginary safety of their doorway. Robson pushed McDonald out.

'Take Mamie, you idiot. I'll stay with Madelaine. The raid will be over in fifteen minutes. I'll get a cab.'

A gendarme trotted down the street, blowing his whistle and calling on the driver to stop. Mamie and McDonald were seized and bundled into a mass of bodies as the car moved off, without any lights.

'You'd have been safer with them,' he said to Madelaine. Her reply, muffled by the way she had her head buried inside his British Warm, was drowned by the noise of the first explosion.

The Gotha was bombing from high up. Two or three thousand feet, Robson guessed from the noise of the engines. He watched the flashes of the explosions march in a straight line towards them and wondered why he was not frightened. The wine and brandy he had drunk seemed to have put a sparkle into his veins. He hugged Madelaine close.

The bombs were not falling in a direct line for them as he thought they might because the last one hit a house at the bottom of the street in which they were sheltering. It must have gone through the roof before exploding because the wall on the top floor seemed to move out before sliding silently into the street below.

All the guns were firing now. Bullets and shell fragments were pattering down like light rain.

'Shall we make a dash for my hotel,' he said. 'The blighter's gone.'

Hand in hand they ran down the street.

'It's silly of me,' she said. 'But I can't stand it when I'm doing nothing. It's the same with shelling. I'd rather drive through it than sit in shelter waiting...'

Suddenly Robson saw the second Gotha; he had forgotten there were two. This one had come down in a glide with his engines ticking over, letting the guns concentrate on his colleague. He saw it silhouetted against the glow of a fire about 500 feet up, flames spurting from the exhaust as the pilot opened his throttle.

A column of flame rose from beyond the shielding houses on the other side of the street. Then he saw the flash a hundred feet in front of them on the other side of the road. A hot wind lifted him off his feet and threw him down.

He could only have been knocked out for less than a minute because when he opened his eyes he could still hear the unsynchronized howl of the Gotha as it climbed away. Madelaine was on her knees beside him. She had his tie off and one cold hand inside his shirt feeling for his heart. But apart from a bump on the back of his head he was all right.

'If you can walk to the hotel I will get a doctor,' she said.

'Don't be silly. I reckon any doctors will be needed elsewhere.' He stood up, shaking in every joint, and dusted himself. 'I only did it to take your mind off the bombing.'

The bombing had not affected the party going on in the bar at the hotel. Robson suggested that Madelaine should use the bed in his room to get some sleep. He would stay in the bar until the bombing was over and then take her back to the hospital.

The lights flickered on and off, a plume of dust started in the room as another bomb went off. The next raider had arrived.

When they got to Robson's room they stood by the window sipping brandy from cups, watching the flames leap high somewhere near the station. Within minutes another raider arrived to stoke the fire. As Madelaine huddled in his arms he kissed her. She kissed him back, her fingers undoing the buttons of his tunic.

'You should be in bed,' she whispered. 'That knock on the head might have given you concussion.'

His heart thumping, Robson groped backwards onto the big bed. He had sufficient sense to pull her down beside him.

'Lock the door,' she whispered. 'And take your clothes off. I bruise easily and your buttons are so cold.'

There were either two bombers or else one of them came over twice, low. The howl of the engines seemed to be just over their roof. The windows rattled from the engine noise and the exploding bombs as she pulled him over on top of her, nipping the loose skin of his neck with her teeth.

They came over again about an hour later, high up this time. She whimpered in her sleep, called out and huddled closer to him. He turned to hold her.

'Who is Ben?' he asked, kissing her bare shoulders.

'Ben, Ben?' she murmured. 'You must have been dreaming. Perhaps you did get concussed?'

It was broad daylight when he woke from a deep, drugged sleep. Only a rumpled pillow remained to show where she had lain, and a note.

'Dear Chris,' it read. 'Thank you for a lovely air raid. Do see your M.O. about that crack on the head. I did not realize it was so bad until I saw your shiner by the cold light of dawn.

Love Madelaine.'

He looked in the mirror. His face, bisected by a crack and a mildewed growth obscuring his chin, stared back at him. He had a black eye and a purple bruise running back under the hair line. Suddenly his head began to ache and he felt faint.

McDonald burst in as he was gingerly shaving himself.

'Show a leg, you sluggard. I've seen our driver. He'll pick us up in an hour. Do you think they'll serve ham and eggs? By Christ, Robbo, that's a whale of an eye you've got there. I thought Madelaine was joking when she told me you were knocked out and she had to put you to bed.'

They had commissioned the driver the previous night to pick up the furniture. McDonald had plumped for plenty of cheap serviceable chairs that could be broken easily and cheaply replaced after a squadron guest night. Robson had insisted on three armchairs. Now, McDonald was singing 'Any old iron' as they drove back to the aerodrome in bright spring sunshine with the tender looking like a second-hand furniture dealer's cart.

Robson's headache got worse as the tender rattled over the *pavé* and crudely repaired roads while the driver chattered on about how the Flying Corps were giving Jerry hell and how everybody reckoned that with the losses he was taking this advance he was crowing about would polish him off. Yes, Robson thought spitefully, if our H.Q. staff were as good as their propaganda we would be in Berlin before the end of the year. It was hard to realize, listening to the corporal, that it was the Germans who had advanced over twenty-six miles in three days. From what the two Tank Corps subalterns had said at breakfast there was nothing left of the Fifth Army to stop him marching up to the outskirts of Amiens itself.

A flight of R.E.s were taking off as they motored towards the aerodrome. The ungainly artillery spotters were carrying bombs this time. Two of them roared at the Crossley, deliberately holding the aeroplanes a few feet above the road, making their driver pull into the side in haste.

The third and last one was in trouble. Standing by the car they heard the engine cough and splutter, intermittent puffs of smoke jetting from the exhaust pipes which ran up above the upper wings like stove pipes.

'If 'e drops them bombs, we're done for,' the corporal muttered, before diving into the ditch behind the car.

Robson and McDonald, fascinated by the pilot's predicament, were rooted to the spot. There were trees on either side of the road ahead of the crippled aeroplane. A horse-drawn ammunition limber and a couple of lorries blocked the road.

The propeller stopped suddenly and the nose dipped.

'You goddamned idiot,' McDonald shouted at the plane. 'Keep going, kid. Straight ahead, damn you.'

But fifty feet up the pilot was gingerly edging the plane round trying to get back to the safety of the airfield. He was breaking the first rule taught at flying school: if the engine fails, glide straight ahead and land—no matter what's in front.

The R.E. seemed to stagger suddenly. Sunlight glinted on the cream undersides of the wings as they rotated slowly into a spin. One complete turn of a spin and the aeroplane disappeared into a wood. The flames shot up before they heard the noise of the crash and a couple of huge smoke rings lifted above the trees as the bombs went off.

''Ere, what's happened to your pal, Sir,' the corporal said to McDonald. Robson had fainted.

'He got a thump on the head during the air raid last night. He ought to have seen a doc but the damn fool refused.'

'That's all right, Sir. The Wing M.O.s 'ere today. 'E was in the mess having brekker when I left. I got a box of supplies in the back for him.'

By the time they got to the huts Robson had recovered. Despite his protests, McDonald insisted on looking for the doctor, and on his way to the mess he met Callaghan who was with a tubby army officer wearing the insignia of the R.A.M.C.

'Ah, McDonald.' Callaghan barred his way. 'You're just the chap I want to see. Robson back with you? I've got a job for the pair of you. Take a couple of new observers up after lunch and show them the area.'

'I was told the Wing M.O. is visiting the Squadron, Sir. It's Robson. He got a crack on the head...'

The tubby man looked at McDonald sharply. 'Well, where is the chap? What happened to him. I am the M.O.'

'Just a minute, Doc,' Callaghan said. 'I want to know what happened to Mister Robson too.'

The M.O. looked at Callaghan with a quizzical eyebrow lifted while McDonald explained about the air raid and the flying masonry.

'He was all right in the car and then he fainted, is that what you're saying?' Callaghan asked. McDonald nodded.

'Did he faint before or after that fool in the R.E. tried to turn back?'

McDonald admitted he wasn't sure.

'All right, Mr. McDonald, it sounds as though the patient will live a few minutes longer. I want a word with the Doc. He'll have a look at Robson in a few minutes.'

A rough hand shook Robson into wakedness. Blinking through sleep-drugged eyes he saw a blurred khaki-clad figure bent over him.

'Robson? What's the matter with you?'

Without waiting for an answer the M.O.'s fingers moved deftly over Robson's bruised face. 'Nasty knock, eh. Tender. Bound to be. No special pain. Thought not. Vision blurred? Watch my finger.'

The M.O. put his finger on Robson's nose, moved it back a couple of feet and then returned it slowly to his nose.

'Hold your hands out. Fingers outstretched. Looks all right. How long have you been out?'

'Only about six weeks...'

'Strenuous times, eh. Nightmares? D'ye dream a lot?' Robson nodded.

'Went to Amiens last night, eh. Damn fine place to relax. Good meal, decent wine, eh? Pretty gels, eh?'

Robson blushed.

The M.O. straightened. 'There's damn-all wrong with you, young man. Nothing that an aspirin and some sleep won't cure. Too much rich food, too much vino, not enough sleep. You night flyers are all the same. Far more dangerous to yourselves than the Hun. You need to be fit, get plenty of sleep. Keep off the vino and leave the whisky bottle alone. That way you will be able to hit the Hun where it hurts and go on doing it. Understand, eh?'

Robson nodded. Instinctively, he suspected Callaghan lay behind the M.O.'s rough, almost brutal tone.

'Right. I'll leave you some aspirins. Don't eat any lunch. Get yourself undressed and into bed. Sleep. You'll be fit to fly tonight. I'll tell your C.O. G'day.'

Robson lay back and closed his eyes. Shit Callaghan, he thought. He saw the sunlight flash on the wings of the doomed R.E.

Then he slept, his face and body twitching as he dreamed. Later McDonald came in, loosened his tie and covered him with a blanket.

Another flight from the day flying squadron on the far side of the field took off, rattling the windows, the howl of the propellers cutting through the hut like a knife.

7

They were all assembled in the mess, waiting. And now they had waited so long that each additional minute started another rumour. Armitage and Fenner and a bunch of 'C' Flight were absorbed in a game of pontoon on one side of the room in hilarious contrast to the earnest whist players on the other side. Periodically someone wound up the gramophone but all the records had been broken in the move except for a scratched 'Cobbler's Song' and a Chopin Nocturne with a crack in it, and as soon as it started someone else turned it off. McDonald and Harris were playing ping-pong.

Robson stood behind Uncle Tom watching the whist players trying to control the knot at the bottom of his stomach that had been there ever since he had seen the Battle Order, the type-written notice listing the crews on duty that night. Robson was on with Captain McRae, someone he hadn't met.

The noise and the brittle chatter died away when Callaghan walked in. The Orderly Sergeant pinned a map on the wall and left as the pilots and observers surged round it. A piece of red string bulged out westwards to beyond Péronne.

Someone murmured, 'Christ, they've made fifteen miles. They're halfway to Amiens . . .'

'How the hell do they do it. We spent three lousy months in '16 taking three miles . . .'

'It's the same ground. Fancy going through the Somme again . . .'

'We won't have as far to fly. If we stay here they'll come to us . . .'

'With a battery of "Jack Johnsons" ...'

'And a long sharp bayonet...'

'My dear chap I joined the Flying Corps to get away from the beastly things...'

Callaghan was reading from a piece of paper, trying to be reassuring. It was true that the Hun had made substantial gains—but at a colossal price. Soon he would outstrip his supply lines. Someone interrupted to say that the advance seemed to get faster each day.

The comment was ignored by Callaghan who continued by saying a fierce battle was in progress for Péronne. It would be their job to interfere with the reinforcements the Hun was hustling into the battle area. The weather was good. They would take advantage of this to fly as many trips as possible. He read out a list of targets. Robson and three others were to attack Vermand, a key junction on the road from St. Quentin to Péronne. Another four were to attack the railway into St. Quentin. A couple were to go after a reported supply dump and another three would make the long haul to Le Cateau again.

'Take off is in forty-five minutes,' Callaghan ended.

'It's still light,' said an incredulous voice.

'It won't be by the time you get over the Line,' Callaghan retorted. 'Moonrise is at ten. You'll have it to help you on your second trip.'

'Ach, to hear them going on you'd think the men out there were indulging in a wee spring picnic. You must be Robson.' A voice with the light sing-song cadence of the Western Highlands spoke in Robson's ear. The speaker was a captain wearing the kilted uniform of the Highland Light Infantry, a slender pale-faced young man, a lock of dark hair curling over his right eye in contrast to the broken nose and the scar splitting the right cheekbone.

'McRae's the name,' he said. Robson noticed McRae didn't offer his hand. 'And now we know where we're going we had best be off. My battalion is—or rather was, as I doubt if there's anything left of it—fighting round Péronne. There'll be no sleeping with my conscience if we don't lend a hand.'

It was still broad daylight as they walked out to the aircraft and no one was hurrying to get airborne. A few patches of dying cumulus cloud showed grey in the dusk and over on the horizon the day was dying in a defiant bar of green light. A mechanic, sitting on a pile of 112 lb. bombs, was quietly playing 'Roses of Picardy' on a mouth organ. Robson dragged his feet and looked anxiously up at the sky.

'Would you be waiting for something?' McRae asked him dryly. He was already in his cockpit fitting the front Lewis gun onto the gas pipe mounting. 'Pass me the spare drums would you.'

Reluctantly Robson handed the ammunition up to McRae, wondering as he did so at the quietness. The bombers were ranged in a slightly curving line outside the hangars. The mechanics stood by waiting. There was only the sentimental wail of the mouth organ. He could hear McDonald arguing with his observer in the adjacent F.E. about the differences in fishing for rainbow and brown trout. The squadron on the other side of the hill were mounting a guard and the distant words of command exaggerated the silence. McRae was staring down at him.

'Man, are you hoping that if you wait long enough the Jairmans will come to you?'

Robson scrambled into his seat explaining that no one else seemed to be making a move. McRae ignored this.

'I want no misunderstanding between us, Robson,' he said quietly. 'When we are dropping the bombs you will fly straight and level unless I direct you to go left or right with my arm. Yes. If you want to shoot at searchlights you can use this.' He tapped the fixed Lewis gun clipped to the left hand side of the nacelle. 'You have one drum for it. This one.' He clipped a drum in place. 'The rest of the ammunition we will use as I please and you will go as I direct you. And...' he stared hard at Robson, 'we will go home when I tell you, not before.'

'Supposing we have an engine failure...' Robson could feel the sweat begin to prickle his hands. Callaghan had obviously been talking to McRae. For a moment his hatred for his C.O. almost swamped his fear. He began to stutter.

'Man it is your job to take us over and bring us back... But should you have a wee spot of bother with the engine make sure there is something wrong for Flight Sergeant Watt to find. He is a very good friend of mine.'

The Scotsman sat down abruptly, almost disappearing into his cockpit and waited with folded arms for Robson to move off.

By the time they climbed to 5,000 feet it was dusk. A mile behind and slightly above them Robson could see the F.E. that had taken off after them, but the ground was a bowl of darkness speckled with a multitude of lights. McRae spotted a flashing beacon and shouted a five-degree alteration of course. The wind was pushing them north.

Robson shivered. The cold was already biting through his fur-lined leather coat, and through his uniform and the woollens he wore under it. Soon his feet would be numb blocks of ice on the rudder bar. That was the worst of pushers, Robson thought bitterly: with the engine in the back there was nothing in front to warm your feet. Even the radiators were behind his shoulders. It was even colder for McRae squatting out of the slipstream in the front cockpit with only a sheet of metal between him and a seventy-five m.p.h. gale.

In front of them to the east, sky and ground merged into one black mass broken by a few wan stars which counterpointed the fires burning on the ground.

A cold draught slapped Robson's right cheek, reminding him that this particular F.E. needed attention by the riggers to cure its tendency to turn left. His left leg was already tired and his numb feet must have relaxed their counter-pressure on the rudder bar. He pressed hard and the F.E. swung slowly back on course.

McRae suddenly popped up and pointed down to the right. For a moment Robson thought that Jerry had brought a fighter aerodrome up into the newly-won territory. But McRae was only pointing to the Amiens–St. Quentin road. Three years of fighting might have reduced the villages of Picardy to unrecognizable humps of brick but nothing could destroy the road arrowing across the uplands south of the River Somme.

Robson stamped his feet gingerly to restore the circulation and, booting the rudder bar, skidded onto a new course crabbing along the road. Over on the left a dump was going up in flames near Péronne, shooting flame and multi-coloured lights high into the sky. A couple of searchlights lit up and wavered about looking for them without success though flashes from the ground showed that one anti-aircraft battery was firing at them. Another two searchlights joined in the hunt. McRae was on his feet now, squinting into the slipstream. He pointed down and lifted his thumb in triumph.

At first Robson could not pick out anything but slowly he was able to separate the jagged chalk lines of trenches from the orderly straightness of the road. He tried to picture the web of roads shown on the map with the fine tracery below.

McRae was calling for him to circle as he pushed a flare into the discharge tube. Seconds later it burst underneath them, a miniature moon swaying under its parachute. The little town below was drenched in its pitiless white light.

The main road through the town from St. Quentin to Amiens, forking right for Péronne, was choked with traffic: guns, ammunition limbers, wagons, team after team of horses, lorries, marching troops, all of them going west.

McRae was signalling for a sharp turn. Robson kicked on the rudder bar; and pushed hard on the stick. The wind slapped his right cheek. They were skidding round. Robson gritted his teeth and told himself: *more bank, more weight on the stick.*

He noticed the airspeed indicator flickering downwards.

Keep the nose down in the turn. It's like wrestling with one of those Army lorries.

McRae's arm was up.

Straighten her up.

The wires were screaming.

Ease the nose up. Where was the horizon?

Right again. Kick the rudder to skid her round. Again. Again. Christ, we're almost stalling.

The A.S.I. was down to fifty-five.

Stuff the nose down. Both hands. Left. Right.

Damn that bloody Scotsman, Robson swore under his breath, why doesn't he drop the bombs. Tracer leaping up in dotted lines, nowhere near them. A searchlight lit up over to the left.

The flare went out. McRae was leaning over the nacelle. Robson, concentrating on flying, relaxed. Now they could go home. But McRae was signalling again: turn again, dropping another flare.

Tight turn. Heave on the stick, kick the rudder, watch the airspeed, listen to the noise of the wires. Was that a misfire in the engine.

Three times they flew over the little town dropped their flares, turned and returned to drop a salvo of 25 lb. bombs. Now there were two small fires, gaps in the long processions blocking the roads. McRae was calling for Robson to dive.

What was he up to? Robson struggled to contain his panic. Christ, there were three F.E.s on the way to bomb this target. Suppose they were underneath ...

McRae turned, teeth glinting, one arm violently motioning Robson down. Robson pushed forward hard, both hands on the stick, knowing he had to use physical violence to force the F.E. into a dive. The rigging wires screamed as they picked up speed.

Ease back the throttle.

Immediately the nose rose and they started to climb. McRae gestured angrily down.

The town flashed beneath them. One of the fires was spreading. Tracer from half a dozen machine-guns flickered up well behind them. The road to Péronne curved northwards. They dipped lower. McRae was firing the Lewis now. Before the flash from the gun dazzled him Robson was vaguely aware of men breaking ranks, a couple of horses rearing up in their traces, then he was relaxing his grip on the stick and they were soaring back into the darkness.

Jesus, that was close.

McRae heaved an empty drum off. Robson watching him, held his breath. If that empty drum slipped it would fly back over his head, along the engine cowling and into the propeller. Even the spent cartridges had to be contained in a bag under the gun. But the Scot did not make any mistakes. His waving arm called on Robson to turn and dive back towards the town.

Four times they dived, machine-gunned, and rose, to dive again until the exploding flare above them marked the presence of the next raider. By the time the machine-gunners on the ground had spotted them, Robson had turned west and headed for home.

It took a long time fighting against the wind to get back. The sweat brought out by fear and by the violent manoeuvres over the target, cooled and froze on Robson's face, and by the time they were over where the airfield should have been he had a stiff neck and cramp in the muscles of the back under the shoulder blades. Robson let the F.E. drift downwards as he searched for the lights of the airfield. But they could not find it. It should have been there. They had crabbed slowly back along the Amiens road as far as Villers-Bretonneux before heading north-west. Twenty miles in twenty minutes—but it was a strong wind. It was a clear night, a star-spangled sky, they could see for ten miles around. But there was nothing. McRae was standing in the slipstream shaking his head. Robson wondered if McRae was wounded—or had he been to sleep? As they circled he tried to stir his numbed mind into action.

'Go back to the road,' McRae shouted at him. 'Fly to Amiens. Then due north for fifteen miles. Are we all right for juice?'

Robson nodded. They were still on the main tank and the gravity tank under the wing was good for half an hour. He turned back and began to climb slowly. At 5,000 feet they would see that much further.

Robson recognized Amiens soon after passing Villers-Bretonneux but kept on upwards. He recognized the big Gothic Cathedral and was mentally retracing his steps with Madelaine when the searchlights lit up and the anti-aircraft guns started firing.

The searchlights and the gunfire were well behind them. Robson started to turn onto a northerly heading, picking out a convenient street at right angles to their course to act as a guide because as usual on a turn to the north the compass was spinning madly in its case. McRae fired the colours of the day from the flare pistol. Immediately the F.E. rocked in the blast of a shell burst and the searchlights weaved towards them as the gunners ranged on the exploding flare. The cockpit stank of cordite fumes.

'Dive, you fool, dive,' McRae shouted.

They raced across the town at roof-top level pursued from all angles by streams of tracer from machine-guns.

Then as they flew north, trying to pick out landmarks that Robson had passed in the tender only a few hours earlier, it became obvious why they had missed the aerodrome. The wind from the west had strengthened and the drift had doubled.

'You took your time about getting back,' Callaghan snapped as Robson and McRae made out their report in his office. The place was packed. The bombers on the long haul to Le Cateau were back and as the tobacco smoke clouded the room a dozen men chattered their reconstruction of the minutes over the target.

'You left twenty minutes before anyone else. How is it you did not get back until the others are ready to go out a second time?' Callaghan was looking at Robson. 'What did you do? Call in somewhere to get an aspirin?'

McRae looked up from his report. 'We got lost,' he said. 'It was my fault. Then we flew over Amiens and our own guns had a go at us. They were nowhere near us until I fired the colours of the day. Then they really zeroed in on us. I think you should remind the O.C. of that battery about the object of firing identification flares.'

'You're a pair of idiots. Why did you have to fly over Amiens? Isn't it big enough to recognize? And as for you, Robson, you should have known how trigger-happy they'd be after last night.'

'Mebbe, Barney, but the lads have got a point,' Tom Cobleigh said butting into the conversation. The rum-laced cocoa he was drinking had washed the grime from around his lips so that he looked like a nigger minstrel from a seaside concert party.

'Those bloody gunners are too bad. There's a battery over here near Cappy.' Turning to the wall map he stubbed a blackened finger on the Somme Valley. 'They gave us a hell of a time tonight. They had no idea where we were until we fired the colours of the day. Next time they'll get a dose of Lewis up their arses.'

'It'd be more sensible to keep well away,' Callaghan replied.

The noise of half a dozen Beardmores running up began to thin out the crowd. Callaghan looked at his watch.

'You can have fifteen minutes,' he said to Robson and McRae. 'Time for a cup of cocoa. Go easy on the rum. If everything goes well the target should be well-lit when you get there...'

'What target?' McRae cried out. 'Man, you must be out of your mind. An aeroplane should bomb Vermond at least once an hour until daybreak. I tell you the road is jammed, jammed solid wi' traffic. Horses, limbers, lorries, men. If we can stop them clearing that junction the day bombers will have a sitting target...'

'McRae!' Callaghan broke in sharply. 'You will bomb where you are told to bomb. We are not split-arse fighter pilots. This is not a game. We get our orders from the Staff and these orders will be carried out. Is that understood.'

Callaghan jabbed the map. 'The Germans have moved up a *staffel* of Hannover C.L.3 trench strafers onto one of our lost aerodromes. The Army does not like being bombed and machine-gunned. You're going to burn out this particular wasps' nest.'

'Where are you going?' Robson asked Uncle Tom, when Callaghan had finished.

'Back to Le Cateau. We left an engine off the rails outside the station. There will be a damned big queue of trains waiting for our attention.'

'That is exactly what I mean,' McRae said. 'That is how the Jairmans do it. Once you have got the target burning we should concentrate all we've got on it. Get things piled up. Then let the day bombers loose on it.'

'My, you are a blood-thirsty young devil tonight,' Uncle Tom replied. 'But you have to remember, my lad, that we are trying to mop up the tide with four sponges. There's thirty miles of Front under attack an' four night bomber squadrons to handle it.'

'Five,' Callaghan corrected him. 'The Navy are putting in a squadron of Handleys. Hop it, you two,' he said to Robson and McRae. 'And don't make a meal of this one. I want you back in time for a third trip.'

Over sandwiches and cocoa Robson and McRae plotted their course. The Le Cateau crews, too, were preparing for their next trip; but their excited chatter as they had reported on their return, had evaporated. They drank their cocoa, munched the curling sandwiches and mentally adjusted themselves to the strain of a return flight to an awakened and waiting target. A few were standing at the bar drinking, under the watchful eye of Armitage and Dick Garbutt. Squadron gossip had it that the Recording Officer knew each man's drinking habits and capacity to the last glass.

McRae sucked on a crumb of bully stuck between his teeth and looked thoughtful.

'Did you hear what that chap in "B" Flight was saying. About their being attacked by a fighter? At night, tch, tch ... I earnestly hope, Robson, that our colleagues have made sure o' them Hannoveranas afore we get there.'

Robson's head ached and a couple of teeth had suddenly started stabbing pains. He hunched his shoulders and morosely watched McRae look at his watch for the third time in minutes.

'Let's away, man, before that deevil o' a foreman, Major Callaghan, has us clocking in and out like the hands in a factory.'

Reluctantly Robson trailed after him. If McRae was right the hangars at the aerodrome would be on fire when they got there. It would be well to bomb from as high as possible. He could imagine the flames from a burning hangar, and the tracers spearing into the silhouetted bombers as they had done a couple of nights ago.

A couple of what looked like sixth-form schoolboys dressed in British Warms were jigging up and down outside the mess to keep their feet warm. They grinned enthusiastically as Robson and McRae passed them. 'I say, jolly good luck,' they chorused. 'Wish we were going. Topping night for it.'

Robson recognized them: Corbett and Harper, the new pilots sharing his room. 'You'll have a job to catch up with Mr. McDonald. He went off half an hour ago,' one of them said.

'Major Callaghan says we might get a flip if there is a spare aeroplane when you get back,' the other added. 'I don't see why we shouldn't go off over the Front with the rest. I've done five hours night flying already.'

McRae let them hold his Lewis as he swung into the cockpit.

'Aye, mebbe so. But if you'll take ma advice you'll no let on. Some o' these new observers are nervous enough already.'

The preceding bombers had made their mark by the time Robson and McRae arrived. Two hangars were burning and a crumpled Hannoverana outside them was adding an oily plume of flame. At 2,000 feet Robson was wondering how best to attack. He had just decided to fly over and then dive back before heading for home when McRae suddenly waved to him to turn away. He leant back over the cockpit. In the moonlight the leather face mask he wore blended with his helmet to make him look like an ancient knight in armour.

'Go away round to the north and come back over the trees,' he shouted. 'You can line up with the flames. With the wind behind us we'll be faster over the ground. Then keep going for a mile or two afore turning for home.'

Robson eased back the throttle and swung round to

the south. His head moved sharply from one side of the nacelle to the other like a wild animal approaching a trap, suspecting it was a trap and yet too hungry to resist taking the bait. The moon-washed landscape that had made the flight so much easier now seemed to him much too bright. Lumbering along at eighty miles per hour in this clear sky made him feel a sitting target. He felt naked and afraid. McRae was standing up now, quartering the sky above and behind.

The burning aerodrome was out of sight as the bleached filigree trees came up to meet them. But a red glow marked its whereabouts and once a host of coloured lights whirled in the sky on a tongue of flame as an ammunition store exploded.

The pain in Robson's head was worse now, and impulsively he tore off his helmet and leant out bare-headed in the icy slipstream. The cold blast of air refreshed him, but his nerves were stretched tight as a drum. This business of flying away from the target, to come in from the east, was only adding half an hour to the strain of watching for an unseen enemy and delaying the moment when they had to dive in on an awakened, burning airfield.

Pulling his helmet on again Robson slowly opened the throttle to stretch his glide and started a slow turn to the left watching the reflected fire in the sky, using it as the centre of the radius of his turn. It was better to get it over with. He saw McRae look at him and shake his head. He ignored it. It was all right for that damned Scotsman. He was brave and he hated the Germans for what they were doing to his regiment.

Robson watched the tree-tops and eased the throttle further open. His world was a silvered pattern of tree-tops and ploughland chequered with roads and hedges rotating slowly round a primeval fire. He saw flames leaping high a few degrees over to the left between a clump of trees.

Throttle right forward, all the way, stick forward, both hands.

McRae clutched his Lewis as the nose tilted down. The bleached carpet of trees resolved itself into bare branches reaching up to pluck them down.

Stick back. Forward again.

The extra speed had made them climb.

Rudder. More rudder.

The wind slapped Robson's cheeks as he skidded into line. He saw three, then four hangars, the last two burning. McRae had left the gun for the bomb release.

Skid right, now left. Boot the rudder hard. Harder.

Tracer leapt up at them from all parts of the aerodrome. Robson could hear it, feel it plucking slits in the fabric. Spang. Something had hit the engine. Oh, God, Robson prayed, let it keep running for a few more minutes. He cowered lower in the cockpit. His legs felt rigid with panic.

McRae was back at the gun. Outlined in flame he lifted his thumb, signifying the bombs had gone. Fire, everything was afire. The flames turned the wings into rosy transparencies, gauze extensions of a moth reaching for the candle.

McRae was shouting, waving one arm as he swung the gun to the left. Robson's gaze followed the gunner's and the F.E. turned with him as his feet relaxed momentarily on the rudder bar.

The flames behind them blinded him when he turned. Where were the tree-tops? Instinctively Robson eased the pressure on the stick. Nothing happened. The controls were solid.

Fight them.

There was a blinding flash from the Lewis. What the hell could McRae see to fire at?

Tracer flickered up at them out of the night. Suddenly, the F.E. bucked and a stink of petrol filled the cockpit as the gravity tank in the wing was torn open.

Oh Christ, they were going to burn, fall through the air like a torch.

The F.E. was still turning left as Robson stared over his shoulder at the engine, waiting for the flames to blossom behind him. McRae shouted something and the sky was blotted out as a biplane suddenly leapt out of nowhere straight into the swinging path of the F.E. Robson kicked at the rudder bar. McRae was whirling behind the Lewis firing point blank. The flash was blinding.

Stick forward. Oh God, where were the bloody trees.

The Hannoverana was gone. McRae was shouting again. 'Turn back. Turn. Not that way, you bloody fool.'

Sky and ground rotated slowly round. The compass was spinning crazily.

Turn, what the hell did he mean, 'Turn?' They were turning. Where the hell was that fighter? Oh, Christ, where was it?

McRae was leaning towards him thumping the nacelle with a gloved fist. 'You are going east. Straighten her when I tell you. Go home. West. Go west. Now.'

His gloved hand lifted and fell. Robson stood on the rudder bar and fought the stick, watching the horizon as it levelled out.

McRae was grinning, his teeth white against his blackened chin. He raised his thumb again as he quartered the sky behind them. 'Home, James,' he shouted. 'We've lost him. But get up to a couple of thousand feet. He might spot us against the ground. How are we off for juice?'

Robson forced his voice to stay under control. 'Should be all right. I think it was only the gravity tank.' He eased the F.E. into a climb and belatedly throttled the engine back to 1,200 revs. He was shaking and his body was sticky with sweat.

He began to look for damage. The engine seemed all right. So did the oil pressure. The water temperature was a little high. Was there a hole in their radiator or was it

through running at full throttle so long? How long had it
been, a quarter of an hour? No, according to the clock
it was four minutes since they dived on the aerodrome.

Jesus.

He forced himself to watch the dials, especially the
temperature. He knew he had to do something, anything,
to overcome the dreadful tiredness that had come down
on him like a blanket.

He was still watching the water-temperature gauge creep
up when they crossed the Line. McRae thumped the
nacelle to attract his attention and pointed to the loom of
Bapaume about five miles away beyond the right wing
tip. A dump to the east of the town was burning. Miniature volcanoes spat fountains of flame into the air.

'How long before we get home?' Robson shouted.

'About forty-five minutes. It's this head-wind. Try lower
down. Is there something wrong?'

They had climbed slowly to nearly 4,000 feet and Robson had no intention of losing any height now. He nodded
back at the engine.

'We must have got a hole in the radiator. She's on the
boil. No water soon. Then, napoo.'

The grinning Scot slapped his arms round his shoulders.
'Pity to waste all that steam. We could do wi' it up
here.'

He held up the map. 'Three north-south railway lines.
There's the first. Then look out for Doullens. There's an
aerodrome fifteen miles ahead—Marieux. Near the last
railway line.'

Robson shook his head. He was too tired and numb to
think. Better to keep going, to land at an airfield he knew.
How long, he wondered, would it take to boil all the water
away? His mouth felt dry. How long would the engine
run without water? The oil pressure was falling. Hot
engine; thin oil; lower pressure.

The two dials, the compass, and the watch clipped to

the dashboard, all claimed his attention. The slow inexorable rotation of the pointers seemed to measure their fate. Robson huddled deeper into the cockpit. Occasionally his tired left leg relaxed and the compass twitched as the F.E. started a left turn, and he would have to kick some life into his feet and turn back onto course.

Fifteen minutes later the pointer of the water temperature gauge was up against the stop, and the oil pressure was five pounds per square inch above the red line and falling. Robson pointed the nose down and the airspeed picked up—eighty five m.p.h. Ten minutes to go at that rate before they reached the airfield. The oil pressure sagged another two P.S.I.

McRae thumped the nacelle again and pointed ahead to a searchlight playing horizontally across a field. Then Robson saw five flickering flares and he knew they were almost home. But as he pushed the nose down they were all extinguished. At the same moment the engine rattled horribly. There was no more water left to turn to steam. The oil pressure was zero. The stink of overheated metal began to creep forward into the cockpit.

'I've got the pistol,' McRae shouted. 'They think we're Jerry. Get ready to flash our letter.'

The green flare soared up over the top wing and a few minutes later the searchlight flashed on again followed one after another by the fired petrol buckets. Some mechanic running between flares was probably cursing us at this minute, Robson thought, and hoping that we will let him get clear before we land.

He had never landed using the searchlight. It conspired with the wisps of ground mist to confuse his judgment of height. Twenty feet in the air he pump-handled the stick to get down. But he'd levelled off too high and the flares were shooting by. There were only five and three of them were behind him. He slammed the throttle open. The clanking heap of metal behind him would just have to go on running for a further five minutes.

Two cylinders failed to fire. The engine spluttered and banged like a machine-gun, and sheets of flame belched from the exhaust. Low on airspeed the F.E. staggered across the aerodrome ten feet above the ground and without sufficient power to climb.

Then one of the missing cylinders chimed in, and the airspeed indicator crept upwards as the mass of trees fringing the airfield closed around them. The massive undercarriage of the F.E. crunched against some branch as they limped through a gap torn in the poplars by an exploding bomber weeks before. As well as trees, every aerodrome had its gaps—expensive gaps.

Gingerly Robson began to skid into a sort of circuit. There was a village ahead with a steepled church, he remembered, and this time he had to do it right. If he didn't the engine would never take them round again.

Too low to see the aerodrome flares now, but the glare of the searchlight told him he was paralleled and downwind.

Get a bit higher. God, the engine sounds rough. Got to pick up more speed. Christ, that was twenty feet lost. Hold it there. Where are those bloody flares? Turn—no, not yet. Too soon and you're a dead duck. Now, slowly kick it round. Watch the ...

The nacelle shuddered violently and the aeroplane twitched to the left as the engine seized up solid and stopped. The silence hurt like a bullet wound. The flares were there, over to the left, tilted at a crazy angle.

Kick on rudder again, push the nose down. How many funeral parties have you been detailed for because of a spin off a turn. Slow march. The last post. Concentrate. Where is that hedge. There. Stick back. Let her float. Wait, wait.

It was like hanging in space: no movement, just resting on the mist. Even the wires were silent and the whistles from the torn fabric, and the flapping cables . . .

Crunch.

The oleo legs bottomed on their stops but miraculously the bomber stayed on the ground, turning remorselessly to the right in a huge circle, leaning further and further over.

Bump, bump, BUMP.

A wing tip grazed the grass. Suddenly they swung and toppled over as the undercarriage legs collapsed on the right side. They stopped with hardly a jolt.

McRae unshipped his Lewis gun and stepped over the side of the nacelle.

'Ach, you should do that every time. It makes for a far more dignified exit. Are you all right?'

Robson sat on in his cockpit nodding his head mechanically. He felt too tired to get out—too tired or too frightened.

'You go ahead,' he said. 'I'll meet you in Callaghan's office.'

He could hear men running and a car engine starting up. The thought of seeing people, answering questions made him feel sick. He climbed down and walked away from them.

McRae was telling them about the flight when Robson walked into Callaghan's office. Half a dozen pilots and observers were there: McDonald was looking green with envy as Garbutt, Armitage and Callaghan watched the Scot manoeuvring with his hands.

'It was after we had dropped our bombs that I first saw it. I caught the gleam of his exhaust in the corner of my eye. And when I looked up there was this Hannoverana with its wee bitty biplane tail formating wi' us alongside the wing tip an' yon Jairman drawin' a bead wi' his Parabellum.

'I yelled and grabbed the Lewis but I thought we were

fini. But not oor man, Christopher Robson. He made a split-arse turn towards the Hun. Never haff I seen a Fee turn like that, split-arsed like a Camel. We damn near rammed him. That put the wind up Jerry—and me. He blew out the gravity tank and punctured the radiator. But we lost him...'

'Where did your bombs land?' Callaghan asked, 'and did you score any hits on the fighter?'

'No idea. I was aiming for the first two hangars, the ones you blighters missed. There were at least three aeroplanes burning on the ground.'

'And the fighter?'

'We put the fear of the Lord into him. I thought I was hitting him, but wi' the flash from the Lewis and Robson split-arsing us onto a collision course I doubt we did any real harm. Here he is, Split-Arse Robson himself.'

Robson stood in the doorway, blinking at the light. He wished they would all go away because he wanted to see Callaghan alone. Stumbling round the aerodrome he had made up his mind. Callaghan could do and say what he wanted but he, Robson, was not flying on the next trip, even if there was an aeroplane to replace the one he had wrecked. He'd had enough.

Someone slapped him on the back and someone else thrust a tin mug of hot cocoa, well-laced with rum, into his hands. Callaghan was speaking.

'How did the fighter pick them up? In exactly the same way that Harvey and Johnson got themselves killed the other day. We are night bombers because the F.E. is too slow and cumbersome to fly by day where we can be seen. Seen, do you understand. If Robson had come in over that aerodrome from the west, straight in with the nose down, full power and the wind behind him, it's unlikely that the fighter would have seen them and caught them before they got out of the illuminated area. And there would not be a wrecked aeroplane out there.'

'And Split-Arse wouldn't have got himself a bloody fighter,' somebody said at the back of the room. 'Now we know what to do. Ram the sods.'

They clustered round Robson, demanding to know the secret. Before he could say anything Callaghan banged on his desk for silence.

'This is an office, not a bear garden. The Third Army are in trouble between Lechelle and Manancourt. According to the stragglers coming back there is a big concentration of troops between them and Equancourt. Staff want us to disturb their sleep. All available aircraft will be used. I have a spare machine for you, Robson, but it will take the mechanics some time to refuel and re-bomb. Take off will be in ninety minutes.'

In the stunned silence that followed someone asked the time of sunrise. Someone else said, as they trooped out to the mess, 'Christ, I thought he said we were night bombers.'

Swept away by the pilots wanting to talk about his night fighter, Robson had no chance to refuse to go, and by the time he had drunk more coffee and had had a bowl of soup he was too tired to protest. As he talked about his anti-fighter tactics he soon forgot that the whole thing had been an accident, the combination of a badly-rigged F.E. and tired leg muscles.

Nine machines were patched up and made ready for the raid on the bivouac area. Eight of them carried 25 lb. bombs and the other one, two 112 lb. bombs. There were no laggards on take-off. The penalty for being late was too obvious.

McDonald was the first off but he had just cleared the trees when the camshaft drive gears sheared and he landed 200 yards beyond the aerodrome finishing with the nose of his nacelle deep in the mud of a ploughed field. Harris, his observer complained bitterly that the fifty m.p.h.

slide over the furrows had done nothing to improve either
him or his trousers.

The pilot carrying the big bombs had half his plugs
oil up as he struggled up to 4,000 feet, and landed gingerly
on the nearest airfield. The last light of the waning moon
helped the other seven to find the target easily despite
the swirls of mist. A tired and over-confident battalion
had been too hungry and cold to mask its bivouac fires.
One of the first raiders started a small fire but no one
lingered too long after dropping their bombs. Even McRae
was content with only two passes over the camp to fire
his Lewis at tents and scurrying figures amid the trees.
The lightening sky in the east hurried them away. Two
more of the squadron fell out with engine failure on the
way home.

It was almost daylight by the time they got back. The
first slivers of light from the newly-risen sun bleaching
the smoking flare pots and gilding the mist swirling in the
trees. There was breakfast for men too tired to eat. The
bombers from Le Cateau were back, two out of the three
that left. Everyone was too tired to care.

But Dick Garbutt scurried round telling them that so
and so had phoned in and was O.K. on the right side of
the Line. It had, he kept repeating, been a momentous
night for the squadron. No other squadron had ever flown
so many hours in one night. They had dropped umpteen
hundred pounds of bombs on so many targets and according to the reports they had done so much of this and
this much of that amount of damage. And without losing
a man, except for the observer who had lost a hand and
the pilot with a broken leg—and three wrecked aeroplanes.

Robson pecked at his congealing egg and bacon and
watched Uncle Tom top up his coffee from a bottle of
rum and suddenly realized that the Flight Commander
was almost drunk. The cold dawn light made him look
an old man.

Fenner from 'C' Flight slumped into a seat beside him. He took the bottle, topped up his own cup and filled Robson's.

'Good old Split-Arse,' he said, nudging Uncle Tom. 'Is this what turns your young cubs into split-arse fighter pilots.'

Robson heard someone behind him saying, '...that's him. Mad young sod. Did a split-arse turn and went for a Hannoverana. Tried to ram him. Damn near did...'

'Silly ass. Ought to use cunning,' the other replied. 'There are old pilots and bold pilots but no old bold pilots...'

Suddenly the stench of the rum made Robson gag in the back of his throat. He staggered out of the mess, went round the back and was violently sick.

8

The sun was hot by the time Robson got up and went to a
half-deserted mess for lunch.

All the Squadrons' transport, the Major and the Flight
Commanders, the Armament and Equipment Officers were
away on an official looting expedition. The great R.F.C.
dump at Candas, the product of three years' continual
growth, was being evacuated and the squadrons had been
told to help themselves.

But Callaghan had left orders with Dick Garbutt to keep
the Squadron busy. Robson and McDonald each flew a new
pilot around the area. Four replacement F.E.s arrived
safely. A fifth flew over too high up then glided in to
land from 5,000 feet. The pilot forgot to clear his engine in
the glide, undershot the aerodrome and, opening the
throttle too violently as the hedge loomed up, the engine
cut out on him. He landed short, bounced on the boundary road, tore off the undercarriage in the hedge and
when the nacelle of the F.E. hit the ground the heavy
engine tore out of its mounting and crushed him.

Dick Garbutt was in his office when Robson and
McDonald reported in after showing the new pilots
around.

'Do you know anyone who can ride a motor-cycle?' he
asked them.

'Sure, look no further than present company,' McDonald said. 'Split and I are experts.'

Garbutt looked at them with the ghost of a smile on his
face. 'I don't know. It is not fair asking you two to go. It
will be a long dusty ride into Amiens and you'd have to

be back before eight. But if you would do it to oblige me...' He explained what he wanted.

Robson walked round the mud-spattered motor-cycle. It was a standard Douglas despatch rider's mount fitted with a wicker sidecar. The spindly handlebars were swept back so that the rider sat upright, and were littered with small nickel-plated levers that trailed Bowden cables in all directions.

'You're a damned liar,' he said to McDonald, quietly because Garbutt was watching them. 'I've never driven one in my life. Always wanted to but my mother thought them dangerous—and a bit *infra dig*.'

'There can't be much to it,' McDonald replied. 'I've watched the despatch riders. Petrol tap, spark, throttle, clutch. Give me a push: Amiens, here we come.'

The engine started easily. McDonald snatched the gear lever into neutral, waited for Robson to wriggle into the sidecar, snicked it into gear and tweaked open the throttle.

The road from the office was a wide cinder path that curved gently to the left towards the hangars. Before reaching them it straightened and turned sharp right to avoid the entrance to the farmyard and ran on for a hundred yards before joining the cobble-and-mud of the main road. The cinder topping was sodden with the rain of the past few days. So when McDonald let in the clutch with the engine running at near top speed the motor-cycle stood still while the back wheel excavated a trench in the loose cinders. When the tyre sank deep enough the wheel gripped and the outfit hurtled away like a bomb—a bomb dragged round to the right by the sidecar. A batman with an armful of laundry shed his load and threw himself under a hut. McDonald pulled on the left handlebar, and as the combination straightened and turned left the sidecar wheel lifted off the ground. Hastily he turned right to drop onto three wheels again but they still went round in a wide circle. Garbutt, clawing cinders off his blackened face, shook an angry fist at them before he was dragged out of the way by an heroic clerk.

There was plenty of room on the airfield and McDonald soon acquired the knack of steering although in doing so he only just avoided shattering the rudder of one F.E. and knocked over a pair of steps by another.

By the time he had found out how to drive it straight they'd arrived at the right turn past the farmyard entrance. The sidecar wheel lifted as they turned. McDonald groped for the throttle lever. Abandoning the turn they ploughed on into the farmyard, splashed through the pond and as the wet drive-belt began to slip they slowed enough for McDonald to glance down in his search for the throttle lever.

He was easing it back when they hit the manure heap. The bike reared up, still climbing, its momentum keeping them going although the rear wheel was spinning like a fan, spraying them, and the surrounding wall, with manure. Then the rear wheel slid sideways, contacted the cobbles of the yard and sent them jerkily into the lane that led to the road.

McDonald's muck-covered fingers slipped off the throttle lever. What he thought was the brake turned out to be the clutch. With the engine screaming they rolled onto the road in front of a horse-drawn G.S. wagon. The horses reared up as the combination climbed the far bank which deflected it back onto the road, scattering a group of Chinese labourers. With the throttle wide open again they sped down the long straight road, leaping from bump to bump towards Amiens.

'What the hell are you doing?' Robson shouted as he attempted to clean his face with a manure-soaked sleeve. 'Find a stream.'

'Nuts,' McDonald shouted back. 'Once we stop we might not get started again. Next stop the hospital. Jeez, feller, say your prayers and hope the girls are home—with plenty of hot water.'

They were. Eventually the four of them had tea together in the huge kitchen of the converted chateau. Robson and McDonald huddled in threadbare hospital dressing gowns while their newly sponged and pressed uniforms steamed gently in half-opened ovens and an orderly threw buckets of water over the Douglas to wash it down.

They were on their way back before Robson realized that the moment he had been dreading, meeting Madelaine again, was over. Ever since he'd awakened and found her gone from his bed, he had tormented himself with the idea that she would not want to see him again. But she had kissed him—after he had bathed—and he now knew where he could meet her. Twice a day the ambulances passed a cross-roads not three miles from the airfield.

9

There was low cloud and the smell of rain in the air when the first of the night's raids took off. South of Bapaume at the juncture of the Third and Fifth Armies the Germans were still pushing eastwards. Six F.E.s flown by the Flight Commanders and their deputies, the most experienced pilots on the Squadron, made the long haul to Valenciennes to attack the railway feeding the advancing army. Another six went on the same errand to Cambrai. The remainder, six of them, including Robson and McDonald and their two new room-mates, Harper and Corbett, had roving commissions to attack bivouacs and transport south and east of Bapaume. Despite the low cloud, and rain that stung like acid, there was no shortage of targets and little ground fire. Robson returned, like the others, with empty drums and not a hole in his aeroplane.

But Corbett, one of the new pilots, had engine failure before reaching the Line. His bombs went off after the crash but he had already been crushed by the engine, and his observer, thrown into one of the shattered tree stumps that had wrecked them, had a fractured skull.

One of the observers on the Cambrai trip returned with a bullet in his shoulder so Callaghan replaced him with McRae for the second raid and went himself with Robson in the 'pom-pom' F.E.

The cloud was getting lower and the rain, mixed with flurries of hail, prevented them from using flares. After an hour in the target area even Callaghan had to give the weather best and return to base with clips of shells unused. But no sooner were they down than the wind changed a few degrees into the south bringing clear sky and a warm hint of the coming summer.

One of the Valenciennes raiders did not return.

Robson was awakened about eight by the noise of a slammed door. A tall youth with red hair and freckles dropped his pack onto an empty bed.

'I say, you, that's Corbett's bed,' Robson said, his mind fogged by sleep and the warmth of the morning.

There was no sign that Corbett had ever existed. The cabin trunk under the bed, the photographs on the chest of drawers and the *pickelhaube* he had bought as a souvenir in Candas had all disappeared.

Robson and the new man stared at each other for a moment. 'Sorry. Forget what I said.'

'I'm Canning, Bob Canning,' the newcomer said. 'I've just got in from the depot. I say, fancy us having to fly old kites like the F.E. I thought...'

Robson grunted, and rolled over pretending to be asleep. He could still hear Corbett saying, '...I say, jolly good luck. I wish I was going with you...'

IO

After a late breakfast Robson walked across fields and through woods sweating in the growing warmth of the sun to the cross-roads that Madelaine had mentioned. He carried a pack with a picnic lunch and a bottle of Burgundy and one of Graves.

McDonald was absent. He had talked one of the pilots on the R.E. Squadron into taking him on the afternoon patrol as a gunner, as they were a man short. Those few people in the Flight who got wind of what he was doing were quite sure that if the Germans did not get him he would wish that they had when Callaghan heard about it.

There was a hump-backed bridge over a stream by the cross-road. Robson lowered the Graves into the water and sat down, his back against the warm stone. The walk, the buzzing of bees and the new warmth in the air conspired to send him to sleep until the noise of the convoy of ambulances woke him. Madelaine had said that they moved up in the daytime and waited just outside the range of the batteries until dusk. Then at last light they went in to empty the forward first-aid posts of casualties and kept driving in and out all night.

But there was no sign of Madelaine. He dozed off again. It would have been expecting too much to meet her the first time.

Something thumped lightly onto the ground beside him. Strong hands rolled him over. He was being lifted and as he struggled to emerge from his sleep a firm strap round the back of his shoulders forced his head down onto rough canvas.

'Poor fella,' a female voice said. 'Shell shock, I'd say. Look how white and emaciated he is. Exposure too. Probably been out all night.'

'Shell shock, my foot. Probably bad gin,' another female voice said.

'Maybe you're right. Either way he's too far gone to have a chance. Seems a durned rotten shame to raise his hopes. I vote we just dump him in the river.'

The strap came off his chest. As he opened his eyes he realized he was on a stretcher that was resting on the bank above the stream. He sat up. 'Here, I say...' He looked round. Madelaine and Mamie Sorensen were lifting the uppermost handles. He slid down, off the stretcher, feet first into the ice cold water of the stream. It came almost up to his knees. Madelaine leant over him. Ripples of sunlight reflected from the water chased over her face and neck, the swell of her breasts. His bones turned to liquid and he shuddered violently. It was not the cold.

'First aid, my sweet,' she said to him. 'We saw the steam coming off your feet and thought you were on fire.'

He scrambled up the bank and ignoring Mamie put his arms round Madelaine and kissed her.

'My, my, the things a body can see on a hot sunny afternoon,' he heard Mamie say in an exaggerated drawl.

After they had eaten his sandwiches and finished the wine Mamie decided to drive on to the rendezvous point. Sooner or later, she explained, someone would start wondering where the two missing ambulances had got to. If she turned up and explained that Madelaine had had a breakdown but it was being repaired and would be along in an hour or so no one would come looking.

'It's not like it used to be,' she said, climbing into the cab while Robson stood by the starting handle. 'This goddam war has gotten too serious to be fun any more.'

She retarded the ignition lever. Robson pulled the engine over slowly. Another sharp pull and it started, tappets clattering, the radiator quivering on the single leaf spring of the front suspension.

'And you tell that goddamned Canadian that if he prefers an aeroplane to my company he can try taking one to tea in Amiens.'

The hand brake on the transmission engaged as she pedalled the foot controls and the rickety old ambulance stuttered away.

'What is the matter with Mamie?' Robson asked. 'I thought she looked rather sad.'

Madelaine hitched up her skirt and sat on the coping of the bridge.

'We're all sad. They are folding us up, shutting down the shop, sending us home. We run on American money. It has always been an informal amateur sort of affair. But though I say it myself we have done a lot of good work. Now the American Army is beginning to build up and they have come over with their own organization. You wouldn't believe it but they are very regimental. So it's officially-sponsored things like the American Red Cross and other bodies now and who the hell are these high falutin' Limey women driving clapped-out Fords in non-issue uniforms.

'The British Army don't want us. The French do but they've no money. Our American sponsors think that now their Army is here the Government can pay. So that's it. Another month and we fold.' She spread her arms wide. 'Our last spring in Picardy. Positively the last, the final appearance of Fred Karno's Ambulance Auxiliaries.'

'The way things are going it might be the last spring for everyone,' Robson said. 'A few more miles and there will be nothing to stop Jerry going right through to the coast.'

'I don't believe it. You men are mad. You and the Germans. This is a war that neither side can win. It will go on and on until there is no one left to fight but the old men. Then the women will take over running things and stop this childish nonsense.'

'Which women? Try walking down the High Street in a civvy suit and see what happens. You are worse than the men. I remember a woman at our training school. Her son had been killed. She came to the funeral and told us how proud she was to have done her bit. Her eldest son had been killed in '16 and she knew the youngest one would be following in his brother's footsteps the following year. I felt sick. She didn't know her son was killed because his instructor was too incompetent to fly and too afraid to let his pupils try.'

'Don't look at me like that,' she said as if divining what he was thinking. 'God help me, I sent two men off to die. I didn't know what I was doing.' She paused, and then said sadly, 'I wonder how many women lie awake at night thinking just those very words: "I didn't know what I was doing".'

She jumped down, took his arm and suggested a walk, as if turning off a painful memory. 'It's your fault,' she said. 'You ought to know me by now. Strong drink may help you seduce other girls but it only makes me argumentative. I had an Irish grandmother.'

They walked on arm in arm along a path on the bank of the stream towards a small copse.

'But don't you worry about driving right up to the Front when things are as they are? You might be cut off.'

His grip on her arm tightened, and she laughed. 'You men, I can tell what you are thinking. Prisoners in the hands of the Boche. Plucky little woman faced with a fate worse than death. I've seen more Germans than you have. They bleed like any other men. And I'd trust them a lot more than I would the French Colonial troops. Ugh. I would not like to be a prisoner. I'd hate it. But rape ... I learned about rape from my husband.'

'Really, Madelaine, what a thing to say. And the poor fellow is dead, killed in action . . .'

'Are you shocked at the word . . . or the deed? When I feel old, very old, like I do now, and I think about the silly stupid little girl I was I wonder how I put up with him.'

'But surely you married him of your own free will? I mean to say, it wasn't an arranged marriage or anything like that. Not in England.'

'Don't be silly. I helped with the arranging. The poor man was lured into the trap. I was the bait, and it was sprung before he knew what was happening. I made the catch of the season.

'He was a Major, a second son, and his elder brother childless. He might have been nearer fifty than forty but, my God, he was handsome. Tall, thin angular face and brown as a berry. He'd just come back from India.'

'How old were you?'

'I'd just come out. My season. That's what made it so marvellous. We scooped the opposition. Everyone was after him.' Her voice seemed to have changed, the accent more polished, the hardness gone out of it. 'I was eighteen when we got married.'

Robson felt his stomach contract into an angry knot. He was visualizing someone like his father taking this beautiful girl to bed.

'The six months before we were married was like being in heaven. I was important. We went out to restaurants by ourselves. We hunted together . . .'

'You said you hated blood sports . . .'

'She was a different girl. Don't interrupt. We went shooting. Everyone said we were an ideal match. And he'd kiss me goodnight. Nothing more. And I'd smell the tobacco in his moustache and I'd go to bed dreaming of how I would look after him—and his career.

'We were too well matched. That six months we were

like brother and sister. It must be hard to change from being a brother to being a lover.'

She shut her eyes and hung onto his arm.

'That first week I thought I would die. He would drink in the bar. Dutch courage I suppose. The stink of whisky came to bed with him. He wanted a son so badly. Poor man, I don't think he got much fun out of it. It wasn't so bad when we got home. Once a month then. He'd come into my bedroom and clear his throat. Ahem, ahem. And put out the light before he took off his dressing gown. It was when we were living in Town that I hated it most.

'He used to come to me smelling of the woman he'd been with. Oh God forgive me, I hated him then. But, at last I produced a son for him and it was over. I never slept with him again...'

She was crying now, stumbling blindly along the path supported by his arm.

'A son? What happened to him? Where is he now?'

'His grandfather has him.'

She tore herself free of his arm and ran ahead to the edge of the little wood. The trees had been splintered in some bygone battle but now a new growth was beginning to climb upwards. As he caught up with her she flopped down in a chalky hollow like a shot rabbit and pulled him down beside her.

'Love me, Christopher, love me,' she cried, her hands searching for the buckles of his Sam Browne. 'Love me. I feel unclean, a murderous bitch. Love me, darling Christopher, and tell me I'm not unclean.'

Instinctively he started to look around but she pulled his face down to hers to kiss. The intensity of her desire was infectious. His hands plucked at her shirt, the waist band of her skirt. They made love suddenly, violently, her back arched upwards like a bow as he entered into her.

'I have shocked you again,' Madelaine said, smoothing down her skirt. As she rolled towards him he could see

the smooth white mounds of her breasts through the unbuttoned khaki shirt.

'Give me a cigarette, one of those Turkish ones.'

She kissed him lightly on the cheek as he fumbled in
his left breast pocket for his cigarette case. His mother
had given him a pocket Bible to carry there. His father
had produced the heavy silver case even though he knew
that his son seldom smoked.

She smiled at him as he lit their cigarettes then wrinkled
her nose at him and pouted, a gleam of mischief in her
eyes. 'You are supposed to enjoy making love to me. Or
do you think it is something that should be done only in
bed, at night, with the curtains drawn?'

'Yes, er no, I mean, of course I like making love to you.
It's just, well, I never know where I am with you. I thought,
you know, after what you said ... Well, what your husband did...'

She lay back, her head pillowed on his chest and blew
a plume of smoke into the sky. 'I told you, it's your fault,
you make me talk too much. The girl that was me. She's
dead now, along with the world that bred her, dead a long
time ago...'

He kissed the top of her head. 'After the war, when we
are married, we'll drink wine every night and you can
talk and talk...'

She shuddered and turned suddenly to hold him tightly.

'After the war, after the war. The words frighten me.
Don't you understand why I feel so guilty about the whole
revolting bloody mess. I carry men, what's left of men,
night after night. I get my nose rubbed into the pain, the
stupid waste of it. And I know that it was the war that
made me. If it hadn't been for the war I'd still be a brood
mare, a hostess ... With a mouth like a rat-trap. An auto-
matic smile, one eye on my husband and the other on his
bank balance. Oh God, I'm getting morbid again. Give
me another cigarette.'

She puffed at it, inhaling deeply.

Eventually he said, 'Who's Ben?'

He felt her stiffen. Then, as if making up her mind, she relaxed again. 'Who was he, you mean. Ben Leben. He was a journalist, a pacifist socialist, a Jew.'

'He's dead?'

'Yes. He was the other man I sent off to die.'

He smoothed her hair. 'We'll have to go,' he said. Madelaine sat up and looked down at him. 'I never thought I could love anyone else after Ben,' she said slowly. Then more briskly, 'Yes, let's go back to the war. I know about it. I've got a job to do ... For a few weeks. I can cope. I'm frightened about what comes after.'

As if he was not there she loosened her skirt, smoothed her underwear down, brushed the dried grass from her uniform before pulling her skirt again. As they walked along the bank she buttoned up her shirt and remade her tie.

Overhead a flight of D.H. day bombers clawed for height as they swept south towards the Lines.

II

He was back in the mess in time for tea. As he walked in, someone going out said, over his shoulder, 'Better give the Orderly Room a tinkle, Split. Old man Garbutt has been looking all over the shop for you.'

Before he could sit down to his tea of sardines on toast, two others told him that the Recording Officer had been looking for him. He realized with a warm glow of satisfaction that suddenly he was accepted. He was Split-Arse, the nut who had tried to fight a Hannoverana and got away with it; positive proof to the fearful that the old F.E. was not just a sitting duck. It had teeth. He saw a couple of the replacement pilots staring at him. Now, he was one of the Squadron characters, a beacon of hope. Uncle Tom and Tim Keegan came over to join him.

'Dick Garbutt was looking for you,' Uncle Tom said. 'H.Q. want some more guff about your fight with that Hannoverana.'

'What fight? All I did was get out of the way in the shortest possible time.'

'Suit yourself laddie, but if you'll take a tip from an old hand never look a gift reputation in the mouth. He's got a pile of mail for you too.'

'Have you seen your fire-eating Canadian friend yet?' Keegan asked. 'He'll not go scrounging flips in Harry Tates again in a hurry. Talk of the devil, here he comes.'

McDonald came over to join them. Someone raised an ironic cheer. The Canadian stood for a moment on tiptoe, straining upwards, his hands clasped over his head like a boxer. His right eyelashes and eyebrows were missing and the side of his face was an angry red, flecked with spots of black as though he had been hit by a charge of buckshot. A long strip of plaster laced the edge of his jawbone.

'It only hurts when I laugh,' he said as he sat down. 'The thing that gets my goddam goat is that it was all over so damned fast I never saw the bastard. Me, the eagle-eyed wonderboy.'

They had dropped their bombs and strafed a machine-gun nest, he told them. With his ammunition drum for the Lewis gun empty he had ducked inside the cockpit for a new one. At that moment a fighter coming from out of the sun had caught them broadside-on and the new ammunition drum had partially exploded in his face just before he took it from the rack. Before he had recovered from the shock a couple of Camels had shot the marauder down. He did not even know what type it had been.

Uncle Tom started to say something but McDonald cut in. 'I know, I know, Callaghan wants to see me. Callaghan is going to have my guts for garters. He's welcome. For a minute or two I didn't reckon on having any left to give him.' He turned to Robson. 'Garbutt wants to see you. Here's your mail.'

He dumped a pile of magazines and letters on the table. As Robson picked up the letters the others attacked his magazines.

'Heli, *Illustrated London News*, *Blackwood*, *Punch*, no copy of *The Strand*. Why don't you tell your people about *La Vie Parisienne*, Split.'

Robson grinned as they ripped the covers off his magazines. He put the letters in his pocket, six from his mother, three from his sisters and a couple of cards from his brother. They could wait. He took out his cigarette case and took one of the Turkish that Madelaine liked. Those letters came from another place in time. This was home.

'Why don't you get some decent cigarettes. Gaspers.' Keegan said, helping himself. 'These things make the place stink like a Port Said brothel.'

'Wing want you to amplify your report,' Garbutt said. 'The one about shooting down the Hannoverana.'

'We didn't shoot it down. At least, I don't think so. McRae would know better than me. He was firing at it.'

'You'll have to sort that out with Wing. The I.O., a Captain Something-or-other, is coming over after dinner. I wouldn't argue. That fight saved your bacon ... and the Major's. Depot has just woken up to the fact that you are here. They wanted you back. Got you posted as a deserter. Or at least A.W.O.L.'

'Is that why my mail came in a heap?'

'One of the drivers saw it lying in the Orderly Room. That's how they tumbled to you. But you are on the strength now ... officially.'

Robson looked at the freshly-drawn charts that lay on Garbutt's desk, new maps with a spider-web of tracks radiating eastwards from this and their previous aerodrome.

'Special instructions from Wing. I suppose they have to dig up something for the newspaper johnnies to crow about,' Garbutt explained. 'So we get put on show. I hear they are sending some journalist along. Not before time. We flew more night hours and dropped more bombs than any other squadron last week.'

'Two more charts and one more coloured pencil and you'll get the Major his D.S.O.,' Robson said, thinking of the conversation he had overheard at Wing H.Q.

Garbutt looked up sharply. 'How did you know? Keep it to yourself. It's not official yet. Between you and me he is not very pleased.'

Robson stared, his mouth agape. He cleared his throat. Garbutt scowled at him. 'Doesn't make sense to you, does it? But then you haven't been out long enough to get this medal nonsense into perspective. You will ... If you are with us long enough.'

The weather had changed again and the sunshine of the afternoon was replaced by a cold driving rain. It was too bad to risk the new pilots. Anyway, luckily for them, there were no aeroplanes. The activities of the past two nights had seen the mechanics worked to a standstill. Flight Sergeant Watt was able to deliver only six F.E.s for the night's work.

To mark his new status, and to McDonald's loudly expressed disgust—the Wing M.O. had grounded him for the night—Robson was to go with the other five to Valenciennes. McRae was his observer again with a 112 lb. bomb under the fuselage and four incendiaries under the wings for company.

Uncle Tom Cobleigh was having a night off but he came along to see them leave. Robson was the only pilot who had not been there before. Uncle Tom took him to one side while the mechanics ran up his engine.

'It's a long trip, seventy miles or more going and seems twice as far coming back. You'll have the usual stiff headwind so watch your petrol. Keep out of cloud. Keep her steady and trust your compass. If you get caught by searchlights, sideslip and let McRae hose them with the Lewis. Keep as high as you can. They've got machine-guns on top of some buildings. If you get a chance make a note of the traffic about the station. Engines, trucks, coaches and so on. God only knows why, but that sort of stuff makes Wing happy. Gives the I.O. something to write about, I suppose. If it wasn't unlucky I'd wish you good luck.'

It was a long cold trip. At 4,000 feet they flew through scattered snow showers that knifed into their exposed cheekbones. The cold was an enemy as real and tangible as the Hun, an enemy that crept up on you insidiously, an enemy that pierced the thick sidcot suit, the fur-lined boots, the leather helmet, and froze the grease on Robson's face until he was numbed into the stupor of a hibernating animal.

He had picked up his drift from a lighthouse before crossing the Line but there was no co-ordination between his numbed feet and cold-fogged brain. The compass spun idly like a child's toy and each time he picked a star to steer on he lost it in a snow shower. He was too cold to risk leaving the meagre shelter of his windscreen to unfold his map. Seeing McRae slapping his arms across his chest and stamping his feet on the floor of the nacelle only made him more angry. The compass swung worse than ever. He tried to remember something he had been taught about 'northerly turning error'. But the pain in his head shut out all power of recall.

He cowered deeper into the cockpit watching the illuminated hands of the watch on the dashboard, waiting for them to tell him when they were over the target, willing himself into believing that at any moment they would see the bulk of Valenciennes, with the black outline of the station, and the minute sparks from signal lights and the glow of an open firebox reflected on steam.

It was not there. The time was up but there was no town. There were woods and roads and farms and, once, a little village, empty of traffic and seemingly lifeless as they circled. Robson was angry, at the weather, at McRae and the country and the war, and the railway station at Valenciennes that should have been there and was not.

McRae banged on the coaming between them. Robson glowered at him. Why the hell didn't he get down out of the slipstream and go to sleep? Why didn't he find something moving, some traffic they could bomb and justify their going home? Reluctantly his eyes followed the line of the observer's outstretched arm and his frozen feet booted the nose of the F.E. into a slow turn.

Away to the north, right on the horizon a dozen search-lights criss-crossed in a moving tableau of light. It had to be Valenciennes. He opened the throttle wide and pushed the nose down slightly. The speed built up and the old pusher began to get hard to hold on the target. The nose kept sliding off to the left. He began to beat his hands one after another on the leather padding round the cockpit. Then it was the turn of his feet. Swearing at the pain as feeling returned, he thumped them clumsily together and banged them on the floor. All the while the waving pencils of light grew nearer until he could see them grop-ing for the aeroplanes that had left before him.

Now he should climb, turn east and swing round to attack in a gliding turn, throwing off the searchlights and gunners with a silent approach. But he was too cold and too relieved at finding the place to bother.

A F.E. in front of him, escaping after its bombing run, writhed in a cone of half a dozen lights, ringed by show-ers of sparks and strings of flaming onions. Robson closed his mind to the sight as he ruddered into line with the tracks running into the station 500 feet below.

McRae raised his arm as the big bomb dropped away. It overshot the station but hit the lines amid a huddle of wagons. The observer signalled for them to go in again to drop the incendiaries. The air stank of cordite. Some one had started a fire at the south end of the station.

He did not see the incendiaries fall because one search-light and then a second caught them, bleaching out the darkness. He was not sure whether he was going up or down. Shell fragments plucked at the fabric, and spanged off a strut fitting. He thought about that big twirling pro-peller and how a splinter could shatter it and how the broken blades would rip apart the four fragile booms, and he felt the vomit rising up his gullet. McRae fired a long burst down the beam of one searchlight and it went out. A church tower shot by under the right wing. Robson heaved on the stick. The F.E. began to climb.

McRae had left the gun. He pointed under the right wing, held up two fingers. The incendiaries had hung up. If they fell off when they landed … Robson went round again, heaving and pushing on the stick, kicking the rudder from side to side trying to shake the bombs loose. They fell away third time round, disappearing into the darkness beyond the fire.

A searchlight picked them up, turning the wings translucent, exposing the frail skeleton of ribs and spars. At 500 feet machine-gun tracer reached out for them. Robson sideslipped into the beam. McRae leaned over the side firing the Lewis. Something plucked him away from the gun and threw him against the far side of the cockpit. He slid down out of sight as Robson, desperately trying to escape from the blinding glare, pushed the nose down, holding the stick forward with both hands. At 100 m.p.h. they screeched across the town at roof-top level, weaving and jiggling to escape the blinding light.

They were half an hour out of the target on the lonely drag home when, first a hand and then McRae's head emerged from the front cockpit. He was wearing a field dressing high up on his left arm. After letting Robson see he was alive he disappeared to get what protection he could from the biting slipstream.

It took them over two hours to get home, four and a half hours for the round trip. For the final half-hour the engine rattled increasingly as the oil pressure needle slipped out of the bottom of the gauge. They landed accompanied by the stench of overheated metal. The propeller, booms and tailplane were black with oil.

'Ach, ye were borrn to be hung, Sirr,' Flight Sergeant Watt said as he looked at the damage outside the hangar by the light of a naphtha lamp. 'I was to tell you, Sirr, there's a wee mannie to see you fra' Wing H.Q. You leave

Captain McRae tae us. We'll get him off to the M.O. right
away.'

Rolling like a drunk Robson plodded across the airfield. The pain from his legs and arms as they came back
to life competed with a splitting headache. He pulled off
his helmet before he went into Callaghan's office, looking
back with mild surprise at his zig-zag tracks outlined in
the wet grass.

Four pilots were making out their reports in Garbutt's
office while their observers huddled over the stove clutch-
ing mugs of cocoa. They looked up as he stood blinking
in the smoke-filled light and grinned at him. Garbutt
poured a mug of cocoa from the pan on top of the pot-
bellied stove and laced it with rum before handing it over.
He poked his head through the connecting door leading
to Callaghan's office.

'He'll see you in a minute. The Wing I.O. is with him
and ...'

'Come back to the mess, Split, and tell us what it's like
to be a hero,' one of the pilots said.

Robson stared blankly at him, his ears still deafened
and his mind half-frozen.

'They'd better clean you up before the photographers
get here. Gallant British aviator be damned, you look
more like one of Mr. Christie's minstrels.'

Garbutt handed him a grubby towel to wipe the grease
off his face and as he did so he caught a glimpse of
himself in the cracked mirror behind the stove. A smoke-
blackened face blotched with lumps of grease and
white-rimmed eyes where his goggles had been, with raw,
inflamed eyeballs. He forced a grin after he sipped the
cocoa, feeling the rum warming him inside and the heat
of the stove reaching his body. Another pilot, Fenner from
'C' Flight, looked up as he laid his pen down.

'Good luck, Split. Any idea why we are getting the
treatment normally reserved for our brave scout pilots?'

The telephone stuttered and as Garbutt reached across his desk for it the conversation stopped as if it had been cut off at some main power source. Garbutt was shouting as though the volume of noise he made could speed up his connection. One of the observers asked Robson about McRae. Apparently Flight Sergeant Watt had rung up the office as soon as they landed. The sixth F.E. was still missing. Robson vaguely remembered the pilot, Whitehead, an Australian. Archie Harris, McDonald's favourite observer, was flying with him.

'... Where are you?' Garbutt shouted. The room came to life. Someone asked Robson if McRae's wound was a 'blighty' one.

Garbutt was scribbling on a piece of paper. '... All right, I've got that. North-east of Arras. We'll get a tender out to you as soon as possible. Make sure you get the watch off the dashboard.'

He replaced the telephone and scratched the inside of his ear with a pencil. 'I believe French telephones were invented by a different man. That was Mr. Harris. They are down in a meadow by the Scarfe. Engine trouble.'

'How about Whitey?' one of the pilots asked.

'He's all right. According to Mr. Harris he was knocked out in the landing and is only just recovering. But as they are being entertained by some Australians I suspect that he is just about to go down with alcoholic poisoning...'

Callaghan put his head round the door, saw Robson and beckoned him in.

Besides Callaghan there was a captain wearing red tabs and a uniform so well cut that it made Callaghan look as though he had just crawled out of a trench, and a civilian, a short pale-faced man wearing thick glasses and a Norfolk suit in thick tweed. For the shooting, no doubt, Robson thought.

'Gentlemen, this is Mr. Robson. I think you know Captain Jones, the Wing I.O., Robson. And this is Mr. Charlton, a newsp ... er, er ... a writer. Mr. Charlton has been commissioned by the Air Board to write a series of articles on the work of the Front Line squadrons.'

There was a wintry smile on the civilian's face as Callaghan finished the introduction. As he shook hands Robson realized why he resented the man. This interloper had two men to whom Robson gave grudging respect, as individuals and symbols of rank, fawning on him, although he was sure they had nothing but contempt for the man and his profession.

'Major Callaghan's first thought was the right one,' Charlton said. 'I'm a plain common-or-garden newspaper reporter, Mr. Robson, an honest scribbler. An honoured scribbler, Sir, that I should be the one to tell the people back home about your feats of daring...'

Robson, his head still ringing from the cold and the engine noise, took the offered cigarette and wondered about the brash little man in front of him. Little only in height, for without effort he seemed to dominate the room. Did people still talk like this or was the man a cynic quietly making fun out of them? The rum was suddenly warm inside his empty belly. He wanted to go to sleep instead of listening to this silly idiot mouthing platitudes. Did he hate the Hun? Not so far as he was aware. How would the little man like that for an answer? The empty tin mug dropped out of his hand, and clattered onto the floor. Robson jerked back into awareness. Charlton's baby-blue eyes were beaming at him as he slid a chair across to him. He felt as though his trouser buttons were undone.

'Mr. Robson has just returned from a raid on Valenciennes,' Callaghan said. 'On the railway station. Six aeroplanes. Four and a half hours for the round trip, most of it behind the German lines. The head wind, from the west, is our worst enemy, you know. This station, of course, is a vital link in the supply chain to the German armies engaged in the current battle.'

'Yes, Major, I can see you have been well coached. Not forgetting Lille, Le Cateau, Lens, Cambrai and St. Quentin,' Charlton replied with a bite in his voice that Robson had not suspected was there. 'And what have you got, four squadrons? Cast-offs from 1916. Birdcages. The Hun seems to be well-supplied with Gothas, where are all these Handley Pages the Navy keep bragging about?'

He turned to Robson. 'Four and a half hours, eh, a long, cold trip. And did all your comrades get back ... safely?'

'One of our aeroplanes...' Jones began, but a glare from Charlton quietened him.

'We heard just before I came in that the last of the boys was down safely up north,' Robson said quietly. 'He found the Scarpe and put it down on the bank.'

'The result of your having to fight your way into enemy territory. How far, a hundred miles?'

'About sixty,' Robson replied. 'He had engine trouble.'

'Those old Beardmores must be getting past it. Suppose he had had a Handley with two Rolls Royces?'

Robson shrugged his shoulders wearily. The man sounded like one of the replacement pilots. What was the use of wishing for the moon. You could only fly the aeroplanes that equipped the Squadron and he did not like the way this fellow went on about the F.E. What did he know about it?

'He was lost. Two engines means twice as much chance of trouble. You won't get very far on one.'

'Was the raid a success?'

'Well, the station was on fire. Our bombs exploded among some trucks at the north end. The line must be out of action.'

'How many bombs did you carry. What size were they?'

There was something about the way Charlton phrased his questions that made Robson uneasy even as the man's prattle relaxed him and induced him to talk more freely.

He sounded more like a man out to prove some pre-conceived thesis than someone being paid to tell people back home what their sons were doing to win the war.

'What happened on the night you had the fight with this, er, this whatjermacallit?'

'Hannover C.L.3. We call them Hannoveranas. Two-seater trench strafer. They are good. That was why we raided their aerodrome. We destroyed...'

Charlton raised his hand. 'My dear chap, no matter how laudable your efforts may have been they mean nothing to our readers. The ordinary chap, the man in the street, he knows that bombing is easy. He sees it happening to him and his family every day of the week. Gothas or Zeppelins cruising overhead dropping bombs where they will and there seems to be nothing we can do about it.

'And no matter what you may think, Mr. Robson, we are not allowed to assume that the Hun can do anything better than we can. So, night bombing is easy and safe ... for the pilot. So the man in the street thinks.'

Doggedly the reporter ploughed on, ignoring the pro-tests of Callaghan and Jones. Robson was speechless.

'There is only one bombing raid your man in the street wants to read about. That is the one when bombs are dropped on the Boche in his own cities. Berlin for choice. Two of our bombs for one of theirs.

'Now you, young man, come along and shoot down a Boche. At night. How good are these whatjermacallits?'

'Oh, one of the best,' Jones said hastily. 'It's the latest design. Fast for a two-seater. One of them will take on two of our scouts, all other things being equal. Of course the new designs coming from our factories are much better...'

'Spare me the propaganda, old man, I have to write it.' Charlton turned back to Robson. 'Now can you see why your story is news. Old man bites young dog. Tatty old factory-built bomber, designed before the war, wasn't it, pre-war birdcage bomber attacks and defeats, at night, the latest Boche warplane.'

Callaghan started to speak but changed his mind. He let Jones bear the brunt of Charlton's scorn as the I.O. tried to defend the one-time Army standard fighter which was now the Army standard night bomber.

Half an hour later Robson realized that he had not been able to explain that, as far as he knew, they had not shot down the Hannoverana. They were outside the hangars being photographed. The only two serviceable F.E.s had been pushed outside and festooned with bombs. In and about them Robson and Charlton, now resplendent in a helmet and sidcot suit, posed for the photographer.

Then the bombs were removed and the photographer, risking life and limb on a plank hastily thrust between two ladders, snapped Charlton crouched over the front Lewis. Flight Sergeant Watt marched up to Callaghan, stopped at attention, and waved his right arm in a ragged salute.

'Sirr, the Hun is on his way over. An observation post in the Line report that they have observed rockets of various colours being fired for the past twenty minutes and now they can hear the sound of heavy aero engines proceeding in this direction.'

Callaghan pursed his lips and stared up at the sky. The last rainstorm had moved east twenty minutes earlier and although there was still cloud it had lifted and broken. A star shone feebly through one break. The Germans used multi-coloured rockets as a navigational aid in the way the R.F.C. used flashing beacons. If the weather was good enough for the Germans to fly, it was good enough for the Squadron.

'How many aeroplanes can you let me have, Mr. Watt?' Callaghan asked. 'Say, in an hour's time. We'll wait for Jerry, follow him home and get him when he lands.'

Watt shook his head. 'Sirr, ye know the position as well as I do. Ye canna go on worrkin' machines and men night after night the way ye're doing...'

Robson climbed down from the cockpit to join the amused group of pilots and observers watching the circus. Charlton continued to lean over the rim of the cockpit, engrossed in the argument between Callaghan and Watt.

'Tiny' Jerome, a six foot two giant who seemed to sit on a F.E. instead of inside it, was standing with McDonald when Robson joined them.

'I wouldn't take your helmet off, old chap,' he said to Robson. 'Poor old Watt hasn't got a chance. Not with a bloody newspaperman watching our noble Commander waging war against the frightful Boche. Any minute now his gallant aviators will be off to harass the Hun.'

A flash of light exploded as the photographer took a picture of Callaghan haranguing Watt. Callaghan would come out well, Robson thought. His tall slender figure, best uniform, the wings and medal-ribbons, and the mobile fingers explaining away the deficiencies, made a marked contrast to the stooped shoulders of the Flight Sergeant in his grubby blue overalls, the chevrons on his sleeve almost obliterated by a splash of oil.

'... These two here, the "pom-pom" and the one with a splinter through the float chamber. Surely you can do a plug change and fit a new carburettor in under an hour...'

'Aye, Sirr, if you say so, Sirr. But I'll no be responsible for the consequences...'

'I am not asking you to be, Mr. Watt. That is the privilege and the curse of being a Commanding Officer...'

'Jesus H. Christ,' a voice with an Australian twang murmured. 'Why'n hell don't they give him his D.S.O. and let some poor bloody observers get some bloody shut-eye.'

'Mr. Garbutt,' Callaghan called for the Recording Officer. 'What are our orders for tonight? The alternative bad weather targets?'

'Free-lance attacks on camp sites, billets, ammo dumps and any other activities likely to harass the enemy.'

'That's good enough,' Callaghan said. He called to Charlton, still sitting in the gunner's cockpit. 'This is why we were moved down from the north last January. To attack the German bomber aerodromes. This we intend to do. I would like you to step down now, Sir. The men will be loading these machines with bombs in a few minutes.'

The first two F.E.s took off twenty minutes later. McDonald—his being grounded forgotten when he appeared helmeted and ready to fly—in one, and Fenner from 'C' Flight in the other. Immediately they were off, the flares were extinguished. Callaghan's plan, expounded in detail to the pilots and observers under the approving eye of Charlton, was to follow the German bombers back to their base which was believed to be south-west of Valenciennes. The first two aeroplanes would patrol a line east of Amiens, the most likely target for the Gothas. The last three F.E.s would wait until the Gothas had passed over flying west. They would then patrol just under the cloud base waiting for the signal, a two-star red Very light, that the bombers were on their way home. Two of the Flight Commanders would be stationed, each one a mile north or south of the aerodrome so that the signal would indicate roughly the track of the Germans.

'Tiny' Jerome stood with Robson listening to the dying engine noise of the first two F.E.s on course for Amiens and the growing unsynchronized growl of the twin-engined Gothas.

'I think the whole thing will be a washout,' Robson said sourly in reply to Jerome's query about the stunt. 'Have you ever tried to find another aeroplane at night? I have. It's hopeless. Anyway a Gotha without bombs is bound to be faster than a Fee carrying a load of Coopers under its wings.'

'You may be right, old man, but if we are within five

miles of the place when the Gothas get home we are bound to see their lights. And if they don't light up, the poor devils will crash.

'I must say that, much as I dislike that bloody "pom-pom"—and I don't care for your bloody-minded flying either—I am glad to be flying with you instead of your Canadian pal.'

'He's a better pilot than I am. And a better shot. If anybody sees those bombers he will.'

'I know. He's also fearfully wound up about your stealing his thunder and getting that Hannoverana.'

'You are worse than that damned reporter fellow. I didn't shoot the flaming thing down. If it went down, which I doubt, it was McRae who did the shooting and deserves the kudos.'

Robson scowled anxiously up at the sky. It sounded as though there were three Gothas coming over.

'I hope Frank doesn't do anything silly,' he said. 'These Gothas are not sitting ducks. They have guns in the queerest places. There's one firing under the tail, for instance. I saw a fellow in a Bristol Fighter catch a packet from that while I was on Home Defence.'

Charlton came over to join them. Jerome made his excuses, he had to get into his flying kit. Robson and Charlton stood, wreathed in cigarette smoke, listening to the approaching bombers coming in from the east.

'Do you know a man, or did you know him, he's dead now, a man called Ben Leben?' Robson asked suddenly, to break the silence. 'He was a journalist.'

'He was indeed,' Charlton replied blowing two smoke-rings in quick succession as he turned a quizzical look on Robson. 'You are a queer fish.'

'Why? I just happen to know someone who knew him, and er, admired him. What was so special about him?'

'Everything, Mr. Robson. As a man, as a journalist, he was a real writer. I was proud to know him even though I disagreed with many of the things he believed in most passionately.'

Charlton lit another cigarette from the one he was smoking and flicked the stub away in a glittering arc. 'Your father is in shipping. Don't look so surprised. I may be a hack but I am a good one. I do my homework. Have you ever talked to one of the men employed by your father? Seen where they live? And I don't mean one of the better-spoken captains. Ever watched one of your foremen pick his gang of dockers out of a crowd of hungry men? It's like picking cattle.

'Well, if you do start thinking about these things you could do worse than read what he wrote. Perhaps if you did that—and you survive this bloody war—there might be hope for the old country after all. He was a Jew, you know,' he added quickly.

Robson nodded. 'But why was he so important?'

Charlton was staring at the cloud-shrouded horizon as though neither Robson nor the bombers existed.

'Cigarettes out, no lights allowed at all, Sir,' a passing mechanic said. 'One of the Jerries is going to pass right overhead.'

Obediently Charlton ground his cigarette under his heel.

'His name wasn't Leben, it was Liebowitz. But Leben looked better as a by-line. He had the idea that no one would take him seriously with a name that sounded like some foreign anarchist. He was a great man for detail. It makes you realize the stupid waste of lives in this futile war. Am I shocking you? We have lost a generation, Mr. Robson, a generation of irreplaceable talent. And when it is over, my God, how we are going to miss them.

'He wrote about men and women and countries in a way that broke down the artificial barriers between us. He made you realize how artificial they are. He was a socialist. He might have made socialism respectable, and

until someone does that, my friend, it will never be of
any importance in England. He was a pacifist who went
to war when he needn't have and got himself killed. It
was like the man to be killed as a private soldier among
a lot of other privates.'

Charlton laughed harshly. One of the bombers was almost overhead now. A long way off, beyond the hangars
two red stars blossomed against the clouds. Someone had
misunderstood their instructions. Robson wondered if the
flare could be seen by the men on their way to Amiens.
There was no way anyone on the ground could influence
what was going to happen now. The action would be
fought, or evaded, 2,000 feet up by men as isolated as anyone
could be. Charlton was still talking.

'A lot of people, those that hadn't met him, hated him.
Why not? He was a Jew, a socialist, he wanted to alter
things. The great English sin. And the class that he disliked most he could not hate. But they got him in the
end. One of their women got him. God, this war has
thrown some unlikely people together. Poor old Ben. He
fell, hook, line and sinker for an empty-headed flapper,
a brittle little bitch with an appetite for brandy and a
wartime interest in "good works". She was a widow. Her
late husband had been a Major in the cavalry, ugh!
She stood for everything Ben had spent years fighting.
Within a year she had him in the army, a few months later
he was dead ... What's up?'

Robson put a finger to his lips and frowned. The Gotha
had passed over and was now west of the field. The heavy,
pour vous, pour vous, of its unsynchronized Mercedes
engines was dying away but there was the noise of a second aeroplane.

'There is another coming towards us from the west,'
Robson said. 'Can you hear it? It's diving.'

Suddenly a line of tracer bullets stitched a silent path
across the sky from one invisible aeroplane towards an-

other. Seconds after they heard the sound of disembodied gunfire.

'Frank, you bloody fool,' Robson shouted, visualizing the Canadian making a classic attack from beneath and behind the bomber.

'What is happening? Who is up there? Are they fighting?' Charlton asked.

Two lines of tracer converged on a point in the sky. Sparks. A red glow that dipped downwards. The glow flared into a long yellow flame that crept down the sky until it suddenly broke into a multitude of smaller flames as the F.E. collapsed into its component parts. The nacelle was still burning as it went out of sight behind the trees.

'We got it, we got the murderous bastard,' Charlton shouted. 'That was the Gotha?' he asked.

'No, Mr. Charlton,' Robson said, walking away, 'that was my friend, McDonald.'

The Gotha's engine sounded loudly overhead, then faded as it continued on its bombing mission.

Over by the hangars a Crossley tender broke the silence and then its own noise was drowned by the clatter of a Beardmore as Watt ran up the first of the aeroplanes he had promised.

At 3,000 feet Robson stubbornly hung onto the tail of the Gotha a couple of hundred feet below him. At this height and distance away, provided he did not take his eyes off it, he could just pick out the exhaust flames from the engine, the starboard exhaust pipe had split and occasionally spat a stream of sparks rearwards, and he could distinguish the loom of the big bomber against the horizon. Another shower of rain suddenly lashed the two aeroplanes, and the Gotha disappeared. He huddled lower behind the windscreen and cursed Callaghan for playing to the gallery and McDonald for following suit and the blasted Germans for flying in such weather. Turning his head to Jerome, vainly trying to compress his lanky frame behind the 'pom-pom', he shouted to him to keep his eyes open as he had lost the Gotha. He did not add that unless he concentrated on flying and not looking they were likely to lose something more important. He could not prevent his hand from stroking the throttle back a fraction. It would be stupid to fly out of the rainstorm and find themselves on top of the Gotha.

Not that it was likely. They had been flying at full throttle for over an hour. The water temperature was up and the oil pressure was slowly falling. The 'pom-pom' F.E. was doing all it could just to keep the Gotha in sight.

As suddenly as it began the rain stopped. A couple of stars appeared in a rift in the cloud. There was no sign of the German bomber. Robson swore again at his aching right leg. The riggers could never get this F.E. to fly straight without holding on rudder. During the shower he must have relaxed and they had turned while the bomber had gone straight on. And now where the hell were they? He stared morosely over the coaming at the featureless black plain beneath them.

Jerome thumped him on the shoulder pointing over to the right, to the east. Away on the horizon a slender pencil of light shone vertically into the sky. Anyone could get lost at night. The Gotha base was beckoning home its brood. Robson pushed the throttle back up to the stop and ruddered into a gentle turn. Now they had to find the bomber without being seen.

Then they saw it, and with the big bomber silhouetted against the aerodrome Robson risked a glance at the flare path. It was no Heath-Robinson arrangement of petrol tins and cotton waste. A row of electric lights marched across the field. On the downwind side a small searchlight with its beam now tilted over the horizontal made an oval splash of light at the beginning of the flare path.

Was this the Gotha that had startled him and Madelaine

into each other's arms in Amiens that night, or the one that had shot down McDonald two hours before? Perhaps it was the one that had raided the airfield and got the Major—what was his name?—the night before he and McDonald had arrived. Robson eased the throttle right back as fifty yards behind they followed the Gotha in a gentle slide. His left hand cocked the fixed Lewis gun in front of him.

'As soon as he crosses the aerodrome boundary,' he shouted to Jerome. The observer nodded. He made a circling motion with his fingers pointing to the black bulk of the sheds on the left.

'Hard left and I'll drop the bombs over there,' he shouted back. 'Then circle back to pick off any aeroplanes we can see, with the "pom-pom". If the damned thing works.'

Robson squinted down the ring-and-bead sight of the Lewis and edged the nose a little higher, bringing it in line with the fuselage of the Gotha. Jerome would aim the 'pom-pom' along the same line of sight as the Lewis.

'Now,' he shouted and opened up with the Lewis. It stuttered, its flash blinding. Ten rounds of tracer arced into the Gotha before the gun jammed. Then Jerome fired. The F.E. staggered as though slapped by a giant hand. Sparks glittered on the centre section of the Gotha. Too high. As he dropped the nose Jerome got off another clip.

The entire top wing of the Gotha broke up, tearing away in three parts, shedding ribs and fittings. The fuselage dropped out of sight as Robson slammed the throttle open. They were too close.

The Beardmore spluttered agonizingly as the plugs, oiled up during the long glide, failed to respond. A fire-ball flared up in front of them towering above the F.E. The engine was picking up power as the oil burned off the points. Three cylinders, four, five. They were too close and too low as they flew through the flames. Robson shut his eyes remembering the load of Coopers on the wing racks. He could sense the red glare through his closed eyelids as he waited for the explosion. It was gone, they were through. Jerome thumped his shoulder, he was shouting.

'Left, turn left.'

Robson opened his eyes, automatically pushing on left rudder. Jerome had his head over the side watching the sheds sidle over to them. A piece of burning fabric hung on the bracing wires between the wings.

'Get rid of those bombs,' Robson shouted. 'Quick, before the gunners see us.'

The fabric flared up into a brighter flame, leaving a ragged trail of sparks dancing between the oil-soaked booms. A couple of machine-guns spat tracer at them. But the fabric was finished before they could take aim, the flame died and the ash slowly broke away.

Jerome thumped Robson's shoulder again, raising a triumphant thumb. The bombs had gone. Robson huddled down, heading for the sheltering darkness. It was ten minutes before he looked at the compass, the water-temperature and oil-pressure gauges, and started to ease the load on the labouring engine for the long drag home.

12

Flight Sergeant Watt showed him the damage after breakfast. The fabric on the underside of the lower wings was blackened and split. There were scorch marks along the underside of the oil-sodden nacelle. Watt reached up to poke the underside of the wing with a stubby finger. Pieces of brittle linen cracked and fell away.

'Mister Robson, Sirr, ye were too close. It's no' worth it. Ye'll be nae use tae that wee lassie under the sod over there. She sent you a letter.'

Watt explained that the letter had been delivered by an ambulance on its way up to the Line that morning. And he added that McDonald's funeral party was after lunch, at 1400 hours.

It had been a disastrous night, and Watt appealed to Robson to witness that he had warned Callaghan about the state of the aeroplanes. McDonald and his observer had been killed. Jenner, the other of the first two away, had seen nothing and had eventually been forced to land alongside the St. Quentin road east of Amiens with a hole in the engine where a piston and its connecting rod had departed. The two of them were back now, liberally decorated with plaster and bandages due to the bombs under the wings going off during the fire that followed the removal of their undercarriage by a ditch. Of the other two, Harper and his observer had survived engine failure at fifty feet immediately after taking off; and the other chap had seen nothing, had got lost and, after bombing some transport, had got back over the Line only to smash his undercarriage landing on a strange aerodrome without lights, fifty miles north of Arras.

Robson went back to his room to read Madelaine's letter but his batman was there packing McDonald's belongings. He had to promise to go through the Canadian's personal effects before he could get rid of the man.

Dear Christopher,

Things are changing so quickly that we will not be able to meet again at the cross-rodes. I did not like to think of you waiting in the rain while we carry on miles away in the other direction. I will go to the *estaminet* at Hesdincourt cross-rodes for lunch today but much as I would like to see you I will understand if you are unable to get there. We will be disbanded at the end of the month so there is little time left. Darling, do be careful. I love you but I do not think I am good for you. Two of my men have been killed. I do not think I could stand another.

Love Madelaine.

A hastily-scribbled pencilled addition expressed her sorrow at the news about McDonald.

He read it through three times. It was the first time she had said she loved him. He realized, looking at the writing and the misspelled words, how little they knew about each other. The writing was almost like that of a schoolgirl; plain, distinct, with an immature lack of character. The words might have been copied from a school primer on copperplate.

While he went through the small bundle of letters, photographs and souvenirs that were the only tangible remains of McDonald he kept wondering how he could possibly get to that *estaminet*. He did not think McDonald would have been offended.

*   *   *

Unknown to Robson, the apparently unending advance of the Germans towards Amiens was settling his problem of how to meet Madelaine. As the Fifth Army collected a scratch force of stragglers, wounded discharged from hospitals, engineers, teachers and some U.S. Army Railwaymen, to bolster the defences of the city, sixteen squadrons of the R.F.C., flying from first light to darkness, harassed the advancing Germans with bombs and machine-guns at trench parapet height. But Wing H.Q., allocating targets for the night, found that its one night bomber squadron had only three serviceable aeroplanes.

'You are for the Depot, m'lad,' Garbutt told Robson when he reported to the R.O.'s office. Half a dozen pilots were there with him. 'The Crossley leaves in half an hour. And no larking about on the road and spending the night in town. Those machines have got to be here this afternoon. You'll be flying them tonight.'

'Our Mr. Watt will not approve of that, Dick,' Robson said. He went on in a mock Scottish accent, 'Ay'll have you know, mon, that ay'll no ha' ma peelots fleein' wi' yon aeroplanes straight fra' yon place. Ah wadna trust a cackie hen to yin o' them Deepo mechanics.'

'Watt is too damned busy to appreciate your inane sense of humour, Robson,' Callaghan said from his doorway. 'While you were sleeping, he and his men were working. He has rebuilt a machine that was supposed to go back to the Depot. You had better test it. When you have finished, one of the men will run you to the Depot in a sidecar. You had better not waste any time.'

Sullenly Robson watched a mechanic stack bags of lead shot in the nose of the F.E. to replace the weight of the absent gunner. Watt fussed around the machine as though reluctant to see it fly. The wings were patched in a dozen places. A new boom, glittering with fresh varnish, emphasized the oil-blackened state of the other three. New bracing-wires showed the clean, blued look of oiled steel, and the unpainted brass of a new radiator on the port side glowed against the matt black dope of the nacelle.

Watt kicked one of the wheels and joined Robson. 'Ye'd be doing the Squadron a favour, Sirr, if ye could hae yerself a nice wee crash wi' yon coo. Ach, ther's no' a thing tae choose atwixt her an' that monstrosity wi' the "pom-pom". They're waeful bodies these bliddy cranky yins. They will na fly nor crash ... Nae use tae man nor beast 'till they tak the notion in their heeds tae kill some puir body.'

'What have you done to it?' Robson asked.

'Ach, no' half enough. She ought tae have a new engine only there isna a spare twixt here and the Deepo. Ye'll find she's maybe twa, three hunnerd revs doon but the old coo was never nae better. She's patched in a place or two but there's nae damage tae the spars. More's the pity, else we might hae had a chance of scrappin' her.'

The engine was warm because Watt had been testing it and now it lived up to its reputation and failed to start until the fourth attempt by the cursing mechanics. Sitting in the cockpit with the air stinking with unburned petrol, Robson watched the Crossley with his fellow pilots go off to the Depot. He twirled again the handle of the hand-start magneto. Reluctantly one cylinder fired, the engine twisting in its bearers until the others joined in, shooting streamers of flame at the tail as the petrol lying in the exhaust manifold burned.

He took his time taxi-ing round to the far corner of the field to get the engine hot. Then he had to wait while three bombed-up R.E.s took off, and to make up for that he ran the engine at nearly full throttle for five minutes, a couple of wind-crushed mechanics hanging onto the tail-plane. He was taking no chances with oiled-up plugs.

At first it seemed his precautions had had the right effect. As Watt had forecast, the revs were down but without bombs or guns aboard the F.E. picked up speed quickly and Robson lifted her off soon after passing over the hump in the middle of the field, holding the plane a few feet above the ground until the trees on the boundary drew closer when he started to climb. Then at fifty feet the engine coughed with a shudder that shot Robson off his seat, and died. The only sound was the chop-chop of the big propeller slicing past the booms and the quiet whistle of the wind in the wires.

Automatically Robson's hand pumped the throttle backwards and forwards while he scanned the trees for a break. 'Never turn back, never ever turn back,' his instructors had chorused. Had they ever been at fifty feet with no power and a wood looming up? And there was all that expanse of aerodrome behind. But if you turned at low speed and little height you would stall, he knew that. With no lift the aeroplane would fall out of the sky. And that motor behind, 160 non-existent horsepower at, say 4 lb. a horsepower. That's 640 lb., a quarter of a ton of metal that would inevitably tear loose and lurch forward squashing...

He steered towards a gap between two trees, eased the stick back a little, pulled the throttle shut. As he reached for the ignition switches the engine started firing again. Not smoothly, for one cylinder was still dead. Too low and too slow, too. He managed to get the throttle open and, dragging the wheels through the tree-tops, the F.E. clawed for the sky.

He climbed slowly up to a thousand feet before he dared turn back. Then he checked the plugs and magnetos, switching each one off in turn. There was nothing wrong apart from the usual small drop in revs. One cylinder was still out. He looked at the shining brass radiator by his shoulder. Probably overheated on the last trip, he thought, and an exhaust valve has burned. Poor old Watt.

He started a gentle turn back towards the aerodrome

and realized he was passing over Hesdincourt; down there Madelaine was waiting for him, he thought, as he craned over the side to watch the traffic below. There was something on the road he had not seen before: groups of refugees straggling, blocking the road, breaking up the traffic heading for the Line and by the side of the road a litter of people and their belongings, those who had come too far. A couple of ambulances, faded red crosses on their tilts, caught his eye. He reached for his map, that *estaminet* could not be far away. He tucked his knees up to hold the stick, letting the bomber fly lazy circles as he orientated the map with the countryside below.

He found the cross-road, and saw the *estaminet* with an ambulance in the yard behind. The nose went down as he ruddered the F.E. into a diving turn. She would know he had got her message when he jazzed the engine at chimney-top level.

At fifty feet he could see white faces turned upwards to locate him, the instinctive flinching of shoulders. The house was a blurred mass of yellow brick, the detail resolving as the needle on the A.S.I. flickered round towards 100 m.p.h. He could pick out bullet scars on the brickwork and the peeling paint on the crooked window-shutters, when he relaxed his pressure on the stick and let the nose come up. As the *estaminet* swept under him he slammed the throttle open. The engine howled. The third time he dived on the *estaminet* the engine started playing tricks again, spluttering and banging when he opened up. A long trail of blue smoke whipped behind him. He pumped the throttle, clawing for height now as the engine went on misfiring, frantically searching for a field big enough for a forced landing.

With a sudden bang the engine packed up completely and from 400 feet he had no choice but a ploughed field next to the road.

Which way was the wind blowing, he wondered. Across

the line of the furrows? Was that shadow the remains of a hedge or a ditch?

He slid over the downwind hedge, crabbing into the wind, and as the noise in the wires died away he kicked the F.E. into line with the furrows and tried to hold it there a couple of feet in the air.

Whump! The belt cut into his belly, his head swung forward to thump into the leather padding as the wheels touched and sank into the soft soil. A piece of chalk ricocheted off the wing and plastered the right side of his goggles. But the F.E. was running straight and slowing fast. It lurched. That shadow *had* been a ditch. The nose went down, a strut cracked and quite slowly the bomber pivoted to the left smashing the rest of the undercarriage until the bottom wings skidding over the mud wrenched it level.

Robson pulled off his helmet, his head still ringing from the impact of the leather padding round the cockpit. He looked at the left wing. Whatever Callaghan might think, Flight Sergeant Watt would be pleased. Both booms were broken and the torn fabric showed a buckled wheel firmly wrapped round the splintered ends of the main spar.

A panting mud-bespattered soldier threw himself at the nacelle and tried to drag Robson from the wreck. Brushing off the helping hands Robson stood erect in the cockpit before stepping over the side.

'I always land like that,' he announced. 'It makes it so much easier to get out. Where's the nearest telephone?'

This remark, he told Madelaine when they met at the *estaminet*, was a standard ploy with instructors faced with the inevitable question after a crash as to how well they felt.

'I think your black eye is very becoming,' she said. 'All you need is a bandage round your forehead. Get that man you were telling me about to take another photograph. I hope no one thinks I was responsible for that swollen lip.'

The lunch was not a success. The two of them sat by a window eating an omelette washed down with a bottle of rough red wine trying to make brittle chit-chat as though their meeting was a casual one between neighbours in an English hotel. Robson's head was still ringing from the blow and he felt cold sweat on his skin each time he remembered the fearful moment when he thought the engine was going to tear out of its bed and crush him. He drank too quickly and when Madelaine's forced vivacity could not carry the strain for the two of them she seemed to crumple inwardly, her eyes dark-shadowed, pale blue veins throbbing beneath the transparent skin around her temples.

Robson commented on her wearing a wedding ring. In reply she unfastened a shirt button to show him a red weal above the swell of her breasts. It had been round her neck on a gold chain with her identity discs, she explained. But the previous day her Ford had lost a front wheel when it lurched into a half-filled shell hole. She had been thrown onto the steering wheel.

'It was Ben's mother's,' she said. 'Poor Ben. His family never forgave him for wanting to marry me. It was worse for him than for me. You've no idea how close Jewish families are. But none of his friends had any time for me. My God, we were both pariahs.'

'I'm surprised you ever met,' Robson said, to break an awkward silence. 'I cannot imagine how two worlds so completely different ever coincided.'

She put her hands on his. They were grubby with in-grained dirt round the knuckles and he could feel the calluses at the base of her fingers. The nails were bitten.

'My sacrifice,' she said staring down at them. 'My mother would have a fit if she were alive to see them. The war threw us together, the war separated us. War, war, we sit here and we can't stop talking about it.

'It was after Arthur was killed. Early '15, I think. A few of us became factory girls for a few weeks. I worked a machine making cartridge-cases. You should have seen me, wearing a ghastly overall and a mob cap like a kitchen maid. All grease and grime and smell. How little we knew. Then we left because we were taking jobs away from girls who needed the money. But the firm asked me to stay on as a kind of welfare worker. Me! You have no idea what that did for me.

'I had made a Lady-of-the-Manor sort of gesture right at the beginning and the girls never forgot it. One of them was going to have a baby and the father had made himself scarce. When I found out he was in my late husband's regiment I saw the Adjutant and that was that. Poor kid, she was a widow a month later. Anyway, after that I could do almost anything with them. So I stayed. I got to like them, that was another surprise.

'Ben was writing some articles on ladies playing at helping the War Effort. I don't think they were meant to be complimentary. He took me out to dinner one night because he was curious about "the kind lidy wot looks arter ah troubles". I learned all about happiness that year. I had never realized that you could be miserable because one person was away for a few hours...'

'Every time we meet,' Robson said, 'we talk about nothing but your husbands and lovers.' They both laughed.

She looked at the fob watch carried in the breast pocket of her uniform and raised the ghost of a smile.

'You frighten me, Christopher Alan Robson. Perhaps we should stop seeing each other.' She shuddered. 'Someone walking over my grave. We are fools to think about love. I couldn't bear it ... I'd feel guilty ... You know ... If anything happened to you. Perhaps it is as well I'm going home next week.'

She stood up and began to pull on the heavy gauntlets she wore for driving.

'Poor Chris,' she said, kissing him on the lips before climbing into the driving seat. 'You are in love with a woman who ceases to exist at the end of the month. Come and see me at home on your next leave. See what civilian life makes of me. You may hate me. I shall loathe it.'

He swung the starting handle twice, the engine fired and the band brakes chattered as she pressed the pedal and the ambulance moved off. She lifted her hand as she went by but her eyes were firmly on the road ahead.

13

Flight Sergeant Watt found him an hour later at the *estaminet*, half asleep, with an alcoholic smile on his face. The stamp of feet as Watt saluted woke him up. The Scot was grinning as Robson had never seen him grin before.

'Ach, Sirr, ye did a grand job o' getting rid o' the ol' bitch. The Squadron will be in your debt, you'll see. As soon as I heard yon engine missing as you were taking off I guessed you'd be putting her doon away fra' the field. But are ye no hurt, Sirr? Yon's a fearsome clout ye had across ye're een.'

Robson stood up, stretching his arms out and yawned. He could see the Crossley tender outside and he looked at the Flight Sergeant with new respect as the real reason for his being here occurred to him.

'You are a flattering scoundrel, Watt,' he said as the pair of them got into the tender. 'Since when have Flight Sergeants had the time to collect pilots after a forced landing. I'll bet you Mary, Queen of Scots to John Knox that if I had not wrecked 985 there would have been an unfortunate accident.'

Watt concentrated on weaving the Crossley through the gap between an ammunition limber and a refugee family with all their belongings piled on a cart pulled by a plough horse. Robson wondered what story of influence and local jiggery-pokery lay behind their retaining their horse.

'Ach, Sirr,' Watt said when they were finally clear. 'Ye wouldna hae me admit tae being aboot tae destroy his Majesty's property, would ye.'

When Watt dropped him at the mess Uncle Tom

Cobleigh was waiting in the doorway to shake hands.

'You don't have to tell me, Split. You wrecked the old cow. I could tell by the look on that craggy Scottish face. I've never seen him look happy before. The Squadron will vote you get a putty medal. But in the meantime get across to the hangars. Callaghan has been called to Wing H.Q. There's a big flap on. He is going to fly you to the Depot. He is waiting and, like her late Majesty, he is not amused.'

But between the mess and the hangars half a dozen others congratulated him on having got rid of the squadron's barnyard relic without injury. As he walked over to Callaghan by the waiting F.E. he felt as if his feet were six inches off the ground. It was starting to rain and the Major did not seem overpleased at having to wait for him but Robson did not care. He was home among friends. He was crashproof, immortal, suddenly convinced that he was going to survive this stupid war and go home to live happily with a radiant Madelaine.

'You are the only man I know, Robson, who looks happy after smashing a perfectly good aeroplane,' Callaghan grated as he swung impatiently into the cockpit. 'You'd better bring a good one back from the Depot; you'll be using it tonight.'

Not many of them arrived back at the aerodrome for the night's work. The shower that soaked Robson in the exposed gunner's position slowly worsened into a rainstorm that lashed the Depot from cloud at hangar-roof level.

Six of them set off with the new F.E.s as soon as the rain slackened and the cloud lifted. One of the 'B' Flight pilots was left behind when his engine refused to start. The number was made up by a replacement pilot, making his fourth flight in an F.E. The cloud frustrated their intention to fly back in formation. The tendrils of mist snaking between them at 300 feet scattered the new pilots. Only Robson and Fenner stayed together. It was not until they landed, faces whipped raw by the rain, that they found out about the rest.

A blocked fuel pipe put one of the old hands down with a dead engine in a field barely ten miles from the Depot. Two of the new pilots got lost, one of them landing at a Naval aerodrome on the coast near Dunkirk, seventy miles to the north. The replacement pilot, completely lost and running low on petrol, found the aerodrome at last light. Coming in across wind in his haste to get down he bounced, tore a tyre off crabbing into wind and spun round until the undercarriage collapsed.

Callaghan, who had landed on his return from H.Q. a few minutes earlier, looked on from alongside his aeroplane. The mechanics furtively watching waited for him to launch a tirade at the crestfallen newcomer. They were disappointed.

Someone brought the pilot in from the wreck in the sidecar of the Douglas combination.

'What's your name?' Callaghan asked.

'Mathews, Sir,' the pilot replied, standing to attention as though on parade waiting for his buttons to be cut off.

'All right, you can stand easy, Mr. Mathews, you're on a squadron now, not a parade ground. Sticking your chin out and sucking in your belly will not repair that aeroplane. How many hours have you got on the F.E.2b machine?'

'Seven and a half, Sir, including the time to get here, Sir. I flew one out ...'

'How many landings on the F.E., and I do not call your recent arrival a landing? What service aeroplane did you train on?'

'Four landings, Sir. I was trained on the R.E.8s but they wanted a pilot to ferry an F.E. so ...'

'So you volunteered. And then you told the Depot you were an F.E. pilot. You are a damned fool, Mathews. But the people who let you come here are worse. All right,

I need pilots even more than I need machines. Report to Captain Cobleigh after you have seen the Recording Officer. Tell him that my instructions are that you are to put in at least five hours' day flying and ten landings at night before you go near the Lines.'

He turned to the watching mechanics. 'Have you got nothing better to do than stand there gawping? Get that wreckage moved. If it cannot be made airworthy before tomorrow night you'd better cannibalize it for spares. Until further notice the squadron must be kept ready to move within twenty-four hours of getting the signal from Wing. The Hun is still snapping at our heels.'

He walked off slowly towards his quarters in the farmhouse. Watt watched him with a puzzled look on his face. Why wasn't he going to his office to brief the Squadron for the night's work?

'What's up with the Major?' a mechanic asked. 'He looks ten years older.'

Watt stared after the retreating figure. 'They've grounded him,' he murmured. 'That's what they must have done.'

'Lucky bastard,' the mechanic growled. 'I suppose it's not before time.'

'They've grounded him,' Watt said again in an incredulous way. He suddenly realized that he was talking to a mechanic. 'Shut y're mouth and stop gossiping aboot ye're orficers,' he snapped. 'Get on with your work and don't be a bigger fule than you can help. It'll kill the man.'

'Phew,' Second Lieutenant Mathews pulled off his wet helmet and wiped his forehead with a shaking hand. 'I thought I was for it then. Sent home, at least. I was told he was a bit of a fire-eater.'

'Aye, he is that. You got off light. Not that ye're no a blessing in disguise. I'll ha' the engine oot o' that pile o' scrap within the hour. Repair it, he says. Man, yon's the answer to ma prayers. Brand new spares.'

Within fifteen minutes the entire Squadron knew that Watt's guess had been correct. Major Callaghan was at long last confirmed in his rank and was leaving for home shortly to form a new Handley Page Squadron which would join the new VIII Wing at Nancy to carry the war home to the German towns along the Rhine. While Captain Cobleigh took temporary command of the Squadron, Major Callaghan's first order, as he sprawled tieless on his bed, was for two bottles of whisky.

It was Uncle Tom who gave the orders for the night's work. The big battle for Amiens was about to begin. A Brigadier-General was struggling to improvise a new defence line fourteen miles east of Amiens, with Villers-Bretonneux, a village on the St. Quentin road, forming the keystone. A scratch force of three thousand men —Royal Engineers, American railwaymen, Musketry School instructors, clerks and batmen—were digging in as the Fifth Army doggedly fought to give them the time they needed.

That time was running out, Uncle Tom said. The big attack would come the following day. Eleven German divisions, six of them fresh from the reserves, waited to attack. H.Q. had asked for a record total of bombs to be dropped on the roads, Somme bridges and railway lines.

Incredibly, Watt and his men had managed to get twelve aeroplanes ready, and from the R.E. Squadron on the other side of the aerodrome had come four aeroplanes and crews. The artillery observation crews, turned into bomber crews for the night, were to work just over the Line along the road from Péronne to Amiens. Six of the F.E.s were to attack the bridges across the Somme at Ham. The remaining six, including Robson with the 'pom-pom' F.E. were to bomb Cambrai.

To Robson, keyed up with his new sense of his own invulnerability, it was exhaustion, not fear, that turned the

night into an unending tunnel. The F.E., laden with the
gun and its shells, and a load of Coopers under the wings,
took twenty minutes to claw up to 5,000 feet. It took them
an hour to reach Cambrai, skirting the probing searchlights around Bapaume, watching the airspeed (lazily
flickering at seventy-five), the oil pressure and water temperature gauges, his ears straining to catch the first sound of
a failing engine. They were the last to get there, but then
the 'pom-pom' was notorious for being the oldest and slow-
est in the Squadron.

A train was burning in the station and as Robson followed the railway line in from the south-east a dump
blew up on the other side of the town. Jerome did not
need to drop their flares to see the transport, horsed limbers and the occasional lorry, moving nose to tail across the
canal. His bombs missed the bridge but a terrified team of
horses slewed a limber across the road to leave someone
else a target.

Robson's orders were to attack trains with the 'pom-
pom'. In a shallow dive he closed rapidly on a goods
engine coming in from Valenciennes, betrayed as usual
by the reflected glare of the firebox, giving Jerome an
ideal target. The locomotive seemed to swallow shells unharmed, but as Robson climbed over it, with the 'pom-
pom' jammed after two clips had been fired, he saw a
couple of trucks skewed across the rails.

They crawled home at 2,000 feet, bucking the inevitable head-wind, Robson slapping his hands alternately on
his knees to stop them from going numb, the throttle
inched up just a little more than was prudent.

They were tenth back. The R.E.s had already set off on
their second trip. Harper, the new man in his room, had
got lost but was down safely, out of fuel, near Arras.
One of the 'B' Flight had his engine fail as he flew over
the Line but he had had enough height to glide back to
safety and a black eye. And one of the new pilots—the

name meant nothing to Robson—had flown back with a fragment of 'Archie' in his thigh.

Uncle Tom took the wounded pilot's place when the ten of them straggled off on a return trip to Cambrai. They rekindled the fire in the station, peppered the bridge without breaking it and shattered a column of transport in the middle of the town. Robson and Jerome, arriving long after everyone else had gone, could find no locomotives. So they made three attacks on the blocked bridge, getting fifty rounds off before the inevitable jam. They left a blazing lorry, and took back with them a nightmare vision of plunging horses breaking their traces and running amuck, through the lines of marching men.

Seven of them got back. One of the missing had engine failure soon after take off and landed safely with his bombs still under the wings. Another new crew got lost and someone in 'C' Flight flew back with a shattered radiator until the Beardmore got tired of running with molten white metal lubricating the bearings, and gave up the ghost ten miles from the aerodrome, forcing the pilot to crash-land.

Uncle Tom used his orders to destroy the bridges as an excuse to send them back to Cambrai again. It was an opportunity, he told his tired crews, to do as the Germans did, and concentrate on one good target. One of the seven had got back with a wing structure that quivered like a jelly so there were only six on the third trip. The R.E. crews had retired for the night as they would be flying the following morning. The first of the six was about to go when Robson landed.

On the third trip Robson was flying like an automaton, despite the black coffee and curling sandwiches served in the mess while the mechanics rearmed, refuelled and patched up the aeroplanes. There was no finesse in his flying now. On the earlier trips he had carefully skirted around searchlights, skittered away from the occasional

'Archie' and flaming onions. Now he hunched his shoulders, huddled deeper in his cockpit and flew on, watching the dimly-lit clock and compass with only an occasional apprehensive glance at the eastern horizon.

He did not reach Cambrai. Fifteen minutes before he was due there—he could see the flames in the sky—the engine spluttered and began to run roughly, a couple of hundred revs low according to the tachometer. The oil pressure began to go down.

He had been heading south of the town again to pick up the railway line. Now he turned north looking for the Bapaume road. A column of horse-drawn wagons scattered as Jerome dropped their bombs. But the 'pom-pom' jammed again after five rounds. It was a wonder it fired at all, Robson thought. After all the work it had done the rifling must be worn out.

Then there was nothing to do but crawl home, eyes on the engine gauges, ears tuned to the ever-roughening engine note. He thought a couple of exhaust valves had gone, and both of them, pilot and observer, watched the grey light of a false dawn strip away their protection. All the Lewis ammunition had been fired at the column. If a fighter attacked them, Robson thought with a wry smile, they would be back to the situation of early '16 of throwing shells at the Hun. Luckily the wind had died but in its place a ground mist was getting up. He did not dare fly too low in case the engine died, so they flew on at about a thousand feet.

Dawn had broken by the time they finally landed. Robson was too exhausted to respond to the lugubrious look on Watt's face and the way his engine fitter shook his head and clicked his tongue. The noise of the engine, the whistle of the wind in the wires still seemed to envelop him as he dropped onto his bed. Someone said that Uncle Tom was missing but he was too tired for the news to register. He stretched out, undressed to the extent of kick-

ing off his shoes and removing his tie and coat, and fell
asleep at once. Half an hour later, when the first flight of
bomb-laden R.E.s took off over the hut, he did no more
than twitch and grunt and turn over in his sleep.

It was raining when the sleep-drugged crews met for lunch
in a subdued mess. Uncle Tom being missing had come
as a shock to men who could not remember the Squadron
without his being there. Now they grouped round the bar
watching to see who turned up, wondering whether so-
and-so had failed to return, or had simply overslept.

Dick Garbutt erupted into the mess like a drunk singing
in church. They had, he announced to an apathetic audi-
ence, dropped a record total of bombs, more than any
other Squadron. Wing were pleased to be able to convey
their congratulations and the thanks of Army H.Q.

Then, as if to kill any hidden complacency, he reminded them that the Squadron was still on twenty-four hours
notice to move and that all officers would have their kit
packed accordingly.

Someone said that if the Squadron would desist from
dropping record numbers of bombs on the German rear the
Germans might stay there instead of advancing.

Garbutt ignored his heckler. Remembering his days as
the star of his regiment's Dramatic Society he had saved
his *piece de resistance* for the end.

'I am sure you will all be glad to know that Captain
Cobleigh,' he announced—and suddenly he had the attention of everyone in the room—'has safely made a forced
landing on the right side of the Line with nothing worse
than a broken wrist.'

In the hubbub that followed no one seemed to hear
him say that unfortunately his observer had broken his
neck. Somebody thrust a glass of sherry into Garbutt's
hand. In a matter of minutes the bar was thronged with
groups of men now able to talk about what had happened

to them the previous night and to ask what had happened to the silly fool flying at nought feet gunning the burning station and who was the idiot who'd dived into that searchlight east of the canal bridge.

It had not, after all, been such a bad night. They had dropped all those bombs, Garbutt had said so. And now there were less than half a dozen serviceable aeroplanes left. The missing men were all laboriously making their way back to the aerodrome. And it was raining, a heavy drenching downpour from clouds that seemed to have settled on the hangar roofs. All those things in combination seemed to add up to a night on the ground and an excuse for a party.

By the time Uncle Tom arrived, the white bandage and sling contrasting with his mud-stained uniform, plans were afoot for a raid on the mess of the R.E. Squadron over the hill. Robson and Fenner were despatched by tender to Amiens to replenish the Squadron's cellar, with strict instructions about the time at which they were expected to be back. Over by the hangars Watt was giving thanks for the respite given him by the rain and driving his tired mechanics to make the most of it. If anyone noticed the continuous rattle of the mess windows from gunfire he did not comment on it.

Robson was not sorry he could not stay long in Amiens. He rang the Hospital only to be told that Madelaine's ambulance was not back nor was it expected for some time. So there was nothing there for him. The city was hideous with the frantic ant-line stirrings of a place about to be besieged. It was the railhead for reinforcements, with two divisions a day pouring in now that the new Commander-in-Chief, Marshal Foch, had declared that there would be no more retreating. And it was a departure-point for those who did not believe him and had the money to go. It was also a gathering place for bewildered peasants, uprooted again before the advancing German armies, drawn into the old centre of the province only to be channelled out again to some new refuge. And it was a place for those temporarily freed from war or about to go to war, to steal a few hours' release. Hot baths, clean linen, select houses for officers, not-so-select houses for other ranks; cafés and restaurants to suit all pockets.

But it was no place for Robson when the one woman he wanted to see was nearer the Front Line than he was. Freshly bathed, and fortified by an early dinner at Josephine's, he and Fenner went back with the loaded tender. In his breast pocket he carried a ring. Perhaps if she had something of his to remind her of him she might begin to forget, in a small way, about the two previous men in her life.

At nightfall the rain stopped and although the clouds hanging low promised it to be only a temporary respite three aeroplanes were hastily bombed up to attack reinforcements moving up the Péronne–Amiens road. Robson took 'Mimi', the 'pom-pom' F.E. Despite its defects it was serviceable but he realized, with a feeling of disgust tinged with affection that even his new-found confidence would not suppress, that he was now firmly linked in the other pilots' minds with the oldest aeroplane in the Squadron.

They flew low, under a thousand feet, skirting trailing clouds of cold rain, their eyes straining to see the faint change in tones of darkness that marked the horizon. Robson was the first one off, but 'Mimi' was so slow that the others were already strafing the road when he got there, attracted by the flares someone was dropping from just under the cloud base.

For once the 'pom-pom' behaved itself. After Jerome had dropped the bombs Robson turned and flew back downwind, his engine throttled back for quietness, spraying the road and sheltering blobs of darkness under trees that resolved as he whistled over them into terrified horses, lorries and huddled columns of men. Twice, half-blinded by the flash of the 'pom-pom,' he narrowly missed trees or the remains of a tottering chimney.

One of the others was not so lucky. As Robson pulled out of his final dive, all the 'pom-pom' ammunition spent, he saw one of the other pilots during a sudden shower of rain, misjudge his height. The wings clipped a tree and the flaming wreckage cartwheeled into the sheltering column.

They were late getting back. Both of them got lost and Robson scraped in with only enough petrol to get him to the hangars before the engine died. It was not until he spoke to Keegan, the 'B' Flight commander standing by his F.E. in his rain-sodden sidcot, that Robson realized that the ball of fire splattered along the Amiens road had held his companion of a few hours earlier. Fenner would make no more light-hearted trips to Amiens.

It started to rain heavily again as the four of them trudged to the mess. The gramophone was blaring a selection from 'The Maid of the Mountains', an overturned table lay in a litter of bottles and four pilots were fighting a vigorous duel with soda syphons. The party with the R.E. crowd had started.

The following night the weather was again too bad for flying. Uncle Tom sent six of them off to the Depot to collect new aeroplanes. Because of the weather they were allowed to stay overnight in Amiens. No one had seen Callaghan for twenty-four hours, and Uncle Tom, his arm in a sling, the colour returning to his drawn features, was in charge. According to Robson's batman Callaghan was locked in his room. He had, so the rumour had it, been drunk for a night and a day.

'What the hell has it got to do with you?' Keegan asked when he heard Robson discussing it as the Crossley jolted slowly along the crowded road. 'You ought to know better than to retail servants' gossip. None of you looked like blue-ribboned boys last night.'

'It's not just servants' gossip,' Robson's room-mate, Harper, chipped in. 'Everyone on the Squadron knows that the Major is drunk. You can't hide the number of bottles his batman takes in. I say it's a dashed bad show. I mean to say, getting pie-eyed at a party is one thing but sitting in your room swilling it down is a very different kettle of fish. Of course, with a man like that what can ...'

Keegan was beginning to get angry. 'For God's sake stop yapping until you have been out here long enough to dirty your britches,' he snapped. 'I never liked the man but I respect him. Do you realize he has not been home since the summer of '15. He was flying Fees when you lot were still at school. And he went on flying them all last year across the Line by day, long after the antiquated bathtubs should have been retired. And let me tell you, it's harder on a man like him to send other people to do a job than it is to do it himself.'

'All right, Tim,' one of Keegan's pilots chipped in. 'So he is entitled to get blotto. But you must admit that he did flog the Squadron to death to get his D.S.O. And what is this blot on his record that everybody talks about in whispers?'

'What do you mean, "flog the Squadron to death for a medal"? He was doing his job, fighting a war. He never asked anyone to do anything that either he had not done or was not prepared to do. As for the other thing, what happened a couple of years ago is his business. If you want to know, ask him. All I'm saying is, by my standards, he did nothing to his discredit.'

The words, earnestly delivered and slightly pompous, took Robson back to his schooldays. People like Keegan, a Captain, a Flight Commander, a man who had survived an initiation at the beginning of the most bloody month the R.F.C. had known, April 1917; and who had lived through a tour on Martinsydes, and then come back to fly an aeroplane that was obsolete when the big 'Tinsyde' was introduced—men like that looked, Robson thought, old because of the authority conferred on them by their rank and confirmed by their experience. Then they said something, something that made you look again at the man who had spoken, and you realized that Keegan, who looked so old and seemed so experienced, was probably nearing his twenty-first birthday.

14

Robson got away from the others after a quick drink with them in Amiens. Ignoring the freely offered lurid advice he made his way to the little hotel at which he had stayed on the night of the air raid. He got the same room. There was plenty of time; Madelaine was not supposed to meet him at Josephine's until seven. But he was buttoning up a clean shirt, tieless, braces dangling, when she came running up the stairs to his room half an hour early. Mamie Sorensen trailed along behind at a discreet distance.

'Don't know whether you can afford to take two lonely, hungry women out to dinner,' she gasped. 'But I had to bring Mamie along. It's her last night. She's off to gay Paree at eleven.'

He grinned and made a show of counting the francs piled on the dressing table.

'I dare say we will manage. Provided you don't eat too much. How did you know I was here?'

Mamie giggled. 'Bless you, honey. I've been dying to ask her that question since she dragged me outa the cab.'

Madelaine looked at him smiling, and he felt his knees turn to water. She turned to Mamie. 'Now see what you have done, you hussy. You have made the boy blush.'

The reaction to his excitement at seeing her made his head ache and the little room suddenly seem frowsy. Like the whole affair, he thought miserably. Then he bundled them out of the room while he finished dressing.

After dinner they dashed through the rain to Henri and Babs' studio to dance until it was time to take Mamie to the station. Their styles of dancing were as different as their appearance. Alternately he was briskly hustled round the room by Mamie, or smoothly by a feather-light Madelaine. There was something going on between the two of them, he suddenly realized, that they were keeping from him. Madelaine was too excited, and he was soon sure, without her actually saying so, that she was staying in France. Mamie did not mention McDonald. To Robson it seemed as if that night had happened three months ago, not three nights. He wondered if McDonald had liked Mamie as much as the American girl had liked him. Perhaps it was just as well their friendship had not developed as quickly as his with Madelaine.

At the station Mamie leaned out of the carriage window and firmly kissed him on the lips. 'Dammit,' she said in a pseudo-military voice. 'If the wench wasn't going to be here to look after you I'd do the job myself. Happy landings.'

Then he left the two girls to cry their good-byes and stood under the shattered canopy at the entrance wondering how Madelaine had wangled a job in France. After what Mamie had said he was sure of it.

'A drink?' he asked as the train blasted out of the station in a cocoon of steam. He was wondering what to do next. She had guessed where he was staying. Did that mean she was going to stay with him, or would he have to ask?

She sniffed and shook her head. 'I hate good-byes. I always cry and I look a frump with my eyes red and watery.'

She took his arm and pulled herself close, hiding her head in the crook of his elbow as she yawned. 'Sorry. We were on the road at six. 'Vacuating Villers. I'm dreadfully tired.'

He nodded, licking his dry lips and swearing at himself for being such a selfish fool.

'And besides,' she went on. 'I saw you had a bottle of

cognac in your room. We can have a picnic in bed. Biscuits and brandy in tin mugs.'

They walked and ran through the rain back to the hotel. As they ran, she told him, too excited to hold it back any longer, that she was staying in France. She was going to help run a convalescent home south of Paris.

'And I did not have to ask for it as a favour. They asked me. A friend of Ben's heard that our unit was disbanding, remembered me, and offered me the job. They are Quakers. He said he remembered my work as a Welfare Officer at that munitions factory.'

She giggled. 'I have an affair with a Jew, meet a Quaker, and between them they keep me near to ... what are *you*, darling?'

They were at the entrance to the hotel now. He stopped, grabbed her arm, and pulled her roughly to him.

'I thought we might go one night without your mentioning one of them,' he snapped as he fumbled in his pocket for the ring. 'Here, take this. I want to marry you.'

'Christopher, let me go, you are hurting my arm. Darling you're jealous!'

Sullenly he let go her arm.

She made a face at him and tucked her arm back in his. He did not move. She looked at his face, white and solemn.

'Oh dear,' she said. 'Arthur went down on his knees in the conservatory. I thought he'd never get up.' She stopped and smiled. 'No one has ever asked me to marry them standing in the rain with a water-spout jetting down my neck.' She pulled herself up to kiss him.

'I know you think I'm a kid but I'm serious,' he growled.

She drew him into the hotel. They walked upstairs in silence, leaving a trail of puddles behind them. He went to the bathroom and when he got back she was already in bed holding two mugs of cognac. He put out the lamp, flicked up the window blind, and joined her.

She raised her mug in salute. 'Darling, I didn't say I would not marry you sometime. But not now. For **my** sake. Don't you see that if anything should happen to you I would feel like a woman with a curse on her. You go home in six months, don't you? It's not so long to wait. And there's no need to be jealous, darling.'

She was lying on her side. The sleeve of her nightgown sliding down her arm exposed one breast almost to the nipple. There were tears in her eyes. He drained his mug and turned to her.

15

The rain cleared in the morning and after lunch the six of them flew back in vee formation through bright sunshine. It was hard work. None of them, except Keegan, had ever flown in formation before. Robson's F.E. was badly rigged so that his left leg was soon aching from the strain of holding on rudder to stop the brute turning into the man on his starboard. Despite this he was happy, sitting in the sun watching the black aeroplanes slowly rise and fall, pull ahead or fall back like horses on a roundabout.

Despite Watt's protests the six new aeroplanes were used to make up the dozen detailed that night to break up troop concentrations along the road to Roye.

Uncle Tom had had a new idea. Two of the F.E.s would carry extra flares and they would light up the road for the others to attack. Each bomber would call for light by firing a blue Very flare. And as Tom pointed out, if they left at five-minute intervals this would reduce the time the flare droppers had to stay over the Line and with that amount of light about there would be no excuse for anyone not finding the target.

Half an hour after last light a long line of F.E.s rocked gently on their wheels. A light drizzle washed the wings, coalescing into large drops that sizzled as they fell onto the exhaust manifolds. Over by the hangars a laggard with a reluctant engine toiled on amidst the stench of spilled petrol. Flames flickered irregularly from the exhausts of the idling engines. At the head of the line Robson impatiently raced his engine to burn off any oil on the plugs. He wiped rain off his goggles and looked at his watch again. The flare droppers had left over ten minutes earlier and still Uncle Tom held them on the ground. Freed for one night from the eccentricities of the 'pom-pom' F.E., Robson was eagerly awaiting the chance to fly something as fast as the rest of the Squadron.

A green light flashed across the aerodrome signalling to the mechanics crouched by the flares to light up. Robson ran up his engine again, fortunately unable to hear the curses of the two mechanics hanging onto the tail-booms in a hail of propeller-driven rain.

The green light splashed onto Robson's nacelle, clicking his letter. He flashed a reply on the lamp on his underside. The mechanics ran out onto the wingtips, swinging him round onto the flare path. He opened the throttle slowly, confident in his new aeroplane's ability to get off quickly. The F.E. trundled off into the darkness. It was ten feet up before they passed the last flare and it soared easily over the red lantern fastened to the tip of the tallest poplar. Every few minutes the others followed until only the crouched mechanics by the flares remained swearing mindlessly as Watt and his men tried to cure the misfiring engine on the last of the dozen.

It was a wasted night. The rain got worse as Robson flew south-east. The broken cloud solidified and the base got lower. He saw no flares or any other aeroplanes. He found a road going somewhere on the same bearing as the road to Roye on which there were marching troops and horse-drawn wagons. Jerome's aim was bad and the bombs missed the road but in the light of the explosions Robson saw terrified horses breaking out of their traces. That, he decided, was enough for one night. Without horses the road was effectively blocked by the wagons and if the Imperial Army spent the night chasing frightened animals over rain-sodden fields they were unlikely to have much stomach for fighting in the morning. They went home.

He always felt relief when he found himself back over the aerodrome, the line of flares spread out beneath. He could relax, confident that there was nothing between him and the first drink in the mess but the exercise of his skill as an airman. Tonight was no exception. It was a black night but his eyes were attuned to the darkness. The wind must have swung because the flare path was slightly out of line. But he was relaxed, confidently crabbing towards the line of lights, the engine almost silent, the only noise the wind in the wires and the chop-chop of the big propeller lazily turning between the booms. Suddenly a flash behind him lit the F.E. like a searchlight. The bomber shuddered and seemed to drop out of the sky, touching on one wheel before Robson could slam the throttle open. Only a few feet above the airfield they staggered drunkenly, on the verge of stalling, the engine screaming as it tried to accelerate the bulk of the F.E., the flare path a line of light at a crazy angle. Gingerly, Robson sorted things out and flew a wide circuit, making gentle turns. It was not until he had landed and examined the rents in the tailplane that he realized that one of his own bombs had failed to drop away—until the moment he had started to land.

'Ach, if ye were sentenced to hang they'd ha' to starve ye to death,' Watt said as they looked at the damage. Uncle Tom was less sympathetic, confining himself to a pungent comment about what would happen to airmen who were in such a hurry to get home that they neglected to check their bomb racks.

Robson forced a wan smile and tried in vain to think of something smart to say. One of the R.E.s landing at dusk the previous day had had the same trouble. But the pilot and the observer had died in the ensuing fire that had engulfed two other Harry Tates as well as their own.

The following morning, he could laugh at what had happened as one more proof that he was not meant to be killed in this stupid war. And it was another anecdote about him that would grow with the telling and retelling. Mechanics looked for him, saluted, and, as he passed, turned to stare and whisper the latest variant of his previous night's adventure; and in the mess there was the usual banter and leg-pulling. As he went in to the mess for breakfast Tim Keegan and two of the 'B' Flight pilots beckoned him to their table, telling him to hurry. The chef had some special hard-boiled eggs for him—in cast-iron cases. The new pilots and observers joined in the laughter and then turned to whisper among themselves about him. Robson suspected his batman of inventing most of the tales.

He was becoming the Squadron's star turn. Good old Split. There was always something happening when Split-Arse was about. Dick Garbutt told him that a couple of the new observers had asked if they could fly with him. He was their living proof that death could be cheated, a man born under a lucky star. He was beginning to enjoy the rôle. He even agreed to take on one of the new observers as Tony Jerome had contracted pneumonia and was at base hospital.

'The thing I like about night bombing,' he said to Keegan, 'is the way it leaves you with a healthy appetite for breakfast.'

'Each man to his own taste,' Keegan replied through a mouthful of bacon and egg. 'I'm satisfied to be here to eat it.'

The weather was too bad for flying that night. Robson played whist with Uncle Tom, Armitage and Tim Keegan, happy to sit smoking with a glass of vermouth while a small party brewed up in an adjacent room.

Dick Garbutt joined them about ten as they yawned and started talking about getting an early night in bed for once. As Uncle Tom handed Garbutt his brandy and soda, he asked how Callaghan was.

Garbutt wrinkled his nose. 'I thought he was beginning to dry out but he's off again. He's getting back to his usual form though. When he was in the office a couple of hours ago he saw the orders against flying tonight. He played hell. Wanted the entire Squadron over the Line. As it happened, it had stopped raining, but only the trees were holding the cloud off the ground.'

He drained his brandy and called for another. 'He'll be all right tomorrow. Now he has got that maudlin nonsense out of his mind.'

'Changed your mind now,' Armitage asked, 'about going to this new Squadron with him?'

Garbutt smiled, and shook his head. He tapped the bowl of his pipe against his heel, methodically blew down the stem and slowly filled it from an oilskin pouch.

'I've known him for three years. It seems much longer. No wonder. He is one of the extinct breed, the best type of Regular army N.C.O. We'll not see their like again. After the war we are going to need men like our Major Callaghan. I'll be more use to him than to Tom Cobleigh there...'

'Wet-nursing a drunk.' The words slipped out even though Robson regretted them the moment they passed his lips.

Garbutt nodded; he did not seem to be offended. 'You'll understand one day, Robson. When you have been out a bit longer.' He patted his pockets, looking for matches. Armitage pushed a box to him. He went on through a cloud of smoke. 'He was making a name for himself when I first knew him in early '15. He was a marvellous shot. Latimer-Needham, the Wing Colonel, he was O.C. "B" Flight then, used to go off with him in our Vickers Gunbus. This was in their spare time. Between them they shot down a couple of Huns. They weren't so numerous then.

In the summer we got B.E.s and at the same time Jerry got the Fokker Monoplane. He got the best of the bargain and by autumn we couldn't keep new pilots. They went west before they had a chance to find out how to look after themselves.

'That was when Callaghan got his Military Medal. Those two damn fools used to go off in a B.E. to look for Fokkers while everybody else was getting killed avoiding them.'

He wasted another couple of matches relighting his pipe. 'That's one reason why I'll stay with him. Then, after he got his wings, Latimer-Needham got him out of a spot of trouble. He came out with the Squadron on F.E.s. We had a bad time last year. Trying to go on using the poor old F.E. as a fighter against Pfalzes and Vee Strutters and Triplanes. By God it was an expensive business.

'We had a hundred-per-cent casualties twice in a couple of months. Callaghan was acting C.O. and we lost two of *them* in five weeks. Until we were put on to night bombing.

'The way Callaghan looks at things he has killed nearly a hundred young men—on our side. Are you surprised he gets drunk?'

On the following day the Fifth Army found that their new general had brought reinforcements with him; Americans and Australians. From a vantage point on the River Luce, General Hutier, seeing the smoke of Amiens on the skyline only eleven miles away, urged his men forward for the final attack. Capturing Amiens would eliminate that fifty mile long exposed supply line from St. Quentin.

H.Q. had looked at that line and had a new idea to further aggravate the torment inflicted on the attacking Germans by the day bombers and scouts. Robson's Squadron was given orders to keep the Amiens–Roye road under continuous attack for ten hours. Thanks to the respite granted by the rain of the previous night there were sixteen F.E.s fit to fly although four of the pilots and five of the observers would be making their first trip over the Line.

It was as good a way to take the plunge as any, Robson thought, as he sat listening to Uncle Tom giving them the orders for the night. The weather did not look too bad. There would be no searchlights, and if the cloud-base was high enough the machine-gun and rifle fire was unlikely to do much harm. Unless, of course, you were after a quick medal and went in low . . .

Of course there was always the threat of engine trouble —or getting lost, which meant the same thing—and being able to find a field big enough and sufficiently smooth to get down safely, always remembering that damned great engine sat on its flimsy mounting waiting to pulverize you . . .

There were simple errors of airmanship to be made too. The horizon would not be very clear for one thing, and there would be fires all over the damned place, and little lights, camp fires, motor transport, wiremen using torches, little sparks in the darkness all of which could be confused with a star. And the more you looked the less sure you were whether you were climbing or diving. You were a fish in a bowl. It was like being hypnotized. If you were lucky the rising scream from the wires woke you before it was too late. He shuddered.

'Gets you by the short and curlies, don't it?' said an Australian voice beside him. 'This bloody waitin'. If there was a bloody quack here I'd go crook before you could say "stone the crows".'

Robson grinned his agreement, pushing his fears behind him. Waiting was tough on everyone, but more so for the new men who had not yet found their feet. But not for him, he was an old hand now.

At last light they went off one by one at twenty-minute intervals. It was going to be a long night, Robson thought. An hour to climb to 2,000 feet, find the long straight road and select a target. Fifteen minutes to bomb and empty the Lewis gun into the chaos below. Then an hour and a half beating back against that infernal west wind. By the time they had drunk the scalding-hot coffee and swallowed a couple of sandwiches, just as the warmth was at last penetrating down to the toes, it was time to go back again.

One of the new pilots misjudged his landing after the first trip and was burned to death against the upwind hedge. On the second trip someone hosing the sheltering trees at the edge of the road with the Lewis pulled up too sharply and spun in off the stall. The wreck lit the target for the next man. And there were two engine failures from which the crews walked away with nothing more than cuts and bruises. Two of the new pilots got lost.

By the time he was returning from his third trip Robson was totally exhausted. The culmination of the cold, the strain of listening to the engine note, looking for the horizon, watching the blurred outline of fields and woods; the physical effort of lugging the F.E. round to dodge a stream of tracer, of diving to attack with the Lewis, had taken the last of his strength out of him like water wrung from a sponge. It was all he could do to get the nose down below the horizon and head more or less in the direction of the aerodrome. He let the F.E. fly itself. That was the reverse side of the coin, he thought gratefully. You had to work like a coal heaver to do anything with the F.E. but, properly rigged like this one, she would take you back, straight and level on her own.

The sky was lightening in the east as he apathetically watched his new observer rise and beat his frozen hands against his chest. He began to take off the spent ammunition drum from the Lewis. Neither of them was in a state to concern themselves with the chance of meeting an early-rising German scout, and anyway there was no ammunition left.

The F.E. lurched. Robson was slow to correct. The new observer, his frozen fingers clumsy in the big gauntlets, clutched at the gun for support. His hands slipped and grabbed the concertina-like bag beneath the breech that collected the empty cartridge cases. The fabric split and a stream of empty cases flew back, clattering on the windscreen, cutting Robson's exposed cheeks. Something bulky whistled over his head. The unlocked ammunition drum had flown off and was being whipped back over the cowling into the propeller blades.

Robson was instantly paralysed with fear, and his numbed muscles were too slow to respond to the danger as his mind pictured what was going to happen when the cases and the drum hit the propeller.

He had seen it happen once before, on the Home Defence Squadron. One of the Flight Commanders had been happily looping a D.H. single-seater, pulling out of the dive at 200 feet and slowly getting lower. He had been playing in the sky to celebrate his return posting to France. The last loop had been too slow and, as the little fighter stalled inverted, the watchers below had seen the pilot make a frantic grab for a loose ammunition drum as it flew past him. The shattered propeller had sliced through one of the booms and as the fighter slid sideways the tail structure had peeled away like a cast-off banana skin. Robson shuddered as he remembered watching the pilot, thrown out of the gyrating nacelle, clawing at the air as he fell.

Somehow his groping fingers managed to switch off the ignition a split second after the propeller broke and before the screaming engine vibrated out of its mounting.

Robson stared wildly over the side looking for a place to land, his stomach muscles knotted, waiting for the lurch that would tell him the tail had gone. But the booms held and he side-slipped over a stone wall into a small shell-pocked field. The undercarriage splintered as the left wheel dropped into a shell-hole, twisting sideways. The left wing took the impact and folded up, in a hideous screech of splintering wood and ripping fabric.

Half a dozen soldiers ran out of the rising mist.

'Are you orl right, Sir?'

'Put that damned cigarette out,' Robson screamed, suddenly aware that they were alive and that the wreck stank of petrol. Hastily he tore open the strap across his thighs and stepped out of the broken nacelle. A couple of soldiers were already lifting out the limp figure of his observer under the supervision of a sergeant.

'I'm afraid he's a goner, Sir,' the Sergeant said. 'Your observer, Sir. Looks like he broke his neck.'

A noise like an approaching express train was beating on Robson's brain before he realized it was a shell. He heard the explosion and the whistle of the next before starting to stumble for the cover of a copse on his left.

He heard the Sergeant call out and stopped and turned to see him lighting a cigarette. As he strolled up to Robson he held out the tin, cupping his Tommy lighter in his other hand.

'S'all right, Sir. I reckon you must be shook up by that crash. 'Tis only Jerry saying, "Good morning" like. He's registered down the road, nigh on 300 yards off. Napoo cross-roads. He'll not reach us here. Not this morning. I reckon you'd best see the M.O. There's an F.A.P. half-left by that copse, right-hand side.'

By the copse was a shattered farmhouse with a sandbagged entrance leading down to the cellar. The M.O. was leaning against the sandbags, a bloodstained, once-white smock loosely draped over his uniform. Beads of moisture, sweat or the morning mist, speckled his hair and eyebrows.

'You all right?' he asked when the Sergeant left them.

'Too bad about your observer. You'd better let my clerk have his name and number.'

Robson nodded dumbly. He was trying without success to remember the name. He could picture the face, round, ruddy-cheeked, flecked with pimples. His Christian name had been Frank but the surname escaped him. He started to giggle. All night they had fought and flown together and all he could remember was a red-faced boy called Frank.

The M.O. glanced sharply at him. 'You'd better sit down here.' He nodded his head at the cellar behind. 'I shouldn't go down there. It's a bit thick after a night's work. You can have whisky, or strong sweet tea. I recommend the tea, it'll do you more good.'

He shouted down into the darkness of the cellar and a few minutes later an orderly appeared with half a pint of strong, almost black tea in a tin mug.

It was noticeably lighter now, nearly full daylight. Robson sat and sipped the tea while the M.O. laconically described their position. Robson barely understood what he was saying. A couple of tired stretcher bearers brought in the body of his observer. A corporal clerk handed Robson the contents of his pockets, a wallet, a watch, a pipe, a pouch of tobacco and a pocket bible. He looked at the identity discs. Frank Osborne. Now he knew. It did not matter. The clerk had taken the details.

'He'll have to be left here,' the M.O. said abruptly as though expecting Robson to protest. 'There's little enough transport for the living. The Germans will bury the dead.'

Robson looked at him blankly.

'I told you,' the M.O. said irritably. 'We'll be pulling back soon. There's an ambulance convoy coming in to evacuate us. They'll be here in a minute or two. You might get a lift. I could give you a ticket. Shock following your crash.'

Robson was about to nod his acceptance when he saw

the men approaching. A round dozen, hobbling like freaks, gross distortions of the human frame coming out of the mist.

'Walking wounded,' the M.O. said, turning to call down into the cellar.

Two men with their arms in slings, their faces as grey as the chalky mud on their tunics, supported a man with one boot and a muddy bandage on his other foot. Behind them, his right hand resting on the shoulder of the man in front, limped a man with a field dressing round his eyes. One by one they stumbled by, uniforms in their head-to-toe coating of mud splotched with black, the dried blood of themselves or their fellows.

'Jerry's morning strafe,' the M.O. said. 'Must go, no rest for the wicked. Watch out for the ambulances. They'll come in over there and circle round the yard. We start loading as soon as the first one is in position here.'

The mist was beginning to lift although it still swirled like smoke amongst the trees. A breeze stirring an over-hanging branch sprayed Robson with water condensed on the newly-opened spring growth. He saw the Sergeant who had helped him to the first-aid post, and asked him to mount a guard over the wrecked bomber. As they strolled over to the F.E. the first of the ambulance convoy rolled into the farmyard.

The Sergeant rubbed his chin. 'Well, Sir, I don't know as I can, even suppose it were worth it,' he said. Robson noticed that he was newly washed and shaved, but his eyes were red-rimmed with exhaustion. 'I've got no more than sixty men digging in on the other side of them trees. They've been digging and wiring all night. There's a third of them asleep, the rest are either getting something hot to eat or on watch. The Captain's asleep, out on his feet. Jerry is no more than a couple of miles away with nought but a handful o' men betwixt us. They'll fall back on us soon as the wounded are 'vacuated.'

He stirred a broken strut with his boot and cocked his head to listen to the shellfire which had suddenly restarted. 'Hark at that. We're promised reinforcements but if they're not here by midday he'll be a couple of miles yon side of us by night. I reckon you'd best take what you can carry and put a match to the rest.'

Robson stood in the middle of the field and stared back at the ambulances. The engines seemed to be kicking up a devil of a row. He and the Sergeant picked up a Lewis gun apiece and began walking back towards the F.A.P.

'I shouldn't light it up yet, Sir,' the Sergeant said. 'It wouldn't do to attract attention. Not till the convoy has gone. I'll do it for you.'

Robson nodded. He wondered if Madelaine was one of the drivers and, remembering the shellfire earlier on, hoped that she was not. A patch of blue sky the size of his hand splintered the mist and looking up he realized that it had thinned to no more than a veil of vapour at tree-top level. He stood for a moment, his head craned to one side, listening. The noise he had heard was getting louder. It could only be from aeroplanes, a lot of them.

'Aye, your lads have done us proud,' the Sergeant said in reply to his comment. 'Knocked the stuffing out of Jerry yesterday. Pity there weren't more of them. There was one of them, if he'd a gone any lower he'd a taken their heads off with his wheels.'

Robson followed the noise in a half-circle, wondering why they were going the wrong way. Suddenly the engine noise grew louder and as he saw them coming in from the west in line astern he recognized them. The smooth cowling over the Mercedes engine, the fat fuselage ending in a biplane tail unit. There was no doubt, they were Hannoveranas.

'They are Jerries,' he shouted to the Sergeant. He began to run before he saw the flames spitting from the front gun of the first Hannoverana. Swerving round the rim of a shell-hole he tripped and fell heavily. Behind him the Sergeant, legs astride, lifted his rifle to his shoulder. Robson swore and ran, crouched double, for the shelter of the farmhouse.

The first bombs—they looked to Robson like stick grenades—tumbled in a long line from the leading Hannoverana. Robson threw himself flat behind a wall. As they exploded a man standing at the entrance to the cellar screamed and toppled over the sandbags.

The turf by the Sergeant rippled as machine-gun bullets cut a swathe to one side of him. He was unhurt, and, continuing to swing his rifle at each Hannoverana, firing like a farmer after wood pigeons. The wreck of the F.E. burst into flames as the last of the Germans swept overhead.

Robson ran to a broken wall by the cellar entrance and had to take cover as the leader of the formation came round again. The engine roar, the rattle of gunfire and the sharp crack of the exploding grenades turned the clearing into a whirlpool of noise. But not much else, Robson thought, as he began to look at the attack with a professional eye. The grenades were too small to damage the building, and the surrounding trees prevented the front guns of the Hannoveranas from bearing on anything unless they were attacking the trench line beyond the F.A.P. There was noise but no danger, provided everyone kept their heads down as the ambulance drivers were doing. Robson could see them huddled behind their Fords.

Then, as if to prove that the Hannoveranas' actions were not to be taken too lightly, a grenade bounced off the cobbles and landed on the canvas tilt of an ambulance. When the smoke of the explosion cleared away the ambulance was ablaze. Another pair of Hannoveranas dived in lower than before. The noise was deafening.

From under the ambulance next to the one on fire a slight figure crawled out, stood up, put her hands over her ears and began a frantic dash for the shelter of the cellar.

There was no doubt in Robson's mind about who it was.

He leapt into the broken wall shouting, 'Madelaine, Madelaine, stay where you are. Go back.'

She either heard him or recognized him because she half-turned stumbling in her stride and began to run towards him. He leapt over the wall but the Hannoverana was so low that the slipstream made him stagger. It was like running through invisible treacle, muscle and sinew pounding, but his legs seemed incapable of bridging the distance between them. The last grenade twirled down.

Everything was in slow motion. The grenade struck a cobble and bounced a couple of feet in the air. She seemed to trip, falling over it as it exploded. Something plucked at his sleeve, stung his cheek. The acrid stench bit at his lungs. The smoke hid her momentarily so that he almost tripped over her body.

She had fallen face down but her head was turned so that he saw her profile, brown hair spilled across the cobbles. She was smiling. Her eyes were open so that for one moment he thought that in some miraculous way she had escaped injury. But as he bent down to put his arms round her a restraining hand gripped his shoulder.

'Don't be a fool, Sir,' the Sergeant said. 'That grenade got her in the middle. Alive or dead you'd best not touch her.'

The M.O. joined them. He held her wrist for a moment and then swept his hand over her face closing the dead eyes.

'Damn shame,' he said. 'Another thirty seconds and it would have been over. Sounds as though the bastards have gone. She a friend of yours?'

He loosened her tie and unbuttoned the neck of her shirt to pull her identity discs on their thin gold chain over her head.

Robson nodded. 'We met during an air raid on Amiens. It was the noise and the waiting, the inaction ... Just waiting for the next bomb without anything to distract her that she couldn't stand.'

'Thought as much when she broke. They're as tough as old boots, those girls. Seen them drive through shellfire without turning a hair but it gets them in the end. The strain has to show one way or another. Wouldn't care for a daughter of mine...'

He tossed the identity discs up and down in his hand. The ambulance drivers were clustered round them. Two of them were crying.

'Known her long?' the M.O. asked.

Robson gaped at him, angry at his matter-of-fact acceptance that there was a dead girl at his feet.

He thought, mentally ticking off the days on his fingers. 'Less than two weeks,' he said. Only two weeks. It had been a lifetime.

The M.O. nodded. He handed the identity discs to an orderly. It was a gesture of dismissal. 'Sorry, I had the idea she might have been someone special. We'll look after things,' he said. He turned to the drivers. 'Come along, girls, get these ambulances loaded and away before they come back. Get a stretcher over here for the body,' he shouted to the orderly.

'You can't leave her here, Sir. It's not right,' the Sergeant said. 'Leaving her body there for Jerry. I'm not saying he won't treat her with respect. But it's not right, is it, Sir?' He'd turned to Robson.

The appeal to Robson left him dumbfounded. For a moment his mind refused to recognize that the limp bundle of flesh and fabric at his feet was all that was left of the warmth and vivacity of the Madelaine he had loved. He said nothing, did not move. But the drivers muttered their agreement with the Sergeant.

The M.O. shrugged his shoulders and said to the stretcher-bearers, 'Put her in an ambulance. The last one.' He turned to Robson, 'My telephone is working again.

Would you like to call your aerodrome? Wouldn't like to say how long you'll be getting through but you're welcome to try.' Robson nodded.

A notebook fell from the breast pocket of her uniform as they lifted the body onto the stretcher. A photograph fluttered from the pages. Robson picked them up and handed the diary to one of the drivers.

The photograph showed the head and shoulders of Madelaine and a dark-jowled man with shaggy eyebrows wearing a private soldier's uniform. They were smiling at each other. Their signatures were arranged in a cross. 'Madelaine. Ben.'

The leading ambulances started up their engines. The noise shook him out of his stupor into realizing that, apart from one of the drivers, he was alone in the middle of the farmyard. Someone called to her. He held out the photograph. But she was already turning back to her ambulance. 'You can keep it if you want to,' she said.

He nodded and carefully folded the photograph in two. Half of Ben's signature remained visible. He put the folded photograph in his pocket and went to look for the telephone.

16

It was early evening before he got back to the Squadron. After leaving the F.A.P.—the telephone had been cut—a passing dispatch rider had given him a lift to a Camel squadron. He had stopped there hoping for lunch and transport and a usable telephone. But the scout squadron was pulling back in a hurry and intent on making sure that none of their stores fell into German hands. He was almost drunk before he realized that he had had nothing to eat since the previous evening. By then it was too late.

It was after four when he woke, lying on the floor of a strange hut on a deserted aerodrome with a foul taste in his mouth and his wits scrambled. The smell of burning brought him to his senses and out of the hut at the double. But it was only a bonfire of surplus equipment capped with the guttering frames of a couple of Camels. The fire, the deserted aerodrome, empty huts and hangars suited his mood of desolation. Behind the wrecked bar he found a half-full bottle of brandy. He was beginning to drink himself into a maudlin stupor when an Army Service Corps wagon picking up the last of the stores helped him on his way. Somehow, he was not quite sure how, he arrived back at the aerodrome.

At the aerodrome there was even more confusion. He had already been reported missing and no one in the Orderly Room knew how to put him back on the Squadron roll. Robson had never seen such chaos in a place. But during the morning the Squadron had been ordered to move back only to have the order rescinded by lunch time. And that morning what had been the Royal Flying

Corps, a part of the Army, became the Royal Air Force, neither fish, flesh nor fowl. Because of the proposed move, Dick Garbutt and his right-hand man, Sergeant Thomas, were on their way to the new airfield and because of their change of status Uncle Tom was at Wing H.Q.

None of this affected Robson because as soon as Tom Cobleigh got back from H.Q. he grounded him for the night. With half the Squadron's aeroplanes unserviceable Uncle Tom decided to rest the experienced men and let the new crews harass the Roye road again.

Robson knew he should have been able to sleep because, apart from his drunken stupor after lunch, he had only dozed and cat-napped since the previous morning. But it was only midnight when he awoke from a half-remembered nightmare soaked in sweat. Half an hour's tossing and turning in bed was enough. He got dressed and went down to the hangars, hastily skirting the mess where a few voices raised in song still celebrated their night's respite.

The wind tugged at his cap and the trees soughed and rattled their branches in a melancholy dirge. There was no rain, but the ragged clouds scudding across the face of the moon were too low for comfort, especially for new arrivals making their first trip over the Line.

Watt found him a mug of tea. He cradled it in his hands, warming them against the cold, before sipping it. Dark brown, it was too sweet for his taste through using sugar and condensed milk, but he was grateful for the warmth. And where the hell had Watt found the rum?

The light from the half-open hangar door spilled onto the cinder-paved area outside. Half a dozen mechanics were working on the machines, rigging a new lower mainplane on one, patching up another. It looked as though it was afflicted with some strange disease, with the black doped fabric, flecked with off-white patches, waiting for the colour to be applied. Down at the far end an engine fitter squatted on top of a Beardmore, changing the plugs.

It was only when Watt came outside for the second time, consulting his silver pocket watch, that Robson realized that all of them were quiet because they were listening for the sound of returning engines.

Suddenly Callaghan appeared out of the darkness. He looked as though he was going on parade, his uniform newly pressed, cap on square and a swagger stick under his arm. But standing downwind of him Robson could smell the whisky he had been drinking.

'Evening, Robson,' he said. 'You've got my mug of tea, damn you.'

'That he has not, Sirr,' Watt said as he emerged from the hangar carrying another mug. 'Here y'are, Sirr. Fresh brewed. I had the kettle on the meenit ye left ye're quarters.'

'It sounds as though this is a regular habit,' Robson said.

'It is, Robson. No matter what H.Q. says, this is my Squadron, and it always will be.' He sipped the tea noisily as if he had to get it down while it was too hot to drink. 'And let that remark of Watt's be a lesson to you. Never underestimate your senior N.C.O.s' intelligence system. They know where everyone is—and what everyone is saying about everyone else. For two pins I'd send them along to Haig's H.Q. with my compliments.'

He cocked his head against the wind as a gust blew a spray of crushed cinders in their faces. 'Hear anything?' he asked.

Robson shook his head. 'They'll be late. Watt says the wind has got up a bit since they took off.'

Robson stamped his feet and thought what it was like up there in a F.E. It was bloody cold down here and he wondered what he was doing standing only half-sheltered from the wind in the early hours of the morning when he could be asleep in the warmth of his bed. It was a bad night for a new pilot to be out and about. With at least one more trip to do before morning.

Callaghan chuckled and when Robson turned he saw the Major laughing at him.

'You've got the disease, Robson. I didn't think you had it in you. I was wrong. If you survive another three months —and "star turns" never do; they either kill themselves or they learn some sense and stop being "star turns"—if you do, Robson, you will never again lie in bed and hear an aeroplane pass overhead without turning to listen and wonder where he's going and whether he is all right.'

'From what I've heard, you were a "star turn" yourself at one time—Sir,' Robson said.

'Aye, I was that.' Callaghan's accent, slurred by drink, was as strong as the smell of whisky on his breath. 'You're not the first or the last, lad. But, by God, I was no different from the others, I paid for it.'

He sounded like the regular soldier he had once been. Robson could imagine him on the parade ground snapping out his orders in the stereotyped accent that the Army grafts onto its N.C.O.s.

'You thought I was being hard on you when you first joined the Squadron. I 'ad good reason, by God, I had. I had a kid brother. God only knows what the Old Lady was thinking about when she had him. He was nigh on young enough to be my own son—if I'd had one. He got things we never got. Better schooling, not that I'm complaining about what the Army did for me. Though it was mostly the war and better men getting themselves killed. But the kid was bright. Apprentice with an engineering firm. He'd a made a good engineer...' He broke off to cock his head on one side as though listening, but Robson was sure that his experienced ear had not been fooled by a chance gust. He wished Callaghan would shut up.

'Then they gave me a Military Medal. That was a laugh. Proved something to the civvies back home, I suppose. That there was nothing marvellous about a Fokker if a Corporal could shoot one down. They made me a sergeant and then I was really on the gravy train. Sent home for pilot training, commissioned in the field, oh I was the blue-eyed boy all right.'

Robson nodded. Callaghan, he knew, wasn't talking to him. He was talking to himself.

'It was too much for the kid. He couldn't get to France quick enough. He had to show big brother what he could do. Poor sod. He hadn't been in the Army six months when he went over the top on the third day of the Somme. Poor bastard. Three weeks later the M.P.s picked him up a couple of miles behind the Lines running west. They shot him. The bastards shot him to set an example to the others. A kid barely eighteen.'

Robson lowered his tea mug. Callaghan thrust his face forward. He swayed slightly, making Robson move back.

'Now are you surprised at the way I treated you. Oh, I said my piece. Didn't do the kid any good, nor me. It's a wonder they didn't shoot *me*. Probably would have if it hadn't been for Latimer-Needham. He let me rant on a long rein until I got my senses back. As you must do eventually. The Old Lady never forgave me.'

He blew his nose violently on a spotted red bandana handkerchief. Above the noise of branches slapping the soggy canvas walls Robson heard the steady note of an aero engine. He glanced at Callaghan, uneasy at listening to the man's confession. So that was the blot on the Major's copybook. Was it so terrible to keep hidden? He shuddered as he thought of Callaghan having to send raw pilots out to fight in antiquated ...

'Watt. Get those doors shut,' Callaghan roared. 'At the double. And screen off those damned lights.'

'Aye, but it's one o' oor lads, Sirr,' Watt said, looking at his watch. After the doors had been closed and the lights dimmed, little groups of mechanics materialized out of the darkness. Red and green stars burst overhead. A mechanic carrying a burning rag ran across the field and a line of half a dozen flares (petrol cans stuffed with cotton waste soaked in petrol) blazed up after him. There were more than usual tonight. For the new pilots? Was that Uncle Tom's doing, or Callaghan's, Robson wondered?

The Major let out an audible sigh of relief as the first arrival taxied up with the mechanics trotting by the wing tips. There was another in the circuit about to land.

'How many more?' Callaghan asked.

'Only three, Sirr. Mr. Roberts rang in half an hour ago. Engine failure, sounded like plug trouble. He got it at Marieux. Still got his bombs aboard.'

The flares were put out after the second F.E. landed. An opened hangar door spilled a pool of light onto a pile of 25 lb. Cooper Mk I bombs stacked ready for re-arming. The second bomber came up taxi-ing too fast. The mechanics on the wing-tips were running to stay with it. It turned on one wheel as the pilot blasted open the throttle with his rudder hard over, spraying cinders everywhere. The observer was sitting on the edge of the cockpit, a broad grin on his face, his right thumb raised to the other crew. Robson turned to look at Callaghan, but the Major had gone. The engine of the F.E. howled again as the pilot raced it to burn any oil off the plugs—probably as a gesture of pure *joie de vivre*, Robson thought in disgust.

The engine stopped and the silence surged back, punctuated by the high-pitched chatter of the returned crews. Robson saw Tom Cobleigh and Dick Garbutt striding across to interrogate them. He stepped back into the darkness, unwilling to see them or be seen.

Eventually he went back to the Orderly Room and through it into the C.O.s office to study the big wall map with the known positions of German squadrons marked on it. But the events of the past days had left the marked airfields far behind the Line. That Hannoverana squadron, he reasoned, a *Schlachstaffell* charged with the attack of troops, could not be stationed too far behind the fighting or they might be caught by our fighters before they reached their target. He got a sleepy corporal to leaf through the latest intelligence reports. But the only moves noted were those of the *Jagdstaffeln*, the single seater fighters. So he went back to bed.

One of the new pilots shook him awake soon after dawn and asked apologetically if he was all right. He had been shouting and screaming. Robson glared up at the boy's face. He could see the marks of the goggles round his eyes in the wan morning light. Roughly telling him to mind his own damn business Robson kicked the rumpled bedclothes into shape, rolled over and went back to sleep.

It rained the following day. Robson had lunch with Tim Keegan and Armitage, the armament officer. Halfway through Uncle Tom joined them fresh from a visit to H.Q. At last, he said, there were signs that Jerry was being held. A new general, fresh troops, and the casualties of the past ten days that had thinned the ranks of the picked German storm troops, were now taking effect. The fighting was still fierce round Villers-Bretonneux where the Germans could see, beyond the rim of the plateau, Amiens on the horizon. But H.Q. thought the worst was over.

Tony Jordan joined them, mud-bespattered after a morning trying to salvage a F.E. that had forced-landed just behind the Line. Robson, his mind still occupied with what Uncle Tom had said, was wondering what had happened to the little detachment he had seen trying to hold the wood by the First Aid Post, and he was not really listening to Jordan's excited description of a fight he had seen until the Equipment Officer mentioned Hannoveranas.

'I can't understand how they manage to get up to the

Line without being seen,' Robson said, keeping his voice as flat as though making a casual comment. 'One of the Harry Tate pilots was saying the other day that the Front Line areas are stiff with Camels and S.E.s beating up Jerry. The aerodrome those Hannoveranas were using must be thirty miles or more behind the Line.' Intercepting an enquiring look from Uncle Tom he added, 'You remember, we made a special trip out there last week.'

'Not now, they aren't, laddie,' Jordan replied. 'They have moved up to one of our old fields. Near Brie, I'm told. Probably smoking our fags and flying on our petrol now.'

He was outside in the rain staring up at the cloudbase when Uncle Tom found him after lunch.

'Don't be such a damned fool,' Uncle Tom said to him. 'I know what you are thinking. I heard about your girl. That M.O. rang through to ask us if you were all right. I'm sorry. She must have been a fine woman. From what I've heard from you in the mess she'd have got you converted into a dyed-in-the-wool socialist in another couple of weeks.'

'What's wrong with that?' Robson snapped. 'Maybe she was right. Your lot have made a damn fine mess of things.'

'Easy, easy, simmer down. You can wave the red flag all you want. Dammit, I might join you. But ... this is the wrong sort of war for personal feuds. There is no room for that sort of thing. If there ever was, which I doubt, then that time has gone.'

Robson stared up at the cloudbase again. 'I could take "Mimi",' he said. 'We could knock hell out of them with the "pom-pom" and some bombs and be back in cloud before they knew what had hit them.'

'That relic. I'm getting it struck off charge as soon as I can. It takes Watt and his men more time keeping that thing airworthy than three of the others. Anyway, I absolutely forbid it. If just one of those Hannoveranas got off the ground you'd be resting in a home-made grave before you could yell *Kamerad*.'

Robson shrugged his shoulders. 'It was just an idea. I still think it would work but you are the boss.'

Cobleigh stared at him through narrowed eyes. 'Will you be all right tonight? Same stunt. Transport along the Amiens road.'

Robson nodded. 'I should know the way by now. I'll take one of the new observers. Break him in.' And it'll give me an excuse if we get lost, he added to himself as Cobleigh moved away.

Robson took a much-worn map out of his fur boots and spread it out on the bottom wing of one of the replacement F.E.s—'Mimi' had been withdrawn from service. 'First trip?' he asked.

'No, Sir, er, that is, Split.' (Robson had already told him twice not to call him 'Sir'.) 'I was on last night. It was very confusing. All the different lights and fires and things.'

'You got lost. Don't let it worry you. Everyone does. It's a while before you begin to see things properly.'

His name, Robson had learned as they walked out to the F.E., was Tim Smythe-Browne. He was nineteen and he was terribly bucked at getting onto a squadron at last because he had been training so long he was afraid people might start thinking things about him but it was on account of a crash he had had on an Avro while training as a pilot. After the crash he could not land properly. It must have affected his eyes he explained so he had re-trained as an observer and he could not wait to get in the qualifying flights over the Line so that he could put up his badge, the big 'O' with the half wing. The words poured out like water from a newly-broken dam.

Robson ran his finger along the map. 'All right, Tim, I want to try something different tonight. We'll let the others bottle up Jerry at the north end of the road. We'll go on down and hit the south end. See how long and straight the road is. We fly south-east until we hit it and then we turn and head for home. Can't go wrong. We drop our bombs in pairs unless I say otherwise. Then we'll go down so that you can use the Lewis. Right?'

His fingers traced the Roye–Amiens road while his mind considered what he knew about the one between Amiens and St. Quentin. He was sure that his observer would not know the difference. And somewhere west of St. Quentin was an aerodrome full of sleeping Hannoverana pilots.

'Our orders are not completely rigid. If a target of opportunity presents itself then we use our discretion about whether or not it should be attacked. Airfields, for instance. Because Jerry has moved up so quickly his petrol and ammo dumps will not be properly protected so now is a good time to have a shot at him.' He was amazed at his ability to invent reasons and to rationalize his inventions. 'Difficult to find at night, as you know, so if we do find one make sure you hit it hard. Aim for the hangars. Get a fire going. And then try to pick off the aeroplanes as they drag them out.'

Smythe-Browne looked Robson in the eye and smiled confidently. He would not miss, he said, and he hoped they'd stumble over one. Be a feather in their cap.

Robson hoped so too.

They found the road without any difficulty. Even on a night like this, flying at 500 feet with the rain clouds blotting out the horizon, it would have been difficult to miss the ruler-straight old highway bisecting the Line. He raised his thumb to his observer and confidently swung the F.E. onto an easterly course. After dodging round rain clouds for an hour he was sure Smythe-Browne was too bemused to argue, and because he had deliberately struck the road to the west of Brie the Hannoverana airfield had to be ahead of them. If they could find it. He throttled the engine down to tick-over speed and shouted to Smythe-Browne, 'Keep your eyes open for an airfield. Hannoveranas. You take the right-hand side, I'll take the left.'

The observer grinned at him, cocked his Lewis and craned over the side.

They almost missed it. A flash of light on the periphery of his vision, someone opening a door perhaps, attracted Robson's attention. He started to turn, half-convinced that the dark shapes that bulked against the pattern of chalk grey shell holes, were not hangars but wishful thinking by his imagination. Then he glimpsed the sharp outline of the canvas sheds and knew that they had found an airfield. Was it the right one? His grudge was with a certain Hannoverana *staffel*.

He S-turned back towards the east intending to attack from the direction from which they would least expect him. With the engine throttled back he held the bomber level just below the cloudbase at seventy m.p.h.

'It might be a dummy,' he lied to Smythe-Browne. 'See if you can hit a hangar with a couple of bombs. Mebbe start a fire. I want to see them dragging out the aeroplanes.'

In a gentle dive, throttle right back, he headed for the hangars. They were built on a curve. He went in low, aiming for the centre, opening the throttle wide as he crossed the aerodrome boundary. He saw the flash of the exploding bomb reflected off his wings but there was no gush of flame to follow it. A single machine-gun opened up as they climbed away but the gunner must have been aiming at the sound. The tracer was well behind them.

He swung round and went in again. There were four guns firing now and a cone of tracer followed them leisurely across the field. A fifth one opened up dead ahead, a no-deflection shot. Boot on left rudder, the slip-stream slapped his right cheek as they skidded round in a flat turn. Then he flicked the right rudder, then straightened for the bomb run. He could hear the flick-flick of bullets ripping into the fabric. Something spanged off the engine and a tongue of flame licked out from the smashed exhaust manifold.

Again the splash of flame in the darkness from the exploding bombs. And nothing else. Damn Smythe-Browne, throwing away bombs. He should have told him to drop two. Twice the chance of a hit. Then, as Robson turned just under the cloudbase to go back in again a tongue of oily, black smoke shot with red and green flame billowed out of the last hangar but one. He throttled back the engine to cruising speed, pulled out of the turn and flew east.

Smythe-Browne turned a disappointed face towards him. 'They'll think we've gone home,' he shouted to his puzzled observer. 'We'll give them a few minutes. Long enough to salvage the aeroplanes.'

And if they are Hannoveranas he said to himself, look out for fireworks. We're going to make a bonfire. They're going to burn, burn so high they'll see the flames in Paris.

He climbed as he circled, never losing sight of the red glow to the west of them. At 900 feet the base of the cloud was trailing tendrils of rain that stung the exposed flesh and blurred his vision through his goggles. Lining up the nose with the fire he closed the throttle and started into a shallow dive. The engine backfired in a series of shattering explosions that shook the structure of the F.E. like a jelly. Yard-long streamers of yellow flame flared out of the smashed exhaust manifold. So much for his silent approach. And that tongue of yellow flame spitting from the engine would give the gunners something to aim at, if they were at their gunposts. With both hands on the stick he pushed the protesting F.E. into a steeper dive.

They were Hannoveranas all right. He recognized that distinctive biplane tail. There was one outside the middle hangar and a swarm of men had another halfway outside the end shed. A discordant howl from the F.E.'s Beardmore brought his head back into the cockpit. Water temperature? Oil pressure? But there was no vibration. The wings, the structure, all seemed to be sound. Then he saw Smythe-Browne leaning over his Lewis into the slipstream, a hunting horn at his lips.

He turned to grin at Robson shouting, 'View halloo-oo-oo. Tally ho.'

'Use your Lewis you silly bastard,' Robson yelled. 'I'll drop the bombs. Get that one outside the shed.'

Two fiery stars burst in front of them. He heard the crack as they dived through a cloud of stinking cordite. 'Archie'. Must be motorized 3.5 cm. stuff. Damn that exhaust, he cursed, there was probably a searchlight somewhere.

He pushed the nose further down until they seemed to be plunging headlong into the ground. The fire was somewhere over his head. Every wire on the F.E. screamed and thrummed. A quick glance at the A.S.I. showed the needle creeping over the 105 m.p.h. mark.

Ease back on the throttle. Sod the engine and those damned flames. Ease the load on the stick.

The fire slid back into its rightful place. Tree-tops, black bark gilded with rose, leaped up and swept behind them. A line of tracer wavered across the field like a garden hose, in front of them. Now they were through it. His hand reached outside the cockpit for the bomb toggles. Smythe-Browne was leaning forward against the slipstream, clinging onto the spade-grips as he fired.

Left rudder. Nudge the nose round to follow the curving line of sheds. Now.

He plucked at the toggles, dropping the last pair of

bombs as he raced over the hangars. They would be lucky to get a second chance. Smythe-Browne was firing. The flash from the muzzle was blinding.

Look over the other side. Watch out for trees. Ease back on the stick.

Flick-flick. Something was hitting them. Spang. Was it the engine or a spar fitting, he wondered. The controls were as heavy as lead. It was like lifting an omnibus into the sky.

Rain slapped him in the face and he hastily reversed his pressure on the stick to get out of the cloud, before swinging round to look at the damage. Another hangar, the end one, was on fire. Something else, a dump perhaps, was burning beyond the sheds. Turning as he had, must have thrown the bombs outwards. But in front of the hangar the first Hannoverana was burning.

But the men on the ground had another one, no, another two, clear of the flames. A third poked its nose out of the burning hangar at the end. Robson twirled his finger round his head. They were going back. Smythe-Browne nodded and hastily changed the drum on the Lewis.

The stench of cordite filled the cockpit as they turned. The gunners had ranged on the cloudbase. The needle on the water temperature gauge shuddered and took a noticeable step upwards. Common sense told him that it was stupid to go in again. There would be no surprise this time. But the four Hannoveranas outside the hangars swamped all reason. He could see nothing but the black crosses of the attacking planes with their helmeted observers throwing grenades over the side as they had raced over the ambulances...

A broken wire beat a tattoo on the fabric as they plummeted in again. Four, five lines of tracer arced up towards them. 'Archie' got two bursts in behind them. Smythe-Browne was firing again. The nearest Hannoverana sagged in the middle. Two running men jack-knifed like hit rabbits.

A searchlight in the far corner of the field struck up, swung, caught them, blinding them. There was tracer all over the place. Flame-centred bursts of cordite bracketed them. The F.E. shuddered and kicked like a bucking horse. Bits of fabric, splintered wood, the windscreen and a shower of cartridge cases deluged him. Then they were through and into the darkness again.

But the F.E. was labouring, sloppy on the controls and, as a blast of cold air brought him to his senses, Robson knew they were in serious trouble. Gingerly he eased the bomber round onto a westerly course clear of the burning airfield. Quivering on the brink of a stall he started a slow climb up to the shelter of the cloudbase.

As his dazzled eyes recovered their vision he realized that there was something odd about the nacelle. It wobbled and quivered like a jelly and he seemed to be sitting without protection in the middle of a howling gale. Stupidly he stared at the wrecked instrument panel. The gaping hole where the airspeed indicator had been could not create either the gale or the peculiar noise. Only the left-hand rim of his windscreen remained but the slipstream came from somewhere underneath. And where the hell had Smythe-Browne got to?

He leaned forward into the slipstream to see if his observer was wounded. The gale plucked at his cheeks almost exploding the eyeballs out of his head. His goggles had gone and part of his helmet. A loose strap flapped and slapped at the side of his face.

He leaned further forward wiping away the tears wrung out by the wind. Sitting high in the nacelle he looked down on the thigh-high pulpit that housed the observer. It was not there. Shielding his eyes with his left hand Robson strained to look over the rim of the cockpit. There was nothing there but the pipe-mounting for the

Lewis sticking up out of nothing. No gun. No observer.

There was a hand clinging to the bottom of the pipe, and the dark bulk of a body. Swinging. Another hand, streaked with blood, struck the top of the cowling in front of Robson clawing at the splintered plywood. He saw the white face of his observer, the terrified eyes, as he leaned over and reached out with his left hand to grasp Smythe-Browne's wrist. The observer screamed but he held on.

Now Robson could see that the sides and most of the floor of the front cockpit had disappeared. Smythe-Browne had one knee on the edge of the nacelle floor, the rest of him hung over 500 feet of darkness.

Robson tried to use both hands to pull the observer to safety but each time he let go of the stick the nose went up and the wail of the airstream through holes and wires died away as they verged on a stall. Then, bracing his knees against the stick and leaving the F.E. to circle on its own, he managed after a while to get his right hand under the observer's shoulder. Now he was able to slide his hand down to grasp Smythe-Browne's belt. Then he was able to haul the dead weight of the observer's body up onto the coaming in front of him. With a final jerk Robson got Smythe-Browne's head and shoulders hanging inside the right-hand side of his cockpit. That was all Robson could do if he was to continue flying the aeroplane. Smythe-Browne had obviously passed out.

He pushed the throttle up to the stop. God alone knew how much water they had left. He could smell the peculiar stench of hot oil and metal that came from an overheating engine and guessed that what there was would soon leak away. So there was no point in nursing the Beardmore. Sooner or later when the remaining water boiled away the exhaust valves would burn or the pistons seize and the engine would stop. And they would land wherever they happened to be. Or try to.

Smythe-Browne's body slid sideways as the F.E. lurched. Robson grabbed it with his right hand. They were flying in a big circle and because of the west wind drifting back into German territory. Gingerly he held on right rudder. The body moved again. If he let go it would slip sideways off the rounded coaming, and then he would never be able to hold it.

Now they were flying straight, heading west he hoped, as he tried to concentrate his fuddled mind on the problem of finding the aerodrome, any aerodrome.

Forget about time, he told himself, forget about the ache in your leg, the pain from the strained muscles of your right arm, the numbness in your hand. Hold on. Each minute takes you nearer some familiar light. Just concentrate on the next minute. And don't let go. I order you, finger and arm muscles, do not let go.

The F.E. bucked and shuddered in some turbulence. Each time Smythe-Browne's body twitched and slithered in Robson's grasp as though it were trying to escape.

They seemed to fly on and on into a never-never land of lights and stars and fires and drifting sheets of rain while the engine rattled and banged and stank but kept on running. Robson prayed it would stop. If only it would stop he could land and free himself from this terrible weight on his arm, recover the sense of feeling in his left leg. He prayed that he could get them both down safely without any further injury to Smythe-Browne. Never again, he swore, would he disobey orders again, if only this once, dear God, they were given a safe landing.

Suddenly he started to giggle. It was too funny for words. He had probably just killed a man, his observer, through trying to kill a lot of men who had not killed his girl. The giggle developed into hysterical laughter. He had done all that while the men he wanted to kill were lying asleep in their beds a mile or more away from the hangars. He had killed a lot of men, people like Flight

Sergeant Watt, Geordie, the engine fitter from Middles-
brough, and Chalky White, his rigger. He should have
known better. On a day flying squadron the aircrews
would be sound asleep at this time of the night. So his
revenge for Madelaine's death had been taken on a bunch
of unarmed mechanics.

Was it revenge? He felt sick at the memory of her terror and an aching loneliness at the thought of losing her.
His anger at the Hannoveranas had been instinctive,
momentary. But was it only because of Madelaine that he
had planned and schemed for the last twenty-four hours?

Was it revenge? Or was he fostering a luckily won
reputation, something for the boys to laugh about at
breakfast? 'Have you heard about Split-Arse's latest stunt?
Shot up a Hun aerodrome stacked with those damned Hannoveranas. And do you know what the cheeky sod did...'

Something for the mechanics to gossip about? 'He's a
card is Mister Robson. They call him Split-Arse in the
Officer's mess...'

Was it revenge? Or this confidence in his own immor-
tality that had grown inside him?

Whatever it was he was going to have to pay for it,
and the first instalment was getting Smythe-Browne back.
He wiped the tears of hysterical laughter out of his eyes
with the back of his wrist and dismissed the thought that
he had momentarily entertained: that he could honourably land the crippled bomber and surrender. Would that
save Smythe-Browne's life? Not unless he could find an
aerodrome with ambulances and doctors.

He squinted down at the shifting pattern of light and
dark beneath him—starlight on a river, a burning dump
—and eased the nose a little north of west.

They flew on and on into a sea of unending night
with the F.E. being pushed along just above stalling speed
by an engine lubricated with molten bearing metal. Robson knew there would be a headwind. There always was.

But he had no idea of how strong it was, or how fast the bomber was flying, only that it was too slow from the feel of the soggy controls. Ground features—a road junction, a wrecked bridge over a river, a fire—crawled by and were replaced by more fires. He had cramp in his left leg, a numb right hand and agonizingly strained arm muscles. And he wanted to go to sleep.

Soon he was reduced to reciting Latin tags, learned at the rope-end running round the playing fields before early school, scraps of verse beaten into him by prefects for burning the toast.

One of the lights ahead and to the left of him flickered in a definite rhythm. Mechanically he headed for it, a sign of life in the midst of desolation. Flash, blink, blink, blink. Flash, blink, blink, blink. The whirling red light brought him to his senses. It was an aerial lighthouse, his aerial lighthouse.

Ten miles, steer 295 degrees for the aerodrome. The wind would be south-west. It was always in the west. Allow a bit for drift.

There was no feeling in his legs. His feet were blocks of ice as he watched the compass card swing wildly.

Hold it. Freeze. Let the card steady. Ten miles. Twenty miles. Twenty minutes.

> 'Oh God, our help in ages past,
> Our hope for years to come.'

Oh God, damn and blast, they were flying east. Kick the rudder. Gently.

The card, sensitive to a northerly turning error, spun crazily.

Hold it. Again. And again. And again.

> 'Drake he's in his hammock an' a thousand miles away,
> Captain, art tha' sleeping there below...'

The hands of the watch clipped to his shattered instrument panel waved and shimmered as he stared at them again through watering eyes. It must be time. Where was that damned aerodrome? He remembered the need to identify himself by firing the colours of the day. Slowly, like a drunken man, he searched for the Very pistol. The colours of the day were written on the back of his hand. In ink. One lick of the tongue and they were gone. Red and white. How the devil was he going to load and fire the pistol while his right arm was needed to hold Smythe-Browne?

The F.E. went into a slow turn as he wedged the stick between his knees. Carefully he laid the pistol on his lap before breaking it open with his left hand. Now for the flare cartridge.

The red firework blossomed above him.

Careful. Christ, you nearly dropped the pistol. Get the nose down. Bloody fool, you nearly stalled it then. Up a bit. Where's that damned pistol? Extract the spent cartridge. Now a white one.

The flare rolled off his lap.

Leave it. There should be another. Up above your head. It weighs a ton. Point it forwards. Pull the trigger. Get the bloody nose down. Quick.

A line of smoky yellow flares bloomed in front of him at an odd sort of angle. It took some time for him to realize what was happening and to react by levelling the wings. Oh, God, now he had to land. Suppose the wheels were shot off, or one of the tyres punctured? And that damned great hunk of metal was poised behind him waiting to crush him.

He let go the stick to close the throttle but the moment he touched it the engine let out an anguished scream and seized solid. Now he could hear only the wail of the wind through torn fabric and the slap-slap of broken wires on the wings and struts. The flare path slid over to the left. The F.E. wallowed drunkenly as he corrected too slowly. The controls were sloppy and his mind was working too slowly, as the bomber slid tiredly out of the sky.

They hit, bounced, the wings tilting against the line of lights as the starboard undercarriage legs collapsed. The wing-tips touched the ground and as the F.E. spun round the body of Smythe-Browne was jerked out of his grasp and the world exploded in a medley of splintering wood and tearing fabric.

He was going to have a hell of a time explaining this to Uncle Tom.

The cold touch of rain brought him round, staring stupidly into darkness. He was still sitting in the remains of the nacelle. The right wing was a jumble of formless canvas. Behind him the engine ticked and spat ominously as the overheated metal cooled in the drizzle. He could not hear or see anything. If it had not been for the broken aeroplane and the stench of burned oil around him he might have thought himself dead. He remembered Smythe-Browne and wished that he was.

His head began to clear and he saw the flares guttering out in yellow smoke away to the left and figures running towards him. He could hear the noise of a reluctant Crossley as it was swung into life. The knuckles of his left hand still showed tensed and white through a torn glove. With an effort he released his grip on the stick, undid his belt and stepped over the side.

Weaving on unsteady legs he began to run, retracing his path along the torn turf. Suppose that damned tender ran over Smythe-Browne's body. Hurry. Oh, God, it had to be somewhere around here.

'Stop. Stop,' he yelled. A couple of mechanics caught him by the shoulders. He gasped out incoherent orders.

'Look for a body. Smythe-Browne. Over there. Oh, God, stop that bloody tender. Don't stand there gawping, you bloody fools. Look for a body ...'

Flight Sergeant Watt emerged from beyond the flares to catch him as he tripped.

'Easy does it, Sirr. Ye're in safe keeping now. What's this about Mister Broon?'

As Robson started to stammer a reply somebody shouted over by the flarepath. Watt turned to the mechanics. 'That must be him. Get that tender away over there. Quick. I'll look after Mister Robson. Get a move on m'lad, jump to it.'

Raw spirit gagged in the back of his throat. He sat up, coughing and spluttering, the brandy running out of the corners of his mouth. He put his hand up to shield his eyes from the light and the pain from his shoulder muscles almost made him faint again. He realized he was in the C.O.'s office.

'You do realize that you are wasting the finest produce of France,' Callaghan said, taking the cup away from his mouth. He and Tom Cobleigh were leaning over him. A medical orderly hovered in the background.

'Smythe-Browne, did you find him? I held on as long as I could but when she whipped ... the wheel went ... after the engine seized ... I just couldn't hold on any more.'

He caught a glimpse of his right hand, the bloody pulp where his finger nails had been. He remembered Smythe-Browne's eyes staring up out of that bloody face and felt his stomach heave. Tom Cobleigh shoved a waste-paper basket in front of him as he vomited.

'Go on, you'll feel better afterwards. We found your observer.'

Robson wiped his mouth with a grubby handkerchief and sat up.

'How is he?'

'Dead,' said Callaghan.

Robson put his head in his hands. 'It was my fault. I killed him. I should never have gone back for that last attack. It was seeing those Hannoveranas outside the sheds that did it. I lost my head...'

Slowly, stumbling over the words, he described the attack on the aerodrome while the other two helped him out of his flying suit. A piece of torn metal dropped out of his lap as he stood up to step out of the sidcot suit. Callaghan picked it up, turning it over and over in his hand while he listened.

He held it out to Robson. 'Looks like a nosecap. "Archie". You were unlucky to find heavy stuff like that round an airfield.' Robson shook his head. 'Stop feeling so damned sorry for yourself,' Callaghan said harshly. 'You were lucky. He wasn't. If anybody killed him it's this damned war.'

The orderly returned with a steaming coffee pot. Callaghan told him to dress Robson's fingers. Not before time for the warmth of the room and the heat of the coffee had brought the feeling back into them. Robson felt better after the dressings were on and the coffee inside him. He helped himself to another cup and stood up. 'I'm all right,' he said, hardly able to believe it. His legs quivered like jelly, his right arm seemed to have stretched a foot, and the cramped muscles of his left shoulder as though there was a dagger thrust into them. But he was all right. He reached for his mug of coffee, misjudged the distance, and lightly brushed his hand against the handle. The sudden wave of pain made him sit down hastily. He tried to write his report but his bandaged fingers could not hold the pen. The orderly wrote it to his mumbled dictation while Callaghan and Cobleigh argued quietly in the far corner.

The air was foul with the stench of the spilled brandy, vomit and stale tobacco smoke. The orderly refilled his mug and left with the bloody traces of his trade. Robson sat, wondering where everyone was, why it was so quiet and what Callaghan and Tom Cobleigh were arguing about.

The telephone rang, breaking up the argument in the corner as Tom Cobleigh answered it. When he'd finished he came across to Robson. 'Are you all right now?' he asked. 'I've been trying to get one of the other squadrons off to stoke your fire. It was too good a chance to miss. You know how difficult it is to find their aerodromes at night. But there's no chance. It will be first light in a couple of hours.'

The Squadron, he explained, had at last begun to move to their new aerodrome. The aeroplanes had already gone. There were only a few mechanics left, and it was time they were moving. The Germans were no more than a few miles away. Tomorrow, if they advanced again, the aerodrome would be under shell-fire.

Callaghan joined them, perched himself on the edge of the desk and lit another cigarette from the stub of the last one. He turned to Tom Cobleigh, coughing as he inhaled a lungful of smoke.

'Robson and I will do it,' he said to Tom. 'Do him good. Get his nerve back.' He turned to Robson. 'How are your fingers? You could still fly with them.' It was a command, not a request. Robson nodded dumbly. He stared at the pair of them, wondering what was going on. Just why was the C.O. waiting with a few mechanics for him to return to a deserted aerodrome?

'We've no planes,' said Cobleigh. 'Not one left here.'

'We can take "Mimi",' Callaghan decided. 'It's better than leaving her behind to burn.'

'It's been written off. That relic is unsafe and you know it,' Cobleigh said. 'It's too slow to catch a cold. And you're off the Squadron strength. You are on leave officially. H.Q. would have my guts for garters if anything happened to you now. You are supposed to be in England.'

Callaghan laughed. He stubbed out his cigarette and immediately lit another. Cobleigh turned to Robson. 'He's worse than you are. H.Q. want us to do a recce up north along the roads going up to Arras. They got a prisoner tonight, more likely a deserter, who claimed that Jerry is switching his attack to the Lys.'

'And if that is true, Robson,' Callaghan interrupted. 'We've won this bloody war despite the bloody generals and the bloody frocks at home.' He saw the scepticism in Robson's face.

'It's as plain as the nose on your face,' he said. 'I know Jerry has run riot this last fortnight. So he ought, with troops fresh from the Russian front. But we have fought him to a standstill. They are gone, dead, and he can never replace them.

'But we have the Americans. It's taken them a hell of a long time to do anything but talk but now they are here and there's more coming. They'll need training and we are going to have to give them equipment meant for fighting instead of bullshine on the parade ground. So far their factories have built nothing but wind, but they will. And this feller, Foch, is not the sort of general who will leave half a million trained soldiers eating corn.'

'So we can go home, pack up our troubles and leave them to it?' Robson said.

'Don't be such a damned fool. I didn't say there'd be no more fighting. I said we are going to win the war. It'll be a tough summer and a long winter holding on. Nobody wants a second Passchendaele. But come the dry weather next spring, we'll go through Jerry like a dose of salts.'

Robson looked through the window, licking his dry lips. Was it his imagination or was the sky lightening in the east?

'They could get one of the D.H.4 squadrons to do the reconnaissance in the morning,' he said softly. 'They'd be safe as houses at 20,000 feet.'

Tom started to say something but Callaghan interrupted again. 'Jerry is no fool. If he is going to move, it will be at night. And anyway you ought to know by now what H.Q. is like. They order a recce and they expect the C.O. to have the recce carried out. Why else should they pay you a quid a day?'

Suddenly Robson realized why the man was being so insistent. He was protecting Cobleigh. If Robson volunteered Cobleigh would not have to order him to do the job. He turned to Cobleigh. 'Do I have a choice?'

Cobleigh stared back at him coldly. 'No. My objection was to the Major going. We have an order and an aeroplane which has not yet been certified as non-airworthy. I'll detail a mechanic to act as gunner.'

Robson nodded indifferently. It was hard luck on the mechanic, but that responsibility belonged to Cobleigh.

Callaghan put a nicotine-stained hand over Cobleigh's wrist as he reached for the telephone.

'Don't be such a pompous ass, Tom,' he growled. 'You have to give Robson a chance. We've flown together in "Mimi". If you send some poor bloody ack emma instead of me you are only doing that to protect your own backside.'

As Robson stood up, his sidcot suit over his arm, he saw Cobleigh, a spot of colour on each cheekbone, nod his head.

'I'll go down to the hangar and get the old cow warmed up,' Robson said.

When Callaghan arrived Robson and Watt were running the engine while a couple of riggers finished a perfunctory check. A bundle of flares had been wired into the racks that normally held the 'pom-pom' shells. Callaghan motioned to him to switch off and join him.

'There's no ammo for the "pom-pom",' Robson said to him. 'But we salvaged a couple of drums from the wreck for the Lewis.'

Callaghan spread the map out on the bottom wing. In the light of a naphtha lamp the Major's face was drawn and haggard and as he brushed his hand across his moustache Robson smelled the brandy on it.

He looked at Robson. 'You've changed. What do they call you, Split-Arse Robson? Well, Split-Arse would not have made his C.O. order him to do a job. What's happened? No fun, no adventure in it any more?'

Robson remembered Madelaine running terror-stricken across the farmyard. Had she seen him? Did he call out first? And Smythe-Browne's eyes as he hung onto the shattered nacelle.

'He asked me to do a job. I'm doing it and the sooner we get on with it the better.'

To his surprise Callaghan nodded his approval. 'Good. Don't worry, the ack emmas will soon find another mug to gossip about. In a month they'll have forgotten that stupid nickname. Now,' his nicotine-stained finger stubbed the map, 'we've got an hour and a half to first light, say an hour to be on the safe side. This is what we will do...'

He sketched in a course that took them across the line at the nearest point and swung north in a great arc of a circle that brought them back to safety up beyond Arras. The light and the nature of what they saw under the flares would determine how far north they flew.

Now that it was decided, Robson wanted to go immediately. His legs still quivered at the knees, his arm muscles ached and he felt incredibly old, but there were no more decisions that were his to consider and all he wanted was to implement the one made and to get into the air before his tired mind started questioning again. But Callaghan seemed to be in no hurry.

A group of riggers were dismantling the last of the big canvas hangars. Watt appeared behind them holding a naphtha lamp. He raised a thumb. Callaghan gave an answering wave.

'Hang on, shan't be a jiffy,' he said as he strode off to join the Flight Sergeant behind the sagging canvas walls of the hangar.

Tom Cobleigh appeared out of the darkness, peering at his watch. 'What are you waiting for? The cloud is lifting and you have to be back on this side of the Line before Jerry's dawn patrol can see you. Where's Callaghan?'

Robson shrugged his shoulders impatiently. 'I don't know what he is up to. Watt gave him a wave and he was off round the back of that hangar like a dog with two tails. A couple of seconds before that he was telling me that war, WAR, big capital letters, was a job, not an adventurous lark.'

His fingers drummed impatiently on the fabric sagging between the wing rims. He was looking east. The outline of the trees seemed to be more distinct.

'It's his last fling,' Cobleigh said. 'He'll fight the rest of the war from behind a desk.'

Both of them started as a flare or an explosion lit the eastern horizon. Robson licked his lips and furtively glanced at his watch.

'What the hell is he doing? We've less than an hour and a half to first light and he has to waste time...'

'He knows what he is doing. I wanted a word with you about this reconnaissance. Don't forget he is down on the sheet as an anonymous gunner. You are in command of the aeroplane. Is that understood?'

Robson lifted an eyebrow and nodded. He wondered if Cobleigh had said as much to Callaghan.

'Second, there's a big difference between a recce and a bombing job. On a raid, once you have dropped your bombs on the target the job is done. Whether or not you get back only affects the cost of the stunt.'

'Well, three cheers and hip hooray, thank you, Captain Cobleigh for those encouraging words.'

For the first time since he had told Robson that the recce had to be done, Cobleigh smiled.

'Don't mention it. It's time you young fellers skipped the details and concerned yourselves more with the broad outlines of strategy. You must learn to look at things from the Staff's point of view.'

Robson opened his mouth.

'Stop interrupting. A recce trip or a photographing job is different. You don't achieve anything unless you get back with the information...'

'Well, if that is what you mean by a Staff point of view I agree wholeheartedly...'

The F.E. rocked as someone climbed into the nacelle from the far side. Cobleigh lightly gripped Robson's arm. 'Harken unto your elder and better,' he said. 'However, this is one case where half a loaf is better than none. Don't leave it too late getting back. It will be your decision...'

Callaghan hailed them from above, leaning over from the gunner's cockpit.

'Hey, have you two forgotten there's a war on or have you made a separate peace?'

Robson hastily scrambled into his cockpit. A mechanic ducked under the wing to swing the propeller. The warm engine started at the first twirl of the starting magneto. Robson curbed his impatience to let it tick over for a moment. He turned to Callaghan.

'What's the idea, getting in on the wrong side. Are you asking for trouble?'

The Major grinned but his explanation was cut short as Robson waved the chocks away and trundled towards the far corner of the aerodrome.

Before turning into wind he ran up the engine, flicking the magneto switches on and off, frowning at the expected drop in engine revolutions. Tom Cobleigh was right. It was time the old crate was burned. A movement in the gunner's cockpit caught his eye. Callaghan was fitting a clip of shells to the 'pom-pom'. He grinned sheepishly as he saw Robson staring at him.

'Watt found them on the dump,' he explained. 'It

seemed silly to go off without them. I heard the other day that Jerry is starting to use tanks.'

Robson shuddered, momentarily imagining them attacking a line of tanks with the 'pom-pom' in broad daylight.

'I don't care if the Line is stuffed with tanks from here to Timbuctoo,' he said. 'We are going out to do a recce. So we will go over as planned at 1,500 feet. You will drop your flares and you will write your little notes and as soon as we know something positive we will go home. If you don't like it get out. I can go without you. Is that understood?'

Callaghan nodded, smiled, and went on cocking the cannon. Robson opened the throttle and blasted the tail round into the wind. He could see the outline of the trees silhouetted against the horizon and the solitary red lamp lashed to the tallest poplar. With an effort he stopped himself from looking over his shoulder at the eastern sky. The sun would rise soon enough without his looking for it.

He opened the throttle slowly, alert for the first sign of trouble. As the aeroplane came to life he fed on coarse rudder to keep it straight. He felt the tail lift in response to his pressure on the stick and suddenly he felt his old confidence returning to him. It was ridiculous. His Commanding Officer thought the aeroplane fit only for the scrap-heap; it was so late that dawn was likely to find them at the mercy of Jerry's fighters; there was no rear-firing gun; and his gunner was a drunk loathing the thought of going back to a job he detested. What had he, Robson, got to be so cheerful about?

The wheels struck a bump in mid-field and they were airborne. Robson waved an invisible hand to the unseen men by the half-dismantled hangar and flashed a quick grin at Callaghan.

As they climbed over the trees he grinned again and swore quietly to himself. That bastard, that old fox, Cobleigh, he needed no help from Callaghan to be a good Commanding Officer. That guff about half a loaf being better than none and about the decision to go home being his alone had been a lifeline. Crafty Cobleigh. And a guarantee that the job wouldn't be shirked.

At 500 feet he ruddered the F.E. into a gentle climbing turn, and the bomber's nose swung slowly towards the eastern horizon.

It was then that he remembered the laughter of the scout pilots they'd met in Amiens when McDonald had suggested taking a 'pom-pom' F.E. across the Lines in daylight. There were easier ways to commit suicide, one of them had remarked.

As he levelled the F.E. on their new course he thought he could see the first glimmer of light in the sky ahead of them.

If you have enjoyed this book and would like to receive
details of other Walker Adventure titles,
please write to:

Adventure Editor
Walker and Company
720 Fifth Avenue
New York, NY 10019